Daughter of Dust

Book of the Huntress, Volume One

Joshua David Bellin

Daughter of Dust

ISBN (paperback): 978-1-7348315-0-4
ISBN (e-book): 978-1-7348315-1-1

Cover design by Valued Creations

for R.S., who asked me to

How deserted lies the city,
once so full of people!
How like a widow is she,
who once was great among the nations!

—Lamentations 1:1

Prologue

The boy walked through the city.

He'd been walking for days. His bare feet were torn and caked with dust, and they burned against the heated cement. He'd seen no one else during his journey. No food had presented itself either, and he was ravenous with hunger.

The ruins of the city stretched all around him, wavering in the heat. The tall spires of skyscrapers had collapsed, some coming to rest against others, some falling into shapeless heaps of stone and steel. The path he walked was littered with debris, forcing him to step carefully over jagged chunks of concrete, brick, and wood. The wind had poured the city's ashes over the ruins, cloaking cement and steel in brown dust. Once a geometric design of uprights and horizontals, the city had been transformed into a thicket of curved, broken lines through which the boy toiled like a desert nomad.

The boy couldn't remember his name.

He couldn't remember anything about himself. Not where he was born, not who he'd known, not what had happened to him. It was as if his life had sprung into existence the morning he woke to the endless expanse of the shattered city, the angry brown light of the sky. For all the days he'd wandered this forsaken place, he'd tried without success to recall anything about the time before he'd fallen asleep. The ache in his mind to know who he was felt as sharp as the ache in his belly, both driving him relentlessly onward.

Ahead, he glimpsed an opening in the wreckage, an archway of toppled steel framing a dark cavern. The place seemed deserted, the only sound the moan of the wind as it flowed over the tunnel entrance. But something deeper than memory told the boy he was not alone. His eyes flicked from side to side as he approached the shadowed doorway, hoping to catch a hint of another's presence.

There.

Beneath the tangle of pipes and beams that crisscrossed the mouth of the tunnel, something had shifted, something had separated itself from the dark. The movement was so subtle, the boy was certain that whoever had made it was trying to keep hidden. But the boy had seen it. His pace quickened as he neared the hiding place.

There was a sudden flurry and a sharp noise. An object slammed into the boy's shoulder, staggering but not stopping him. He reached out for the tattered figure who had taken a shot at him, and in that instant the boy was transformed, his feet no longer dragging the ground, his body speeding across the distance like a gust of wind. He caught up to the vagrant at once, and had just enough time to glimpse the terrified face. A refugee no older than himself, armed with a rifle he had discarded in his panic to get away.

"No—don't!"

The boy gripped his victim by the throat, raising him above his head. His body shuddered, his stomach twisting as if it had been turned inside out. His mouth opened wide, and then it was no longer only his mouth that opened; it was all the flesh from his face to his chest peeling back to reveal the cavity within him. It sickened him, this sensation of being pulled apart, but at the same time, he welcomed it. Without thought, without will, without anything but the urgent need to feed, he spread his arms and embraced the vagabond, and as his prey screamed, the boy knew.

He knew his name. He knew his past. The long night of his existence blazed with light, and he saw the life of the one he consumed as if it were his own: the parents he'd loved, the companions he'd lost. He knew his victim's fears, the nights he'd hidden in this den in the city, shaking with cold and terror, longing for a loved one who would never come again. While he feasted, he *was* the other boy, reliving all his joys and sorrows, and it was as if those times were still with him, as if they hadn't been swept away by the bombs that had reduced this city to ashes.

Then they were gone, the memories fading into the twilight.

The boy walked on through the city, wearing a new skin, eyeing the road ahead for his next meal.

Chapter 1

Michelle Simmons was out for a drive on her seventeenth birthday.

She drove her new car, a present from her parents. A Mustang V6 convertible. Lipstick red. The way it responded to the touch of her foot thrilled her like a first lover's kiss.

The two-lane road curled through the foothills of the Laurel Highlands in southwestern Pennsylvania. Stands of maple and oak crowded the road, bright with early spring foliage. As regal as the trees were, they were no match for the towering wall that had been built along the stretch of highway to block the traffic noise. Behind it, circled by an elaborate iron fence, Tudor style mansions rose against wooded hills. In one of those houses, Michelle's mother and father were rushing around excitedly, hanging streamers, directing the caterers, and pleading with Michelle's eleven-year-old sister Rosie to get off her phone and help out. They'd sent Michelle on this drive to keep their activities a secret, though they'd thrown her a party every year and she'd known about this one for weeks. Her parents probably knew that she knew, but it was possible Rosie didn't, and for her sake, Michelle was determined to act suitably surprised.

The Simmons family never skimped on birthday parties.

In past years, they'd invested in tons of food, a towering cake, and—courtesy of Rosie—enough games to make everyone totally silly by nine o'clock. Maybe Michelle should have outgrown the whole thing by now, the way it seemed that Rosie was beginning to, but when she considered that there would be only one more year after this to celebrate her birthday at home, Michelle got a mingled feeling of warmth and sadness.

Today, the thought of returning home made her stomach dance with nervous anticipation, but not so much for the party itself. She was looking forward to seeing her relatives who lived two hours away in Altoona, especially her cousin Dana, who'd started college at Penn State and could always be counted on to tell alternately hilarious and educational insider stories. Then there would be the girls and guys from the track team, along with her best friend Janine and Janine's boyfriend Greg. This time, though, one thing was different about her party. One major thing.

Mark.

Her boyfriend. A middle distance runner, he'd joined the team during winter training. He'd caught her attention right away, with his auburn curls flying out behind him when he ran and his eyes the color of the evening sky. He'd said nothing to her for a solid month, though he couldn't have failed to notice the way she—along with every other straight girl on the team—ogled him when he stripped off his shirt in the weight room. Finally, when she was on the verge of deciding that he was either hopelessly vain or already taken, he'd invited her for a run. That unseasonably warm February afternoon melted more than the mud and slush along the trails in the park. They'd dated since, and she'd spent most of the past two months in a dream of tandem runs, long drives in his car, and late-night texts. She'd never had a serious boyfriend before, but Janine, who'd dated Greg for a year, told her she knew a match made in heaven when she saw one.

No sooner had Janine said that, though, than things started to get strange. Texts went unanswered, conversations grew stilted. She'd spent two entire months losing herself in those gorgeous eyes of his, but now it seemed as if he looked through her, not at her, when she tried to talk to him. The closer she tried to get, the more he seemed to pull away. In the time they'd dated, they'd done little more than kiss and hold hands, and Michelle wondered if that was the trouble— if he wanted more from her than she was ready to give. But when she asked Janine, the conversation got her nothing but embarrassment and more confusion.

"He's not gay, is he?" Janine asked.

Michelle blushed. "I don't think so."

"Is he cheating on you?"

"How am I supposed to know?"

"If Greg tried anything like that on me, I'd know," Janine said. "And *he* knows what I'd do to him if I found out."

That was Janine: always confident, always assertive. Always tough. Michelle admired her, but doubted she could ever be like her.

"So what should I do?" she asked.

"You should learn to stand up for yourself," Janine answered. "And if he's not good enough for you, you should dump his ass."

Deep down, Michelle knew Janine was right. She'd only dated Mark for two months—why was she treating their relationship like such a big deal anyway? But when she thought about putting her friend's advice into effect, she grew uncertain. Janine was secure in her desirability, which made it easier for her to act all blasé. Michelle was exactly what Janine said: too soft, too timid. So worried she'd lose everything, she was afraid to do anything.

She'd texted Mark about today's party. That was Janine's recommendation: make it casual, don't seem needy. He hadn't acknowledged the text. Now here she was, not knowing what to expect from tonight yet feeling that whatever happened would decide her fate whether she liked it or not.

Michelle followed the highway as it climbed higher into the mountains. When a spur road appeared, she took it, thankful for the privacy and quiet. Alone among the trees that overlooked the valley, she put the top down, hoping the wind in her long blond hair might strip her anxiety away.

She wondered if it would be better to keep driving, to wait until after the party started before returning home. Would that make it more likely that Mark would be there, less crushing if he wasn't? She pictured him standing awkwardly in the living room when she made her entrance, his eyes flicking up from his soda to watch her breeze in with cheeks flushed and hair mussed from the drive. Would that show him that she was her own person? That he had to be more mindful of her feelings if their relationship was going to work? Or would it make her look rude and inconsiderate? If she forced him to wait for her, would that make it harder to get him alone so they could talk? Every scenario she imagined had its pros and cons, and she couldn't decide which was best. So she kept driving, hoping the wind would blow her an answer.

Her phone, sitting face-up on the passenger seat, pinged.

She glanced at the gray text bubble. In her quick scan of the message, she caught Mark's name. Michelle's heart skipped and her hand flinched to pick the phone up, but then she remembered the long, painfully serious talk she'd had with her parents the day she got her license. She returned her attention to the road, looking for a place she could pull over to read the text.

Something flashed in front of the car.

She hit the brakes, trying to steer around whatever it was. It thumped the hood and spun past the driver's side door, a blur of brown. Michelle screamed, unable to help herself. The car fishtailed wildly while she wrestled with the wheel, forgetting which way she was supposed to turn it, instinct and instruction equally useless. For a panic-stricken moment, she pictured herself plunging off the mountainside into the valley hundreds of feet below. Her eyes squeezed shut in terror, and she was in complete darkness when the wheels caught on something and the car came to a jolting stop.

Michelle opened her eyes.

Her heart pounded in her throat, and her knuckles were white where they wrapped around the wheel. The car had come to rest on the grassy shoulder on the left-hand side of the road, facing back down the hill. The side view mirror hung by a thread, and the seatbelt she'd dutifully buckled when she left home was pressed so tightly against her chest, it felt as if it were choking her breath away. Fifty feet beyond the hood, a blob of brown struggled to lift itself from the road.

It was a deer. Its body jerked unnaturally as it tried to

stand. Michelle could tell at once that something was wrong with its hindquarters: it couldn't get its rear legs under its body, and so it was lurching around on front legs that wobbled and shook like a faun's while it dragged its haunches behind it. For an instant, its head turned her way, its liquid eyes gazing at her in entreaty and accusation. When she focused more closely, she saw the fan of blood that smeared the road behind the animal, the white lengths of bone jutting from its hind legs like stakes.

Michelle unsnapped the seatbelt and opened the door to lean out and puke onto the margin of the road. The burning chunks of her last meal made her cough, and when she did, snot erupted from her nose. She wiped it off with the back of a trembling hand. To her utter mortification, she realized she'd peed her pants—barely enough to be visible through her shorts, but it made her feel as if she were swimming in a pool of hot, sticky urine. That thought made her sob uncontrollably, shoulders heaving, tears and snot and puke caking her lips with an indescribable taste of salty, bitter vileness. She flung her head against the headrest, hugging herself to get the tears to stop, and closed her eyes to make the flopping horror outside the windshield go away.

When the crying finally dwindled to shuddering breaths, she opened her eyes and saw that the deer had ceased moving. Its head was turned away from her, so she couldn't see its eyes, but she could see the pool of blood that darkened the road around its body.

I'm sorry, she said silently. *I'm so, so sorry.*

Ripping her eyes away from the inert brown mass on the road, she remembered what had made her lose her concentration, and she leaned to the passenger side and shakily picked up the phone from the floor where the collision had thrown it.

The screen was illuminated, the text bubble waiting as if the impact had frozen it there. The message was from Rosie.

mark cant come sucks 2 b u

After that, a snickering emoji trailed a conga line of characters: *HAHAHAHAHAHA*

Michelle gripped the phone and stared at the text until the words blurred. She told herself that Rosie didn't mean to be cruel, that she was trying to play a grown-up game she was too young to understand, but a dark wave of hurt welled in her all the same, so strong she felt as if someone she loved had died. Even stronger was the rush of anger—at Rosie, at Mark, at fate. She knew this was her fault, that *she* was the one who'd taken a day meant for celebration and turned it into a day of mourning, but the mocking accusation on the brightly lit screen filled her with rage, and her hand tightened around the phone as if she could snuff the words out.

She exited the car. Taking a step toward the drop-off, she flung the phone as far as she could, watching it arc over the body of the dead deer and plummet out of sight. For a second, just as the glowing rectangle disappeared, her heart lightened ever so slightly. Then the heaviness descended again, and she turned back to the car with a bleak feeling of dread.

Now that she was outside, she could see the extent of the damage. In addition to the dangling mirror, the car was deeply dented and scored where the deer had crumpled the fender and scraped against the driver's side door. The scratches in the bright red paint looked like claw-marks. The realization that they were from the animal's shattered bones made a fresh surge of bile crawl up Michelle's throat. The car was probably drivable, though she was fearful of buried harm that might cause sparks and fire. The road was empty at the moment, but if she stayed here long enough, someone was certain to drive by and offer to help. But when she thought of heading down the mountainside and returning home, she recoiled in shame—at the carelessness she'd shown, the death she'd caused, the wetness at her crotch she couldn't help thinking everyone would see. All her guests would be there by now, and though they'd be relieved that she was all right, they'd have questions about where she'd gone, what had caused the crash, how she'd lost her phone. Her parents would be deeply disappointed in her, which was almost worse than them being angry. Rosie would probably laugh. Janine might ask about Mark. It was too much for her to take.

She climbed into the car and snapped the seatbelt in place, turned the ignition and heard the motor clunk then roar to life. Slowly and deliberately, as if she were learning to perform a three-point turn for the first time, she redirected the car back up the hill. Once she regained the road and was confident the wheel was responding to her commands, she floored the accelerator, glancing once in the rearview mirror as the mangled shape receded behind her. Then she whipped around a bend in the road, and it was gone.

She drove faster than before, risking speed on hairpin turns, daring something else to cross her path. She came to a Y intersection, and without thinking, she spun the wheel to the right, tires screeching as she joined this new trail. Every now and then, she came to another intersection, and each time, she let impulse guide her as to which direction to take. She didn't stop to think where she was going, didn't question the force that flattened the accelerator against the floor and guided her on this journey into oblivion. She felt like a murderer fleeing the scene of a crime, and she wondered how people managed to put something like this behind them. How could you ever create enough distance to get away from your own past?

The miles between her and home lengthened. The thought skipped through her mind that her parents would be starting to worry about where she'd gone, looking out the picture window at the circular driveway and offering nervous excuses to their guests. The girls from the team were probably trying to make small talk in her absence, stressing over their upcoming meet and checking the time on their phones. Janine must have broken away from Greg's octopus arms by now and started frantically texting her: *where r u?????* For a single moment, she wondered why Mark had decided not to come, why, if this was his way of breaking up with her, he'd left a message at home rather than texting her. And Rosie—was she feeling bad about her impulsive text, connecting it to Michelle's disappearance? Or was she simply getting jumpy at the sight of the idle presents and untouched cake?

All of these thoughts seemed far away, as if they weren't her thoughts at all but those of a complete stranger. She felt oddly reborn in blood and guts and bone, and the only thought that seemed to matter was why, on the day of her second birth, her body felt as dead and empty as the thing she'd left lying on the road.

The mountain trail stretched before her, endless. Twists and turns appeared from time to time, encouraging her to seek places of ever deeper obscurity, and each time she chose such a route, she felt a perverse pleasure at leaving home farther behind. Marked arteries yielded to side roads and side-side roads, the paths she traveled becoming narrower and more poorly paved until finally her wheels jumped onto what was little more than a dirt track plunging through a dense tunnel of trees. A utility road or something like it, with no residences or signs to show she was anywhere near civilization. Still she drove on, sun and shadow flashing by on either side.

Occasionally this path bisected another, similar one, and when the whim struck her, she turned onto the new trail, ignoring other options with just as little logic. The highway had disappeared so long ago it hardly seemed real, and she couldn't remember the last time she'd seen a sign of human habitation. She'd gone skiing in the Laurel Highlands many times, but she wasn't sure she was in the Highlands anymore; this patch of woods was completely anonymous and unfamiliar, the kind of place where you could lose yourself. She pushed the car recklessly forward, climbing higher and higher, searching for an elevation where her old life would drop below the cloud line and vanish entirely from view.

She'd long since lost track of the hours and miles when she became aware of the car making an unnatural sound, a sputtering, clanking noise she at first attributed to damage from the accident. When she slowed to listen more carefully, she felt the vehicle lurching, hesitating under her command no matter how hard she pressed the accelerator. Her eyes fell to the fuel gauge.

Empty.

She recoiled in shock. She couldn't remember whether the tank had been full when her dad handed her the keys this morning, but it seemed impossible that she could have used an entire tank in—how long had she been driving? She glanced at the digital clock in the dashboard, only to receive another shock: it was almost five, which meant she'd been out for over six hours. The odometer showed that she'd put nearly three hundred miles on the car since she'd left home.

She slammed on the brakes, executed a five-point turn and started back downhill, then realized she couldn't remember which way she'd last turned. She passed a break in the trees that gave onto a plunging trail; was that the one she'd taken? The engine protested, shuddering in obvious distress. She tried to will the vehicle farther, to eke out another mile to recover the hundreds she'd lost, but it was no use. She barely managed to steer the car onto the margin of the road, where, with a final unhealthy cough, it died and refused to start again.

She sat behind the wheel, trying to calm herself with deep breaths. The surrounding trees appeared newly ominous. She'd meant to get herself lost, and she'd succeeded. But what was she supposed to do now?

Michelle climbed from the car. The smell of gasoline hung in the air. Could the accident have damaged the fuel tank? Shakily, she walked to the edge of the road and looked out through the screen of trees at the barely glimpsed valley far below. Thick woods swathed the basin and surrounding hills, with no buildings visible on the slopes, no windmills or utility towers adorning the ridgelines. She realized, as if she'd woken from a dream, that while she thought she'd been climbing higher the whole time, she'd actually traversed a series of rises and falls in the countryside. She could be anywhere by now—maybe not even in Pennsylvania. It was hard to see the sky through the trees, but she could tell that the sun was to her left, so that way was west. But west of what? The mountains looming above her formed a barricade she couldn't cross, and with her phone lying at the bottom of some nameless ravine, she had no way to call for help.

Panic seized her when she realized what she'd done. Unless another car drove by—and she'd seen only a handful of vehicles in the hours since she'd left the highway—she'd be stranded here through the night. Her parents would have called the police by now, but she'd heard somewhere that the authorities wouldn't search for a missing person until twenty-four hours had passed. And even when they did start looking for her, how would they know where to look? Whether purposely or haphazardly, she'd taken roads no one would expect her to take, roads that, it now seemed, almost no one else drove. How long of a hike was it back to civilization? Days? A week? As a runner, she'd learned how quickly a person could die from dehydration. But she hadn't thought to take a water bottle with her when she left home, and she knew nothing about how to find food or water in the wild.

Michelle stepped away from the edge of the road, shivering. She fell into the car and looked around her for something, anything, that might help. But there was nothing—no cup, no flashlight, no blanket. The interior was as bare and squeaky clean as could be, with the cloyingly fresh smell of newness clinging to its seats and floor mats. The death it had caused hours before hadn't changed the car's demeanor. It couldn't know that, a mere day after it had been purchased, it would become a death trap for its driver, no less than for the animal it had left rotting on the road hundreds of miles away.

Night fell while Michelle sat behind the wheel, paralyzed with fear and uncertainty. If she left in search of help, she might easily lose her way, but if she stayed, she might die right where she was. She knew her parents wouldn't wait for the police. They would be out looking for her, recruiting her aunt and uncle and cousin and as many of her friends as owned cars. She also knew that none of them had a chance of finding her. Rosie would have dropped her preteen pose by now and turned frantic, and everyone else would assume the worst—an accident, a carjacking, an abduction. Even if, by blind luck, they discovered the dead deer and the tire-marks from her skid, those bare clues wouldn't be enough to trace the rest of her trail. Maybe by daybreak, with the sun to guide her, she could start the trek back the way she came. But that was assuming she could figure out where she was. She couldn't believe that just hours ago, her biggest worry had been whether a boy she'd dated for two months was about to dump her, and now she was facing the very real possibility that she might starve or freeze to death in the woods, where no one would ever learn what had happened to her.

She hadn't said her prayers since she was Rosie's age, but she found her hands clenched tightly together and her lips moving soundlessly as she voiced the words in her mind.

Please, God. Please let them find me. Please. I'll do anything. Just let them find me soon.

Her only answer was a rising wind in the trees. A chill had descended with the coming of night, making her shiver in her shorts and T-shirt. She closed the top, but that didn't help much. Hugging her shoulders to preserve body heat, she closed her eyes and tried to sleep. Neither attempt was successful, as the cold crept into her bones and the eerie calls

22

of whip-poor-wills, shot through with the occasional hoot of an owl, kept her frayed nerves from calming. Something howled in the distance—a coyote, or was it a wolf? There were bears in the Pennsylvania woods, or so she'd heard. Every rustle in the underbrush made her fear one was snuffling in her direction, curious to explore this tin can with its tender meat inside. The thought that she was being punished for what she'd done made her shrink into herself, the way an animal might do once it realized it had become prey.

Just as she'd decided she couldn't take it anymore and was about to leap out of the car and run off into the night, the sounds of the wild stopped.

Michelle opened her eyes and peered into the dark. She could see nothing except the glow of stars through the canopy. The forest had gone entirely still. Her ears strained for the slightest sound of life beyond her own breathing—a bird, a whisper of wind in the branches—but there was dead calm.

As she stared into the darkness, more afraid of the quiet than she'd been of the noise, a pale light bloomed in front of her, outlining the shapes of trees. Her heart leaped, thinking it might be someone else's headlights. But as the light grew, she realized she'd misjudged its distance: it was coming not from the road ahead but from the rim of hills surrounding the valley, a golden glow like the first hint of daylight rising above the housetops when she went out for an early run. It couldn't be morning already, could it?

She was about to exit the car to study the strange light when she became aware of a rumbling noise, something like the sound of a plane flying overhead, except it didn't shift in pitch and volume as it passed by. Instead, it grew steadily louder, becoming first a roar and then a screech that seemed to split the heavens. Her hands flew to her ears, but the sound penetrated through the shield. The car seat trembled, the vibration growing until the entire vehicle rocked on its wheels so hard Michelle feared it would tip over. She was thrown against the door, but when she scrambled to open it and free herself, the noise forced her to cover her ears again. She could barely hear her own mind screaming impossibilities.

Earthquake? Bombs? Is it the terrorists?

As suddenly as it had started, the car stopped rocking, and the night fell silent. The light across the valley brightened, filling the sky much too quickly for dawn. Within a matter of seconds, the light became so intense she was forced to squint and then shut her eyes as if she were staring directly into the sun. Even then, the brightness was unbearable, and her hands forsook her ears to block the deadly glare. Unable to see anything except the blood-red afterimage of the hilltops burned on her retinas, she huddled with her face pressed into the seat of the car, terrified that the ground might swallow her up or that the earth had gone off course and was careening into the sun.

She stayed in a curled position for what seemed like hours, whimpering, wanting nothing except for it to end. At last, the painful brightness subsided enough for her to risk opening her eyes in cautious slits. When she did, she found that she could see.

Trees stood outlined by yellow light. A crackling noise filled the air, and her nose picked up the scent of burning wood. Trembling, she exited the car and crept to the edge of the road.

The valley was on fire.

The flames stretched in a solid band across the horizon, a brilliant yellow wall of fire that looked as if it covered the whole world. It consumed the distant trees with a sound like a giant beast gorging on bones. Every so often, an explosion separated itself from the background roar, and a ball of fire like a meteor in reverse shot into the brightly lit sky. The smell of destruction wafted to her from afar, and though she stood untouched in the shelter of the trees, her face was bathed in heat so intense she felt her brow drip with sweat and her eyeballs smart. She was much too far from the source to see what lay beneath the yellow fire, but she knew instantly that nothing it touched could have survived. Her vision was seared by its light, and she sensed that the world she'd known had been utterly changed, though she didn't know why or how.

She fell to her knees and, for the second time in a single night, lifted her thoughts in prayer. Her pleas were no longer for her. They were for Mom and Dad and Rosie, for her aunt and uncle and cousin, for Janine and Greg— even, though he'd hurt her, for Mark. That injury seemed trivial now, and she prayed for his safety in the same breath as she did the others'. She didn't know what had caused the blaze, how far it spread, how many people were caught in its deadly grip. She didn't know where she was, and at times, listening to a voice she barely recognized speaking words inside her head, she felt as if she no longer knew *who* she was. She only knew that she'd never forgive herself if the fire preserved her, alone and alive by chance, while taking everyone and everything she loved.

"Mom," she whispered above the crackle of flames. "Dad. Rosie. I'll find you. I swear, I'll come back to you. I promise."

She covered her face with her hands, lowered her head, and wept.

Chapter 2

The fire raged through the night.

Michelle stayed in her car the entire time, while thirst and hunger wracked her empty body. When the next morning brought an unnatural glow that supplanted the coming of the sun, she considered leaving, but she was hesitant to abandon this apparently safe place, not knowing where else the fire might be burning. So far, it seemed to be confined to the valley and opposing hills, but her greatest fear was that it would climb the peak where her car had broken down. Her stomach had squeezed into a fist and her tongue had grown so dry it could no longer lick her cracked lips, but much as she wrestled with her decision, she always arrived at the same answer. If the fire burned into another night, she'd have no choice but to leave the car in search of water. For now, she remained in a state of anxious watchfulness, clutching her hollow stomach and catching brief spells of sleep before jerking awake again, staring at the wall of fire that loomed across the valley.

When it finally extinguished itself, she thought she was dreaming.

She stepped cautiously from the car and stretched cramped limbs. The woods were as silent as a grave. Her legs felt weak and rubbery as she went to the edge of the road and peered into the valley. Nothing was visible through the smoke that had collected in the bowl, thicker than the thickest fog. She reasoned that the fire must have burned everything down below and died from lack of fuel. This high up, a haze hung in the air, diffusing the early morning sunlight and making it impossible to breathe deeply. She held the collar of her T-shirt over her nose and mouth and took shallow, tentative breaths through the cloth, and that helped, though she still felt as if she were gagging on the stench of ash. Even the sun, creeping over the mountains to the east, had a smothered look, like a moon haloed in nighttime mist. She blinked, trying to clear away the tears that blurred her vision. She remembered what she'd learned in Physics class about nuclear winter, the deadly dust cloud that would choke the sun after thermonuclear war. The same kind of cloud that, when a giant meteor struck the planet millions of years ago, had spelled the extinction of the dinosaurs.

Could *that* be what had happened the night of her birthday? A series of meteor strikes? If so, had the same prehistoric pall been cast into the atmosphere, muffling the sunlight? If this *was* a meteor strike of the magnitude that had occurred in the past, then it wouldn't be long before the entire world started its descent into darkness.

The prospect of death hadn't been far from her mind since the fire began—her own death, and the death of everyone else. But when despair whispered in her ear that her parents and Rosie were already among the dead, she drew courage from the fact that *she* had survived. She was parched and famished beyond belief, but she was alive. That meant there had to be a limit to the fire's reach, which meant that others must have lived through it, too. If she could find a way off this mountaintop and locate fellow survivors, there was hope that they'd be able to help her search for home.

To stay on her feet at all, though, she needed water. She knew the signs of dehydration, and she had every one of them: stale mouth, swollen tongue, dizziness, headache. Her body felt utterly drained, much more so than she would have expected from a single night without drinking anything. She reeled and nearly fell when she returned to her car, and had to brace herself against the door before her vision settled and her legs felt strong enough to carry her. She swallowed to clear the foul taste from her mouth, but her throat clenched and she ended up gagging instead. She tried to spit, but she couldn't summon enough saliva to do it.

The crazy thought struck her that she should pop the hood. Didn't cars have water in them somewhere? But she had no idea where, and she couldn't risk drinking transmission fluid. Next, she hit on the expedient of chewing a leaf to suck the moisture out of it, but when she plucked one from a maple tree and worked it around in her gummy mouth, she found that it was dry and brittle, more like an autumn leaf than one from early spring. She stooped to scour the ground for morning dew and found the grass withered and cracked, the way it got during a summertime drought. How could that be? Was it possible that even though the yellow fire had come nowhere near her outpost, it had leeched every trace of water from the surrounding woods— the same way, it seemed, that it had sucked the fluid from the cells of her own body?

She stood on trembling legs and surveyed the area around her. It wasn't only the fogginess of the sunlight filtering through the trees that dulled the world's natural radiance; the foliage itself had lost its green tint, the leaves fading to yellow and brown. She grabbed a branch, shook it gently—and fell back in shock when it came free in her hand. Dropping the branch, she studied the ashy residue that had settled in the lines of her palm like black veins. A handful of leaves from the fallen branch left the same chalky film on her fingertips. When she rubbed one of the leaves between forefinger and thumb, it crumbled into powder, insubstantial as smoke.

Michelle snatched her hand away in horror. She could no longer doubt it—the woods were dying. It was nothing like the way the woods died every year, in a blaze of brilliant red and orange mellowing to bronze and gold, the fall splendor she associated with the homey scent of campfires, the annual trip to the pumpkin farm, and Trick or Treat with Rosie first as her sidekick and, lately, as her reluctant ward. This death had come suddenly and completely to the mountaintop where she'd believed herself safe from the ravages of the yellow fire. She would find no water here, and she could only hope she'd find it somewhere else before the blight seeped into her bones the way it had into the surrounding trees.

With determination, she started slowly across the hillside, heading in a more or less westerly direction, away from the valley. Dry leaves crackled and crunched under her feet, sending up a fine spray of ash. When she looked over her shoulder, she could trace her trail by the ghostly footprints she'd left. Other leaves fell around her, twirling to the ground in a slow ballet, heralds of spring that had been green just a day ago now spotted yellow and translucent as wax paper. There was little wind in the woods—that had apparently died, too—but whenever the slightest breeze stirred the branches, a shower of leaves descended, some of them splintering on contact with the ground, others disintegrating before they reached the end of their flight. It was like watching a snake shed its skin. The only difference was that, so far as she could tell, there was nothing new growing underneath.

She'd walked for only a few minutes when she came across a dead bird.

She froze in place, stunned by the small carcass. With the toe of her sneaker, she delicately prodded the body to free it from the leaves that coated its back. The bird was a cardinal, she could tell by the black mask and heavy beak. Its beige-brown plumage made her think it was a female, except its stomach feathers were bright red, like a male's. Decay had thinned its body, turning it into a lean and flattened cavity. Unlike the deer she'd killed, there was no blood, no sign of what had brought it down.

Fifty meters away, she saw another unmoving shape on the forest floor. When she approached, she discovered that it was a bird too, with an owl's large, round head. It was splayed on its back with wings extended and clawed feet raised into the air, as if it had been knocked off its perch and had been unable to right itself in time to fly. Its eyes were gone, and the empty sockets stared at her with a terrible mixture of abandonment and recrimination.

So it went as she walked, shuffling across the desiccated landscape: every minute or two she encountered another carcass, sometimes two or three within steps of each other. Most were birds—woodpeckers, songbirds, crows—but some belonged to mice, raccoons, even an opossum. One was the huge body of a hawk, felled along with the lesser creatures it preyed on. All of the animals had the dulled appearance of their surroundings, but Michelle wasn't sure if that was because they'd been dead for the past day or because they'd suffered the same fate as the leaves and trees. She remembered how silent the woods had gone just before the yellow fire appeared, and she wondered if whatever had caused the fire had stricken the woodland creatures along with their habitat. She was beginning to think that what she had witnessed last night was the dropping not of meteors but of bombs, or of one bomb of unimaginable power. That would explain the airplane sound she'd heard, as well as the fire, the quaking in the ground, the destruction of the valley. The only flaw in her theory was that she'd never heard of bombs that killed in such a strange way: preserving the form of living things while stealing their life-force.

After the first couple of miles, she stopped turning aside to investigate each new corpse she saw. She couldn't stand to confront so much death, couldn't let it weaken her will as much as the fire had weakened her body.

The hillside had risen steeply when she started out, but just when Michelle thought her legs couldn't take one more step, the ground leveled off. After another mile, it changed course again, sloping gradually downhill toward what she hoped might be a hollow where water had collected. But then, the land fell away into a broad ravine that barred any further progress. Not trusting her balance but needing to see what lay beyond, Michelle lowered herself onto her stomach and peered over the edge.

The depth of the gully made her vision swim. From her height at least sixty feet up, she scanned the shadowed floor, finding only more desolation: dried leaves, naked trees, two or three small, dark shapes that might have been dead animals. She was about to inch away from the ravine and seek another route through the forest when her eyes caught something that made her stop.

It wasn't much: a dark wrinkle in the valley floor. She was almost sure she'd seen a dull light playing across its surface, and now that she stared at it, she became convinced. It was barely a foot wide, and its shallow bed was clotted with decaying leaves, but she was positive that it was the sparkle of a small stream.

At the sight of it, any thought of circumnavigating the ravine fled. There was water down there—not much from what she could tell, but water. Whether it was safe to drink was another matter, but she instantly dismissed the worry. Her body was starved for fluid; her mouth and throat felt as dry as the land she'd walked, and her hands shook no matter how hard she tried to still them. She felt certain that if she didn't drink soon, she'd end up like one of the pitiful creatures that lay belly-up on the forest floor.

Michelle craned her neck over the edge of the ravine and looked straight down. The incline was nearly vertical at this spot, clayey soil dotted with rocks she had no faith would support her weight. A scan up and down the length of the cut revealed no change in the angle of descent; the hillside was dangerously steep as far as she could see, sometimes being scooped out past the vertical. She doubted she could manage the climb even in top physical condition. She'd scaled the climbing wall at the gym a few times, but that was only a twenty foot ascent, with a rope cinched to her waist and pads on the floor below. Yet now that she was within sight of what her body so desperately craved, she could feel its magnetic pull in her chest and gut, drawing her like a divining rod toward the floor of the ravine.

"It's the same as the wall," she muttered to herself. "You can do this."

She stripped her shoes off, tied the laces together, and flung them over the edge, watching them bounce in a puff of dust on the floor of the ravine. Taking a deep breath, she lay on her stomach and eased her legs over the brink. She felt for the rocks she'd spotted a few feet below the rim, and when her toes touched them, she sank her fingers into the dry soil at the top of the cliff and carefully let her weight settle back against the soles of her feet. Everything felt sturdy so far, so she took a chance and slid farther back.

The footholds stayed firm. With her right hand clawing into the slope to steady herself, she bent her knees and reached behind her with her left hand until her fingers touched one of the rocks on which she stood. A quick transfer of foot for hand later, she was spread-eagled against the slope, clinging to the clay with her right hand and the rock with her left, her right foot balanced on a rock while her left foot felt below for the next support. She found it, and tested it for strength.

Again, it held her weight, allowing her to drop her top hand to the rock where her right foot rested and release that foot to find the next rung down in the makeshift ladder. The awkward, lurching motion of her descent turned out to be nothing like climbing the wall at the gym, with its conveniently shaped handholds and rubberized surfaces to improve one's grip. Here, her hands needed to dig deeply into the slope to clutch for buried roots, while her feet felt more like hands, her toes curling and gripping in ways she hadn't known they could. Her progress was painfully slow, requiring more concentration than her water-starved brain had readily available and more strength than her quivering arms and legs felt they could provide.

But it worked. Inch by inch, foot by foot—and hand— she descended the ravine toward the feast that awaited her.

I'm Spider Girl, she thought. *I'm using my Spidey Sense.*

Ten torturous minutes later, her feet registered the level bottom of the gully, and she collapsed in a cushion of dead leaves. She lay there for at least as long as it had taken her to climb down, wanting to run to the water but unable to command her legs to support her. Her feet were scraped and swollen from the climb; the fingernails she'd had manicured for her party were broken and chipped, the red polish practically gone, the dirt under what remained of the nails so deeply worked into her fingertips it looked as if her hands would never be washed clean again. She swallowed oxygen in grateful gulps until she felt capable of standing. Then she stumbled to the creek, her stomach growling as she smelled the incredible crispness of water in the air.

She fell to her knees at the water's edge and thrust her hands through the leaf litter into the stream. It was gunky, full of black residue, but here in the shade of the ravine it was cool, and the mere feel of the water made her bruised body ache with joy. She splashed handfuls on her face, letting the droplets slide down her throat in a delicious trickle. She knew you weren't supposed to guzzle when you were dehydrated, so she stripped her shirt off and immersed it in the water, then wrung some of the nastiness out and drank the drops that fell from the saturated cloth. When she'd squeezed out as much moisture as she could, she repeated the process, holding her head back and letting the fluid fall one heavenly drop at a time into her open mouth.

At last, when her parched body felt satiated and she grew worried about overdoing it, Michelle stood and slipped her aching feet into the chilly stream. It wasn't deep, only up to her ankles, but using the shirt like a washcloth, she was able to wipe her skin clear of some of the grime that had accumulated during the day. Bending over, she submerged her head until its crown touched the sandy bottom. She rinsed her hair as well as she could, feeling it regain a degree of suppleness as ash drifted away in the slow current.

She knew she couldn't stay here much longer. Now that the water had revived her, it was time to continue her search for food and other survivors. Maybe she could create a container to carry water with her. She lingered in her private oasis a moment more, bathing in the water and pretending it could wash all memories of the past and all fears of the future far downstream.

"Having a nice swim, sweetheart?"

Michelle jerked upright at the sound of the voice, her wet hair whipping across her face. When she turned, she saw a man sitting on a tree stump not thirty feet away, his smile making it clear he'd been eyeing her upturned butt. She'd been so fixated on the stream, she must not have heard him creep up on her. He was much older than her, her father's age at least, with a scruffy beard flecked with gray and an outfit consisting of an olive-colored tank top, camouflage pants, and heavy hiking boots. His right leg was crossed at the ankle over his left knee, and Michelle's heart skipped when she saw the hunting rifle cradled in his lap.

The man stood, leaning his weapon against the tree

stump while he shook out his legs. He performed the stretches slowly and mockingly, as if to emphasize how long he'd been there and how much he'd seen. When he was done, he hefted the rifle again and took a step toward her.

"You from around here?" he asked, holding the smile. "What's your name?"

Michelle took a step backward, out of the water. She pressed the wet shirt against her chest, covering her bra. The man's smile widened. His face was grimy, as if he'd tramped through the same ash-coated landscape as she had.

"Take it easy, honey," he said. "I only asked you your name."

He came a step closer. She had a moment to decide whether to trust him, but the fact that he'd been sitting there all this time, watching her undress without announcing his presence, made her sure he meant her harm. They were alone in the woods, alone in the world for all she knew. His eyes roamed her body, and he had a gun.

He took one more step before Michelle turned and ran.

The man let out a snarl that ended in the filthiest name she'd ever been called, and then she heard him following. She'd counted on the gun being used only to threaten her, not actually to shoot her, and she must have been right, because he didn't fire. His footsteps kept pace with hers as she scrambled up the hillside on the opposite edge of the ravine. She could hear the crunch of leaves in her wake, but she didn't dare look back to see if he was gaining. Much as the stream had revived her, her legs still felt as if they were filled with sand. She realized she was carrying the T-shirt, heavy with water. She flung it aside as she reached the upper rim of the ravine and took off through the trees. Rocks and branches cut her bare soles, but she didn't slow down, instead lengthening her stride to test his speed and endurance. He shouted another string of curse words, but his breath came heavily, his voice fading as she put ground between them. She pushed herself harder, heart pounding, sunlight and shade flickering in the periphery of her vision. He shouted once again, but this time, his voice was practically lost in the distance, a faint cry barely audible over the sound of her own rushing feet.

Another man dressed like the first sprang from the trees on her right and clutched at her hair, forcing her to brake sharply and veer out of his reach. Through the trees ahead, she saw a third man bearing down on her from her left, and she realized that each man was trying to herd her toward the other. The one up ahead was the fastest of the three, and she didn't know if she could outrun him, especially with her body so low on energy. Her foot struck a hidden rock with such force she cried out, stumbled, then darted to the left just in time to elude the second pursuer. Her chest ached with each breath, but she put on a final burst of speed and leaped past the third attacker, whose bared teeth made it clear what he would do if he caught her.

She'd almost convinced herself she was going to escape when a huge figure stepped out from behind a tree and she crashed squarely into him.

The force knocked her to the ground. In a second, iron hands gripped her arms, pulling her into a bear hug. Michelle wrestled with the man, trying to free her hands to claw his eyes, but he was too strong. A scream rose in her throat, but she choked it back. Who would answer if she screamed?

"Take it easy, girlie," the big man rumbled in her ear.

"Stop fighting me before you hurt yourself."

Michelle turned her head to catch a glimpse of the speaker, and saw a broad, lined face, bushy gray beard, and bald dome. She snapped at the man's nose with her teeth, but caught only air. The man swore, and a new voice spoke from behind him.

"Looks to me like you're the one who's going to get hurt," the voice said with a laugh. "Better let her go, Argus."

To Michelle's surprise, the bear of a man released her. As soon as her feet touched the ground, she tried to run, but her calves cramped, and she sprawled in the leaves.

From the ground at the big man's boots, she saw another man emerge from the trees. He was tall, slim, and dark-haired, wearing camo pants and a black jacket with gold bands at the cuffs. Before she got a good look at his face, he stepped in front of the man called Argus and confronted the original three, who had caught up by now and paused in their tracks twenty paces away.

"Whose idea was this?" the new man called out in a voice that conveyed both authority and anger.

None of the three answered. The newcomer strode toward them, and though the man from the creek was armed, he cringed away, his rifle barrel drooping toward the forest floor. When the man in the black jacket stood face to face with the gang's ringleader, he spoke again in a quieter voice, but one edged with danger.

"I'm going to ask you one more time. Whose. Idea. Was this?"

The man with the rifle seemed unable to look the speaker in the eye. "Come on, Jason, we were just—"

"Just what?" the man named Jason asked. "Having a

little fun? I've warned you about this, Caeneus. But you never listen. You never learn."

This time, the other man's reply was too indistinct for Michelle to hear.

"A week in the box," Jason said in that dangerously quiet voice. "For each of you. And be thankful that's all you're getting."

The other man's head snapped up when he heard his sentence. "A week? For Christ's sake, Jason, we didn't even touch her."

"Only because you were too slow to catch her," Jason said to him. "Two weeks in the box for you, Caeneus. As a reminder that jackals belong in cages."

He turned sharply and was pacing back to where Michelle lay when she saw Caeneus's rifle barrel twitch upward. Her mouth opened in warning, but before she could utter a sound, Jason spun with ferocious quickness and leveled the hunter with a single blow to the head. Caeneus fell, his rifle clattering to the ground, his body sending up a cloud of ashy dust from the forest floor. He was still breathing, but his eyes were closed and blood streamed from his nose.

Jason turned from his victim and approached Michelle. Seeing him up close for the first time, she was surprised to discover that he was much younger than the other hunters: no older than his mid-twenties, whereas the rest of the men, including Argus, were easily in their fifties. His dark hair was cut just shy of military short, and he wore a thin mustache and neat beard along the edge of his jaw. His eyes were an unnaturally light blue, the way some dogs' eyes are. Those eyes were filled with concern as he offered her the same hand that had struck down Caeneus. She took it warily, feeling the strength in his arm as he pulled her to her feet.

"Are you hurt?" he asked.

She shook her head.

"What were you doing out here?" he continued. "This is not a safe place."

She glanced behind him at Argus, who had picked up Caeneus's rifle and was in the process of disarming the unconscious ringleader's companions. Though the big man bore no weapons that she could see, the two hunters meekly handed over the knives sheathed at their belts.

"My car broke down on the mountain," she told Jason. Reluctant to divulge too much, she added, "I'm trying to get home."

He smiled as if he knew there was more to her story than she was letting on. "Lots of mountains around here. Where's home?"

She told him. His smile broadened, and for a moment, her heart leaped at the thought that he was going to offer to take her there. But his next words crushed her hopes.

"That's a long way off," he said. "And we're exposed in this position. We need to get somewhere safe by nightfall."

He turned to check on the others. Argus had hefted Caeneus over one broad shoulder, while the unconscious man's partners stood with their heads bowed and their arms hanging at their sides. Jason nodded and turned back to Michelle, his eerie blue eyes gleaming brightly.

"It's a good thing we found you," he said. "I think you'd better come with us."

Chapter 3

Michelle hesitated as Jason placed his hand behind her back.

"Where are we going?" she asked.

"To a secure location," he answered simply. He kept his hand in the air behind her, not actually touching her bare shoulder, but she felt her skin crawl from the nearness of him.

She quickly assessed the situation. Jason's face was open and unthreatening, but the thought of how quickly he'd turned on a member of his own team made her uneasy. If this was a kidnapping, what chance would she have to escape? Wherever he was planning to take her, it sounded as if it would be far from here, deeper into the maze of the woods, where she'd be hopelessly lost.

But truthfully, could she get any more lost than she already was? Jason *had* protected her from the other men, and he clearly knew the area well. Maybe, after she told him the rest of her story, he would help her find her way home.

Jason must have seen her decision in her face. He nodded, then took off his jacket and offered it to her. Given the choice between exhibiting herself half-naked in front of a group of older men and accepting one of the strangers' clothes, she chose the latter. Jason also held out a string of lumpy brown stuff that looked like homemade jerky. Michelle took it, too ravenous to wonder what animal it had come from or to care that she had sworn off red meat freshman year. Her teeth tore into it, and though it had a distinctly gamey taste, she wolfed the whole string down in three bites. Jason watched her, but said nothing.

When she was finished and had washed down the meal with a swig of cold, clear water from Jason's canteen, he placed his hand on her elbow, steering her back through the forest toward the stream. Argus and the others tramped alongside, the big man handling his unconscious burden as if it were a sack of mulch instead of a human being. Hemmed in between the group's young leader and his powerful henchman, Michelle realized she had no choice but to follow.

They reached the creek bed in a couple of minutes. Jason halted the others for Michelle to put her sneakers back on. She glanced at him once and noticed him staring intently at her bruised and bleeding feet. When she'd tied the laces, he pointed downstream.

"It's a long hike to where we're going," he said. "When's the last time you slept?"

"Earlier today."

"Tell me if you get tired." He started out along the bank of the stream, keeping to the shaded hollow. Despite his apparent solicitude, Jason set a brisk pace, taking long strides that outmatched her own.

Michelle fell into step behind him, with Argus following and the duo of hunters in the rear. Her legs, stiff and sore from her run, loosened as they walked. It helped that Jason handed her another of the jerky strips, along with his canteen.

43

Her headache from the morning had mostly subsided, along with the aching in her hands and feet from her climb into the ravine. She was alert enough now to watch for any indication that Jason or one of the others planned to take advantage of her. She considered trying to start a conversation with him, probing his history or his motivations, but she sensed from his determined pace that she wouldn't get far. If she told him about her family, about being lost, would that elicit sympathy? Or would it make her even more vulnerable? She kept coming back to the one fact she knew for sure: she was surrounded by armed men who knew these woods intimately. She would have to pray that Jason meant her no harm, and that ultimately, after he'd taken her to the safe place he was so eager to get to, she could find some way to convince him to lead her home.

Jason maintained perfect silence as he guided the troupe along the creek, not only saying nothing but stepping in such a way that his hiking boots made no sound on the leaf-strewn bank. What little sense of direction Michelle possessed had been completely thrown by her sprint through the forest, but it seemed from the position of the sun that they were heading west, away from the ridge where she'd left her car. It also seemed as if their surroundings were reviving somewhat as they left the valley behind: the overhanging branches fleshed out with flecks of green among the brown and yellow, while the carpet on which they walked became less brittle and dry. The creek ran stronger and clearer with each mile they covered, and Jason stopped once to refill his canteen and offer Michelle another long swallow. Even with these signs of life, the woods remained silent except for the sound of her own clumsy feet and the two hunters' heavy breathing; where there should have been constant birdcalls, there was a stillness in the air that spoke of death on a scale too huge for Michelle to conceive. But as long as they kept close to the water and she looked straight ahead, at least she was spared the sight of tiny carcasses littering the forest floor.

They walked for what must have been several hours before Jason ordered a halt. Everyone sat by the stream, which now bubbled and frothed over a bed of mossy rocks. Jason handed out strips of jerky and slices of dried root vegetables. Caeneus had regained consciousness well before this, but he stayed as far away from Jason as possible, which meant he kept clear of Michelle, too. If she was unsure what to think of Jason and his strongman, she'd already taken the measure of the three hunters. Their sneaking glances and cringing motions made it clear that while they would have hurt her if they hadn't been stopped by Jason and Argus, they were too cowardly to try anything now that their youthful chief was onto them. That thought should have brought her some comfort, but it was counterbalanced by the realization that the deeper Jason led her into the woods, the more she was at his mercy.

"Is it much farther?" she asked him.

He looked up from his food. "We'll be there by evening."

Her heart sank as she tried to calculate how far they'd walked already, how much additional ground they would cover in the coming hours. "And is where we're going"—she paused, unsure how to phrase her question without arousing his suspicions—"is it close to anywhere … "

"Civilized?" he asked in a sarcastic tone. "Seems to me civilization isn't in such great shape right now."

45

"You saw the fire?"

"Kind of hard to miss. Normally we keep to ourselves, but we knew this was big. It's why I sent out teams"—he nodded at Caeneus and the other two, who ducked their heads into their shoulders at his attention—"to scout the area and collect intelligence. Didn't expect I'd have to spend my time checking up on them to make sure they stayed out of trouble."

He held Michelle's eyes, his expression oddly challenging. That look told her he was hiding something. If he'd sent his men out to investigate the yellow fire, why had he followed them? Presumably, Caeneus and his companions wouldn't have tried to attack her if they'd known Jason was watching, so they must have thought they were on their own. What was Jason's true reason for dispatching his teams? What had he expected, or hoped, to find when he and Argus trailed along?

She dropped her gaze in case he should sense her misgivings. If those penetrating eyes of his detected anything, he didn't let on. Packing up the remainder of their meal, he stood and helped her to her feet. "How you holding up?"

"Fine, thank you."

"Argus can help if you're getting tired. Just let me know."

She pictured herself clinging to the big man's back, and instinctively recoiled. "I'm okay."

"Fair enough." He set off down the creek again, walking even faster than before, as if he were testing her or trying to prove she'd regret not accepting the offer of Argus's arms.

Hours later—she had no idea how many hours, though she did know that she was spared from collapse only by extra helpings of jerky—Jason's tireless march finally came to an end. True to his word, the sky had deepened to a shade of evening blue as they stood on a cliff top overlooking a level area crowded with towering trees. The stream had become a near-river by this point, and it cascaded in a waterfall down the escarpment before flowing in a bend around what Michelle realized was a campground.

Having been given little notice what to expect, she was surprised to find not a handful of tents but seven sturdy buildings of various shapes and sizes scattered among the trees, all of them constructed of rough-hewn logs and roofed with wooden shingles over which nets of leaves and moss had been laid. The trees had lost none of their spring foliage this deep in the woods, and the buildings were huddled beneath their branches, the largest cabin seeming to grow from the base of a giant oak. Rustic as it looked at first glance, Michelle saw evidence of modernity: a large antenna shaped like a cat's cradle jutted from the roof of the building that wrapped around the oak tree, while electric lights showed through the curtains of each building. Though the buildings had no chimneys and thus emitted no smoke, the smell of something cooking made her nose twitch and her mouth water as they headed for a gap in the rocky cliff that stood above the miniature village.

They'd barely taken a step in that direction when a shadow rose from behind a boulder, blocking their way. Michelle jumped back, but Jason merely nodded.

"Arachne," he said. "Caught any flies in your web?"

"If only," the person spoke, and Michelle saw that it was a woman, short and slim with an olive cast to her complexion and muscles visible in her tattooed arms. She wore black pants and a sleeveless black top, and kept her hair shaved practically to the scalp. A sleek black rifle rested on her hip, with a compact body and telescopic sight. Though Michelle didn't know the first thing about guns, she could tell that the woman's weapon was much newer and more powerful than Caeneus's old-fashioned model.

"Circe was wondering when you'd be back," she said to Jason. There was a hint of an accent in her voice, but Michelle couldn't place it. "What's the news from the front?"

"We'll talk later," Jason said. "Radio Circe and tell her to meet me in an hour."

The woman's eyes narrowed at Michelle, but she stepped aside to let Jason and his team pass. Michelle felt her watching them until they turned a corner in the trail and were hidden by a wall of rock.

"Our sentries take their jobs seriously," Jason explained. "And none more so than Arachne. Once you're situated, I can show you around camp to meet the others."

Michelle nodded and tried to compose her face into a pleasant, noncommittal expression, but her heart fell at the word "situated." With armed sentries patrolling what seemed to be the only way out of camp, she might as well be walking into an actual spider web from which she'd never be able to disentangle herself.

Sandwiched between Jason and Argus, she made her way down the bluff. The dirt trail zigzagged between boulders, its ground packed hard and smooth by the passage of countless boots. Michelle's legs quivered so much from the morning's events and the day-long hike, she stumbled after only a few steps. Jason made no move to steady her, but she felt as if he had eyes on the back of his head and was watching her closely all the way down. It was that creepy sense of being inspected as much as relief from her exhaustion that made her thankful when they finally exited the pass.

"Almost there," Jason said encouragingly. "Argus, take care of these three. I want to show our guest around."

The three hunters stiffened at Jason's words, but they said nothing as Argus marched them a short distance from the main body of the camp. Michelle saw that they were headed for a low structure the size of a tool shed, built into the ground on a slant like Dorothy's storm cellar in *The Wizard of Oz*. Unlike the other buildings, it had no windows, and when Argus yanked the door open, she saw no light within. She didn't have to be told what it was: the box. She wondered how they would all fit inside, and whether they'd be given food or allowed to use the bathroom during the week—two weeks in their leader's case—that they were imprisoned there. Despite what they'd tried to do to her, she almost felt sorry for them as they were about to be deprived of light and air and freedom for such a long time.

Jason marched through the trees toward the center of the campground, and Michelle had to hustle to catch up with him. With the apparent ability to put everything out of his mind except his immediate purpose, he ignored what was happening to Caeneus and his crew and began a running narration as he strode through the camp.

"I own this land," he began. "I've got well over a hundred acres all told, but the main camp's confined to twenty. The rest is dedicated to our solar farm"—he gestured toward the curve of the river—"which enables us to run completely off the grid. We've got tunnels leading to underground storage facilities"—another gesture, this time in the direction of the bluff—"so we're well stocked in case of emergency. You could take an aerial photograph if you were willing to fly low enough, but what you'd see is only the tip of the iceberg."

Michelle's ears perked up at his words, and she wondered what was hidden beneath the site's summer-camp surface appearance.

"There are thirty-four of us at the moment," Jason continued. "At maximum occupancy, the camp could house seventy, give or take. But I like to keep our operation on a smaller scale, with people I know and trust."

As if on cue, other members of the camp emerged from the buildings, men and women in camouflage uniforms that blended with the dusk-lit forest. All of them bore rifles similar to Arachne's. As with the sentry, Michelle could tell that these people had lived and trained with their guns for a long time; the way they cradled the barrels and nestled the stocks under their arms made the rifles seem like extensions of their own bodies. They weren't soldiers, exactly—their uniforms bore slight differences in color and cut, and their weapons were similarly diverse, looking more like personal possessions than a standard issue. But they moved with regimented efficiency, and it was obvious that they'd been honed by their leader into a battle-ready fighting force.

Watching them as they went about their business, Michelle felt the beginnings of a plan form in her mind—a plan to escape this place and find her way back home. It would be risky, and it would require her to deceive Jason, but she couldn't think of another way. Everything Jason had said so far suggested that he intended to keep her here permanently, as the newest member of his band of heavily armed desperadoes. If that was true, she would have to give her plan a try, and hope that his gem-bright eyes wouldn't see through to her true purpose.

Jason had reached the front steps of the central building in the encampment, the one whose two wings hugged the oak tree. Though the camp had little ornamentation, Michelle saw from up close that a rough human form had been carved out of the forward face of the tree, making it look as if the figure rose from the roof. The way the building's two wings angled sharply back enhanced its resemblance to a sailing vessel, with the tree bearing its figurehead. None of the men and women had deviated from their routines to investigate the camp's new arrival, but Michelle could tell that they were all watching her curiously as their leader put a hand behind her back and ushered her up the steps to the building's front porch and through the door.

The interior was illuminated only by windows that admitted very little light beneath the trees. The floor and walls were constructed of wood planks, the ceiling rafters visible overhead. She and Jason stood in a central hallway from which the building's two wings diverged. To the right, down a short corridor that led to the wing on that end, there was an open door, which Jason approached. Holding out a hand, he gestured for Michelle to enter. She froze momentarily, realizing that this would be the first time she was completely alone with him. Then, reminding herself that he could have assaulted her in the other men's presence if he had wanted, she steeled herself and entered.

The room was darker than the hallway, and Michelle's heart leaped to her throat when she felt Jason's slim form brush against her arm. She relaxed when he moved past her to click on a light, which revealed a small, square room with no furnishings except a wooden desk, two ladderback chairs, a bookcase full of thick volumes, and a hinged desk lamp in lieu of windows. Jason circled the desk and sat, leaning back on the chair's hind legs. Michelle took the other seat, and couldn't help feeling as if she'd been called to the principal's office for some unknown infraction. She tried to sit straight and meet Jason's unsettlingly direct gaze.

He smiled amiably. "I really should apologize. Things got so crazy back there, I never asked you for your name."

She hesitated, but knew he'd catch her if she tried to lie about something so basic. "It's Michelle. Michelle Simmons."

"Well, then, welcome to the Argo, Miss Simmons."

"Michelle's fine."

He nodded. "You probably figured out that we don't use our old names around here. Everyone gets a code name, like me and Argus."

"Jason," she said, realization dawning. "The leader of the Argonauts?"

"You know Greek mythology?"

"I read Percy Jackson in sixth grade."

He laughed lightly. "What those books don't mention is that Jason was considered a fanatic in his time—an acolyte of the impossible, chasing the mythical Golden Fleece. He was young, too, which made it easier for those in power to dismiss him. The older generation's always complacent. They're too beholden to their own ways to perceive the truth, much less to fight for it."

There was a silence as Michelle tried to think how to respond to that. Probably Jason didn't want a response; clearly enough, what others thought about his beliefs wasn't of much interest to him. She did wonder, though: if this was the Argo and he was its captain, what was his Golden Fleece?

"So, Michelle for now," he resumed after a moment, "tell me about yourself. Tell me how you survived."

Carefully, as carefully as she could in response to a direct question, she told him her story. About the deer, her car, the yellow fire. Everything she related was technically true, though some of it skirted the line between evasion and outright falsehood. She said nothing about her lost phone, reasoning that he must have figured out she had no way of contacting anyone outside the camp, or if he didn't, he could easily learn the truth. She left Rosie and her parents out of it altogether, the doubts she'd felt all day and the plans she'd begun to formulate warning her that she should avoid letting him see how anxious she was to search for her family. Fortunately, he didn't ask questions about her age or home life. He leaned back in the creaky chair with his fingers steepled under his nose, his eyes never leaving hers. When she told him about her decision to head away from the valley and into the woods, he nodded.

"Good instincts," he said. "From what we know, the formerly inhabited parts of this region are no longer fit for human life."

Michelle's heart quailed when he said that, but she did her best to hide her emotions. "Do you know what happened?"

"Not with certainty. We've gathered intelligence via shortwave, and it seems there was an assault of regional or possibly national scope on human population centers, using unconventional weapons we can't yet identify. We have no reliable casualty estimates, but I'd say it's unlikely there are many of your kind left."

Sorrow swelled in Michelle's chest, and she closed her eyes for a second, as if she could block out the world around her. The way Jason said *your kind* made her feel as if he considered her to belong to another species. It didn't sound as if he mourned the devastation he was reporting. It sounded as if he'd been waiting for it to happen, and was pleased to find his prediction confirmed.

"I thought it might be a meteor," she said.

"You mean an asteroid," Jason corrected. "That doesn't fit the available information. An asteroid strike would have been followed by major environmental impacts—tsunamis, earthquakes, volcanic eruptions. And it wouldn't have caused the decay we've seen in the woods just beyond the Argo, not this quickly. This was an assault *on* man, *by* man."

"But why would anyone … ?"

He shrugged in a way that Michelle found particularly heartless. "Why does anyone launch such an attack? Why does our own government stockpile weapons of mass destruction—nerve gas, biological agents—if it doesn't plan to use them someday? And who does it have in mind as its target?"

Michelle tried to respond, but found herself too stunned to say anything. It didn't matter, because Jason talked on.

"This isn't new," he said. "Governments have been waging war against their own people for millennia. Look at Ancient Greece and Rome, the British Empire, the Soviet Union. And every time it happens, there's a pirate ship like the Argo, sailing just beyond reach of the powers that be, trying to warn people before it's too late. But people don't listen, do they?"

"How … " Michelle began, and then cleared her throat. "How do you know all this?"

He gestured to the bookshelves. "I'm a historian. Or was." He laughed humorlessly. "Everything's in the past tense now. Guess it's my time at last."

He fell silent while Michelle's eyes scanned the titles on his shelves. She hadn't read any of them, but most seemed to be about the end of societies. *The Rise and Fall of the Third Reich. The Last Days of Pompeii. Civilization and Its Discontents. The Decline and Fall of the Roman Empire. The War of the Worlds. The Ghost-Dance Religion and Wounded Knee.* Jason let her look as long as she wanted, but eventually, her eyes blurred and her head ached from reading the endless litany of death and doom.

She forced herself to ask another question. "Do you think there will be any more attacks?"

"There's not a doubt in my mind," Jason answered instantly. "That's why I've drawn in my forces, and it's why I'm so glad we came across you. It's not safe out there, for you or for anyone. Whoever did this will have figured out by now that there are survivors, which means they'll be conducting mop-up operations in the coming weeks, targeting any stragglers they can find. Ordinarily, under those circumstances, I'd be reluctant to take in someone I don't know. I've already shown you more of the Argo than anyone from the outside has seen in years, and there are some in my camp who I'm sure are none too happy about that."

Michelle heard the threat in his words, and thought about Arachne's sullen glare.

"But," Jason went on, "I like you, Michelle. I wouldn't have risked bringing you here if I didn't. And I'm willing to place you under my protection, if you're willing to commit yourself to the only safe place we know for sure we have left."

He fixed her with his pale blue eyes. There was nothing inappropriate in his gaze, nothing that seemed to imply she owed him her body in return for his protection. Still, she realized that this was the moment he'd been building toward all along, the reason he'd rescued her and brought her here. Though she trembled at the words she was about to say, she knew she had to say them. "You'll need help defending your camp. Especially with what happened to Caeneus and the others."

He nodded gravely, though his mouth quirked in a slight smile.

"I can run," she said. "I ran a 52.83 in the 400 meters my sophomore year. That's a ... that *was* a state record."

"Yes," he mused, leaning farther back in his chair. "I've seen you run."

"I could be a messenger. Or a scout. In exchange for your ... protection."

He leaned forward abruptly, his eyes locked on hers. "Think carefully about what you're offering, Michelle. Out there, you're either predator or prey. In light of recent events, there are sure to be ... *lone wolves*, let's call them: people with nothing to lose and nothing to fear, scouring the ruins for whatever scraps they can find. Savages like Caeneus who won't think twice about violating anyone they see as weak or vulnerable."

Looking into Jason's eyes, Michelle realized what had struck her as strange before, and she drew an inward sigh of relief at her decision not to tell him anything about her family. For some reason, the survivalist leader had distrusted Caeneus and his companions, and so he'd sent them into the woods to see how they'd act once they believed they were beyond his reach. That was why he and his lieutenant had tracked the three hunters, and why Arachne had been placed on high alert. Jason might have killed the three by himself if the encounter with Michelle hadn't given him a better opportunity: to exhibit Caeneus and his crew as a public example for the rest of the camp, while at the same time luring a new and much younger recruit to his cause. Would the three hunters ever get out of the box alive? Or would their lifeless bodies be found one morning, their deaths apparently at their own hands?

Michelle knew at last what dangerous company she'd fallen into, what a dangerous game she was playing. She needed Jason's aid, there was no doubt about that. She lacked the ability to survive in the woods under the best of circumstances, much less if the world had changed as radically as he said. With a feeling of embarrassment mingled with grief, she remembered the Simmons clan's pathetic charades at roughing it, which involved cozy cabins and frequent drives to the camp store for hot dogs and marshmallows. If Jason was willing to teach her the skills she needed—and who better to teach her those skills than the captain of a group of wilderness survivalists?—then in time, she could attempt to slip away from the Argo and set out for home in search of anyone who remained. But while planning her escape, she would have to play along with his rules to earn his trust, and make sure he saw her as a better investment than Caeneus and his men.

She held Jason's eyes. "I'll work hard for you. And for

the Argo."

He leaned back in his chair. "That's all I ask. Now, if you don't mind, there's one more thing I'd like to take care of."

Michelle stiffened, alert for danger. But Jason simply stood and went to his bookcase, returning with a medical kit from which he extracted a tiny needle, the kind doctors use for finger sticks. Coming around the desk, he sat and reached for her hand.

"This won't hurt," he said. "Circe—that's our camp doctor—can fix you up with any necessary vaccinations later tonight. I'd like to get a blood sample, though. For identification purposes."

That sounded strange to Michelle—why couldn't the camp doctor take her blood?—but she knew she couldn't refuse. She held out her index finger and felt the quick bee-sting as Jason pressed the needle into the fleshy tip. A spot of blood bloomed; he collected it on a glass slide and turned away to store it in his kit. Michelle accepted the gauze pad he offered and pinched it between her thumb and forefinger.

"All done," Jason said. "You ready to go?"

She rose, and he led her to the door, gesturing for her to exit ahead of him. They entered the darkened hall, Jason following silently. Before they left the building, he paused.

"Let me ask you one more question," he said. "When you climbed down into that gorge, how did you know you wouldn't fall?"

So she was right: he'd been tracking Caeneus—and her—all along. "I didn't know," she said honestly. "But I was dying of thirst, and I figured I'd rather die trying to live."

Jason smiled broadly.

"Then you were already thinking like one of us." He held

out a hand for her to precede him into the night. "I'll have you assigned to the women's quarters. Once you're settled in, we can start your training."

Chapter 4

Michelle crept through the woods, her bow held before her.

She walked silently, stepping from heel to toe, keeping her knees loose and hips wide to distribute her weight. Forest undergrowth provided cover as she eased across the ridge to take up her position behind the trunk of an elm tree. She cocked an ear to listen, felt the wind fluttering on her cheek. Her right thumb brushed in anticipation against the feathers of the arrow she'd drawn to the bowstring. Leaning out, she spied into the hollow below.

Jason was there, facing away from her.

She laughed to herself when she saw how exposed he was, how he'd failed to conceal himself behind trees or ground cover. *Careless, careless.* His back presented a perfect target. She mentally drew an x where the arrow would go in, where it would do the most damage, puncturing a lung or skewering his heart. With a shallow intake of breath, she lifted the bow, brought the fletching of the arrow to her cheek, and sighted along the shaft, her fingers itching for the release.

Who's the vulnerable one now? she thought, just as she prepared to let the arrow fly.

His voice floated up to her. "You're going to have to do

a lot better than that if you want to save your skin."

Michelle let out a hard breath of frustration, simultaneously lowering the arrow from her pretended target. Jason loped up the hill toward her.

"I heard you rustling the bushes," he said. "Making enough noise to wake the dead, as usual."

Michelle ran a hand through her close-cropped hair. "Was it that bad?"

"The enemy would have had you in his crosshairs before you took three steps. You were so busy trying to judge your angle of approach, you failed to keep cover the way I showed you."

She returned the arrow to its quiver, then looped the bow over her back. "This is impossible. Every time I think I'm getting the hang of it … "

"That's your problem right there," Jason said. "Overthinking. It's your old self getting in the way, the girl who was always worried about pleasing some authority figure or following some arbitrary rule. You have to let that girl go. Otherwise, the enemy's going to be collecting your scalp as a trophy."

He handed her a piece of his omnipresent homemade turkey jerky, and they headed back to camp in the stark light of mid-afternoon. She was silent while she chewed the tough, stringy meat, but inside she was simmering at the way he baited her. *The good girl*, he taunted. *The dutiful daughter.* She hadn't said a word to him about her family in the three weeks since she'd joined the Argo, but he evidently thought it was his job to wean her from home, to remake her in the image of his favorite soldier, the implacable Arachne. He never missed a chance to remind her how dangerous the world was, how easy it was to die. How good girls like her were walking invitations to be preyed upon by those who lay in wait just beyond the Argo's borders, those who'd unleashed the yellow fire on the world. On and on he'd talk into the dying light of evening, until he finally released her to another fitful night's sleep and another repetition of the same performance the following day.

She couldn't figure him out. It was obvious he was trying to scare her, to keep her from questioning the need for his protection. But if he was so sure she'd been a sheltered princess all her life, did he really think he could turn her into an ice-veined assassin in such a short time? It made her wonder if he genuinely believed the outside world was as bad as he said, or if he was only using that story on her and the others to make them feel cut off from life beyond the Argo. There'd been no attacks on the camp since she arrived, no reports from his scouts of the roving squads of hit-men he'd told them they'd encounter. The woods in the vicinity of the Argo had remained as vibrant as ever, even filling with birdsong each morning. So was he lying to everyone, keeping them close to camp so they'd never learn the truth? Or was she lying to herself, holding onto the hope that the yellow fire had been nothing more than a bad environmental accident and that the people she loved were still out there, waiting for her to return?

Ugh. She really *was* the girl Jason said she was. He could read her like one of his fat, dog-eared books, while he remained almost a complete enigma to her.

That first night, after their meeting in his office, Jason had escorted her across the darkened campground to the women's quarters and introduced her to its inhabitants via their code names: Medea, Calypso, and a blur of others he rattled off too fast for her to remember. He didn't tell them her name, and she sensed that she shouldn't volunteer it. Everyone was much older than Michelle, except for identical twin sisters who even longtime residents must have had trouble telling apart, since they had nametags stitched to their breast pockets: Nausikaa and Aristodeme, stick-thin tweens with pasty skin and hollow eyes who never spoke a word and didn't seem to belong to any of the adults. The ten or so women crowded around her as if she were some kind of freakish animal they'd never seen before, but no one said much of anything or offered to make her feel comfortable until the camp doctor, Circe, returned an hour later from her scheduled meeting with Jason. A small, dark-skinned African American woman, she was accompanied by a little girl she introduced as her daughter Tyris, though to Michelle, Circe looked old enough to be the girl's grandmother. Tyris, whose lighter skin and reddish braids made Michelle wonder who her father was, clung to her mother's side while Circe prepared the shots Jason had promised she'd administer: tetanus and MMR boosters, something for either malaria or yellow fever—Michelle wasn't sure which—and an incredibly painful rabies shot that Circe warned her was only the first of three. Then the camp doctor led her to the cold-water showers behind the sleeping quarters and gave her a nubby piece of soap that smelled like tallow and rubbed like sandpaper. After Michelle had washed off the day's grime—along with a fair amount of her skin—she wrapped a coarse towel around her chest and was subjected to the ministrations of Arachne, who'd been relieved from sentry duty just in time to cut the newcomer's hair. Michelle's eyes watered and she nearly cried out as the woman yanked and hacked, her wiry arms' strength matched only by her gift for inflicting pain. When she was done and Michelle got a look at herself in the beaten piece of tin that served as a mirror, she felt like crying again. Arachne had snipped her hair almost all the way down to the scalp. Seeing her expression, Circe spoke to her in a soft voice.

"Easier to manage. And fewer lice." That didn't make Michelle feel any better, but she gave the woman a smile for trying.

The buzz cut wasn't the end of her ordeal. Arachne handed her a camouflage uniform at least a size too big for her and a roughed-up pair of hiking boots, and when she looked in the mirror a second time, Michelle gasped at the transformation: this bald-headed waif in the baggy unisex jacket and pants couldn't possibly be the girl who'd had a walk-in closet full of outfits to choose from for her birthday party just a day ago. Studying the faces of the women and girls in the harsh light of the bedroom's single overhead bulb, she thought they looked more like concentration camp survivors than anything else, and a fresh wave of sorrow rose in her chest to realize she had become one of them. But the women showed no pity for themselves and—with the possible exception of Circe—no compassion for her, so she forced the feeling down, reminding herself that she'd have to appear a stoical if not enthusiastic convert if she was to have any hope of carrying out her plan.

Exhausted and emotionally drained as she was that first night, it took a long time before she fell into a restless sleep on one of the room's narrow, scratchy bunks. She dreamed it was the day of her party, and everyone was there: her parents,

Rosie, her aunt and uncle and cousin, Janine and Greg, even Mark. They all looked at her in reproach, but when she asked them what she'd done, no one would answer, unless Janine's spiteful sneer was an answer. Michelle glanced at what she was wearing and realized it wasn't her party dress but the drab, shapeless camouflage uniform. She tried to explain, but everyone turned from her and went back to the party. Then the dining room with its crystal and streamers and balloons was consumed in yellow fire, and all the bodies sloughed into ash, Rosie's last of all. When the light streaming through the cabin's sole window told her she was awake, she felt as guilty as she had in the dream.

A woman stood by her bed. Much as Michelle wanted to believe it was her mother, the morning light showed her that it was the small figure of Circe.

"You ready?" the woman asked.

Her deep eyes watched while Michelle rose and tried to clear away the cobwebs. Then, with Tyris holding her mother's hand and skipping along beside them, they took a tour of camp in the shadowed morning light.

The Argo, Michelle discovered, was designed much less haphazardly than it first appeared. Windows provided an unobstructed view of the surrounding area, while buildings were placed at strategic angles to baffle would-be intruders and to provide cover for defenders. There were booby-traps throughout the compound, some of which—like the deep, brush-covered pit in front of Jason's headquarters—were fixed in place, while others—like the garrotes and trip-wires Circe pointed out as they moved from building to building— were portable. The doctor explained that Michelle wouldn't be allowed to walk around camp without a guide until she committed the rotation to heart. When Michelle asked if she could see the underground storage bunkers for food, arms, and other supplies, Circe responded that those were forbidden to anyone but the camp's leadership, with one exception: if an invading force entered the compound, the entire population of the Argo would be moved to the sublevel for a last-ditch defense.

Jason, Michelle realized, trusted her only as much as he trusted anyone: warily, and with plenty of conditions. She'd have to be careful not only around him, but around any of the possible spies—Arachne got her top vote—who'd be happy to report any suspicious behavior by the camp's newest member.

Circe, though, seemed like someone she could possibly trust. The woman was as taciturn as her daughter was giddy, but she wasn't hostile or unkind; if you pressed her, her clipped monosyllables would sometimes turn into complete sentences. Michelle learned that in addition to being the camp's physician, she was the nominal leader of the women's quarters, which made her third-in-command behind Jason and Argus. Her voice lightened and her face became less guarded when Michelle asked her how old Tyris was.

"Just turned five," she said, affectionately stroking the little girl's pigtails. "She's a handful, but then, she keeps me young."

Tyris, oblivious to both the compliment and the reproof, hummed contentedly while she picked flowers by the bank of the river.

Michelle knew she couldn't ask anything too personal, so she tried to play it safe. "How long have you lived here?"

"Six years," Circe answered. "Hard to believe."

"And Jason ... "

"He built the Argo at the bend of this stream ten years ago. Named it the Lethe to fit the theme. Then, once word got out, the rest of us came."

Michelle did a quick calculation, wondering if Jason had been a teenager when he'd founded the Argo. If so, where had he gotten the money to buy and build on the land? Or when he'd told her he owned it, was he using that term loosely, claiming squatter's rights on this out-of-the-way plot of wilderness?

"What about the twins?" she asked. "Did they come at the same time as you?"

Circe's eyes flickered with a hint of suspicion, but she answered. "No, they came later. We're always ready to welcome those who need our help. Those who don't have anywhere else to go."

Michelle didn't challenge this rosy assessment of the Argo's hospitality. "Did you live near here before?"

All at once, a door slammed shut in Circe's face. She looked at Michelle with pursed lips.

"It's best not to dwell on the past," the doctor said. "What's done is done. Tyris!" She glared at her daughter, who'd muddied her jumper squatting by the Lethe. "How many times do I have to tell you?"

Michelle's face burned as if *she* were the one being reprimanded. She offered to help Circe with Tyris, but the doctor politely declined. As she led the little girl back to the women's quarters, she spoke to Michelle over her shoulder.

"You're free to stay outside if you like," she said. "Just don't go wandering. Jason will be by soon to pick you up."

"Jason?"

"To start your training," Circe said, then had to race to catch up with Tyris before the imp tracked mud all over the floor of the women's quarters.

Michelle sat on the grass, mentally kicking herself for her mistake. It had seemed such an innocent question, such a natural part of the conversation to ask someone where she was from, but apparently, that was one of the unwritten prohibitions of this place. The Lethe, she recalled, was the river of forgetfulness that dead souls passed over when they entered the underworld. Maybe that was the whole point of the Argo, the promise Jason had made to its members: that whatever had led them to drop out of society and retreat into the woods, they could start fresh here, without having to deal with outsiders and all their prying questions. And like an idiot, she'd gone and broken that promise with the one person she thought might turn out to be a friend, or at least a sympathetic ear.

Well, so much for that, she thought. From now on, she'd treat everyone as a blank slate and a potential enemy. If the cost of learning this lesson was alienating someone who might have become an ally, she supposed it could have been worse. She could have made a similar mistake with Arachne, and then the sentry, rather than simply looking askance at her, would have hauled her in front of Jason and demanded to know why the new girl was sticking her nose into other people's business.

When Jason himself arrived a few minutes later, wearing the black commander's jacket he'd lent her the night before, Michelle put on the blandest expression she was capable of, hopped up from the bank, and followed him without a word of curiosity about where they were going.

As it turned out, they weren't going far, at least not on that first day. Essentially, he gave her an expanded tour of the campgrounds, taking her beyond the inhabited area to the outskirts. He led her down the bank of the Lethe to show her the clearing where he'd planted the solar farm, then walked her to the other extreme of his property to point out the sentries' positions. She discovered that though the pass at the headlands was the only way to reach the Argo without crossing the Lethe, the entire forest surrounding the camp was patrolled by sentries, the majority of Jason's troops serving in that role. Arachne, with her brutally tough body and matching mind, was the master of the patrols, and based on her own brief encounter with the woman, Michelle had no doubt she kept her minions in line through a brand of discipline verging on terror. Given Arachne's duties, it was Argus who accompanied Jason most often when he had to leave camp. Between his faithful sentries and his burly deputy, Michelle realized why Jason seemed so confident in his position. Only a fool like Caeneus—and even he wouldn't have been foolish enough to defy orders if he'd known he was being watched—would think of challenging the captain's authority.

Jason finished the tour by steering her past the silent box. The smell was unbearable even from the outside.

"As you can see, the Argo is strong," he said, fixing her with his eerie blue eyes while she breathed shallowly against the stench. "But it's only as strong as its weakest link. Our scouts are farthest from home base, which means they're closest to temptation. Sometimes they get unhealthy ideas. It's my job to root out those ideas before they have a chance to infect the Argo as a whole."

She nodded, saying nothing. How much could those eyes of his see?

"Be ready for me tomorrow," he said when he dropped her off at the women's barracks. "First thing."

She watched him stroll toward headquarters. *Message received*, she thought. The point of this initial tour had clearly been to impress her with the Argo's tight security and equally tight restrictions on its border troops. Had Caeneus tried to betray the Argo, to reveal its location or its secrets? If so, the punishment of him and his accomplices might be intended as a lesson for the camp as a whole—but it was specially directed at her, and it clung to her as surely as the stink she feared she'd never be able to wash from her body.

After that first day, Jason must have felt his point had been made, because he didn't waste time repeating it. Instead, he focused on survival skills: tracking, shelter, first aid, and much, much more. His relatively young age belied his experience as a woodsman; he knew everything there was to know about getting by in the wild, from orienting oneself by sunlight and shadow to obtaining water in ways Michelle never would have thought of, like wrapping branches in plastic to encourage condensation. "Especially useful for dry camping," he told her, explaining that you couldn't always count on finding a potable water source. He showed her which plants and roots were edible, which were poisonous, which were useful to supplement the medical kit he always carried with him. He explained the use of iodine tablets to disinfect water, the method to prepare a campfire so it wouldn't smoke, the way to make fire if you were out of matches or flint. Using his walkie-talkie—he didn't allow cell phones in camp, claiming that they could easily be traced or hacked—he reviewed the coordinates that his troops called in from the field to notify camp of their position. Michelle noticed, but as usual said nothing, that he never referred to any location by a name she might recognize; it was all alphanumeric code, which she devoted herself to memorizing but had little faith she'd find useful beyond the Argo. She wouldn't call Jason a patient teacher; he was demanding and short-tempered, the nice-guy façade he'd presented on the day he recruited her giving way to the drill sergeant intent on breaking down a new conscript and winning her over to his way of thinking. At the end of each day, her head was bursting with information, which she recited to herself over and over as she lay fully clothed in her lonely bunk in the women's quarters. She had nothing else to do except listen to Circe read to Tyris, and that only made her pinch her eyes closed against the tears that formed when she remembered story time from years ago with her mom and Rosie.

In their second week together, Jason surprised her by presenting her with a bow and arrows, which he confessed was his weapon of choice over a rifle. "Though I prefer close-quarters fighting most of all," he said with a disturbing grin, his fingers resting on the sheathed knife at his belt. The unexpected gift led to the most awkward moment she'd shared with him, as he introduced her to archery by circling his arm around her, steadying her hand on the bow, and instructing her in a low voice, his breath in her ear. "Nice and easy," he said, and she could barely restrain the shudder that passed through her chest. Thankfully, that scene never repeated itself—because, to her complete astonishment, she showed an instant knack for the bow. She could nock an arrow, sight, and release almost as quickly as he could, and her accuracy, especially over distance, rivaled his as well. He introduced her to the basics of tracking by prints and scat and signs in the brush, and she was pleased to discover that she was equally adept at that skill set. She was less thrilled when her tracking ability enabled her to bring down her first kill, a young buck. The fact that it was actually the second deer she'd killed was a painful reminder of the chain of events that had marooned her here. Jason showed her how to skin the carcass, a process that left her gasping with revulsion, but at least she didn't throw up. He built a campfire while she disposed of the entrails in a pit he'd showed her how to dig, and when she returned after repeatedly washing her hands in the Lethe, he said he had another surprise for her.

"What is it?" she asked dubiously.

"Close your eyes."

She stiffened, but did as he said. He popped something hot and salty and metallic-tasting between her lips. When she bit down, there was a crunch and then a gush of scalding fluid down her throat.

"Fried blood," he said when she opened her watering eyes. "Quick source of nutrients if you're on the move and don't have time to cook the meat."

Michelle nodded, but all she could think was, *A week ago, I couldn't stand the sight of blood. Now I'm letting some guy turn me into a vampire.* Like so many things in recent days, the thought made her heart heavy with grief and shame.

That evening, Jason came to the women's quarters to announce that Michelle had earned her camp alias: Diana, the Huntress.

"Properly, it should be Artemis," he said. "But I thought you'd appreciate something a little less foreign."

For the first time since she arrived, the women showed real interest in her, clustering around her and congratulating her on her new name, which they insisted was Jason's way of bestowing a unique honor on her. She smiled at them, thinking, *You don't even know my real name.* But she went to bed feeling a degree of quiet satisfaction that she'd earned their respect.

She'd discovered in the time she'd been here that the camp women weren't anything like her first impression of them. Their bodies might be wiry, but that only meant there wasn't an ounce of needless fat on them; their eyes might seem sunken under the shadow of their brows, but—with the exception of the blank-faced Nausikaa and Aristodeme—those eyes were vigilant and intense. When she looked into their eyes, she felt a flush of humiliation for the scene that had brought her under Jason's wing; any of the women would have disdained to run from Caeneus when they could have stood their ground to fight. Whatever had brought these Amazons to Jason's camp, they'd been sculpted by their experiences until they were no less strong, tough, or capable than their leader.

And now I'm truly one of them, she thought. The prospect of becoming as lethal as Arachne, or as seemingly dead to the world as the twins, frightened and saddened her. But if that's what it took to achieve her ultimate goal, so be it.

The third week of training put her resolution to the test, as Jason shifted from hunting to what he called, without the slightest trace of irony, "war games." His mantra for the week was simple: "Out here, it's kill or be killed." Goddess of the Hunt or not, she found herself on the receiving end every single time. Her running prowess, which had impressed Jason enough to get her in the door, turned out to be pretty much a non-factor when facing an antagonist intent on taking your life; she'd been "killed" by arrow, snare, deadfall, and numerous other devices during the six days they'd been playing. Luckily, Jason had warned her each time just before she walked into his very real ambushes—but the price of her life was even greater disgrace, since it proved that he could not only set traps she was too stupid not to blunder into, but could keep watch on her without her knowing he was there. As if that weren't bad enough, there was the inevitable, unvarying lecture that followed: she was too distracted, too tentative, too squeamish to strike the killing blow. Hunting animals was easy, he said. With rare exceptions, they weren't trying to hunt you. Hunting humans was something else altogether.

"You think I've taught you how to survive in the wilderness," he said as they headed home after today's debacle. "I haven't taught you anything except a few measly parlor tricks, Diana."

My name is Michelle, she thought, feeling very much like a pouty child.

"The wilderness is no place for weaklings," he continued. "A seasoned adversary won't hesitate for a moment to use your doubts to his advantage. That's why you have to take control. To become the hunter, not the hunted."

You've been doing this for years, Michelle said to herself as she tried to match his silent, confident strides. *I've only been doing it for three weeks.* But that didn't help, as it merely reminded her how far she was from leaving the Argo and its captain behind.

"I've told you I won't let anyone jeopardize what I've

fought so hard to build," his words intruded on her thoughts. "So tomorrow, I expect you to hunt me for real. Put an arrow in my chest if you can. If you're too soft to do that, how will you be able to pull the trigger when it really counts?"

She froze, unsure if he meant that tomorrow *he* was going to hunt *her* for real, too. He couldn't mean that, could he? You didn't train your troops by killing them, did you?

Did you?

Thus far, her fears about the extremes of Jason's discipline hadn't been fulfilled. The first two hunters had emerged from the box after a week, pale and submissive as they took up their new full-time job of emptying the latrines. Their ringleader followed on schedule, looking as if he'd spent two years in confinement instead of two weeks: his skin was gray, his hands shook, and he walked with shoulders stooped, dragging one leg behind him. But he'd been left alive—probably as an example, but still, alive. After trying to desert camp, maybe even plotting to betray the Argo's leader, Michelle knew that he could have suffered a much worse penalty. But then, wasn't she itching to do the exact same thing—to leave the Argo as soon as she felt comfortable enough in the woods to do so?

"Diana!"

Michelle startled out of her reverie at the whispered warning and the sight of Jason's uplifted right hand. She stopped instantly and directed her attention ahead, following his line of vision. The afternoon sunlight fell at an oblique angle through the canopy, sharpening the shadows thrown by trees and brush. Though she couldn't make anything out through the heavy undergrowth forty paces ahead, she heard the rustling and saw the random movement of branches that said some creature was foraging there. From the sound of it, it had to be something big. She nodded as Jason tapped two fingers against his temple in his sign for a deer's antlers. She unstrapped her bow from her shoulder and reached for an arrow, hoping against hope that if she showed sufficient avidity in killing the deer, the captain of the Argo might put aside his planned activity for tomorrow.

Then Jason made another signal, a slashing motion parallel to the ground, and Michelle's heart thumped as hard as it had in her flight from the hunters. The canceling gesture was unmistakable; it was no deer up ahead. Given the size, it could only be one thing.

A human being.

Not one of the regulars from camp. No one came or went from the Argo without its leader's approval, and Jason had told her specifically that he hadn't cleared anyone but her for field exercises today. The two of them were much too far from camp for it to be one of the sentries. And Jason wasn't acting as if the concealed person was friendly; he was fitting an arrow to the string of his bow, at the same time signaling Michelle with a toss of his head to fan left and create a secondary position. She obeyed, her heart racing without pause. He'd just been giving her a lesson on survival against an unknown adversary. Would she have to stand here and watch him send a deadly arrow through a person's throat?

Or, worse, would he demand that *she* fire the shot?

"Show yourself!" Jason shouted, and Michelle flinched at the bark of his voice in the quiet woods. "There are two of us, both armed. Throw down your weapons and come out with your hands up!"

"Don't shoot!" a cry came from the bushes. The voice

76

was husky and weak, and it was followed a moment later by its owner.

He rose from the underbrush, hands held high: a painfully thin man with hair that would have been black if it hadn't been caked in gray dust. His face was covered by several weeks' worth of unruly beard; his eyes, even from this distance, were noticeably bloodshot. His clothes, consisting of nothing but black sweatpants and sweatshirt with a red design printed across the chest, were torn and soiled, and seemed to hang from his body like a scarecrow's suit. To Michelle's eye, he looked like someone who had barely eaten—or slept—in the time since the night of the yellow fire.

He took a wobbly step from his hiding place, and then he fell.

"Diana!" Jason shouted an admonition, but she'd already dropped her bow and sprung to the fallen man's side.

She knelt beside him, fearful of harming him further with her touch. His appearance was even more gruesome than it had seemed from a distance: his face was emaciated, his lips cracked and covered with sores, his color a shocking grayish yellow. He trembled violently, his eyes rolling up into their sockets while cords bulged from his scrawny neck. His bare feet were a mass of bleeding abscesses; why he would be out in the woods without shoes puzzled her until she realized he'd probably been chewing the leather for food. Though starvation and exhaustion had hollowed his body and aged his face unnaturally, Michelle realized with a shock that he wasn't much older than her.

A survivor, she thought. If this boy had survived, then others must have, too. But if their condition was anything like his, they wouldn't survive much longer. And if he died, she might never discover what was happening beyond the Argo.

Jason knelt by her side, leaning close to the boy. He'd discarded his bow and now gripped his hunting knife. Before Michelle could ask what he was doing, he touched the tip of the knife to the boy's bruised and lacerated feet, then even more bizarrely, brought the bloodied point to his lips. With an odd, strained glance at Michelle, he pulled the walkie-talkie from his belt and spoke in a breathless whisper she'd never heard from him.

"Mayday, mayday, mayday. We have located a survivor. Condition critical. Repeat: condition critical. Dispatch emergency team at once. Transmitting Maidenhead coordinates as follows ... "

Michelle gripped the boy's hand, feeling the heat of the fever that raged beneath his clammy skin, and prayed for him to hold on.

Chapter 5

Circe answered Jason's summons within forty-five minutes, bringing two assistants plus medical supplies and a stretcher.

To Michelle's surprise, Tyris tagged along with her mother. The little girl watched, wide-eyed, as Circe assessed the unconscious boy's condition then directed the others to hoist him onto the stretcher while she started an IV. His breathing remained shallow and irregular, his eyes closed and his teeth chattering with fever.

While Circe worked, Jason rummaged through the bushes where the boy had been hiding and emerged with a tattered backpack. That, plus the red design across his sweatshirt, made Michelle wonder if he was a college student, but his clothing was too filthy for her to read what the shirt said.

"Was he alone?" Circe asked.

"So far as we know," Jason answered.

"I'm giving him fluids," Circe said. "But we need to get him to the infirmary."

Michelle held the boy's hand and ran alongside the stretcher as they hurried to camp. She had no idea if her presence comforted him or if he was even aware of it, but with his muscles as rigid as they were, she couldn't have pried her hand free if she'd wanted to.

The infirmary building, she was relieved to find, was well stocked with supplies, including bandages, IV fluids, antibiotics, and a storage freezer with blood for transfusions. Michelle waited outside while Circe and Jason switched the boy's filthy clothes for a clean camouflage uniform, then Circe invited her back in while Jason headed off to alert Argus. Tyris had remained in the room the whole time, the little girl watching her mother work with the same intensity Michelle showed.

"Where did you learn ... " Michelle started to ask Circe, before she remembered that discussing the past was taboo.

But Circe answered. "I was a trauma surgeon," she said as she switched the boy's IV. "For a time."

Michelle would have loved to ask how a surgeon became a backwoods survivalist, but she didn't want to distract Circe while she was working, plus she assumed the woman wouldn't go into details. Right at that moment, the boy started thrashing again, which forced Michelle to hold him down while Circe strapped his wrists to the bedrails.

"What's wrong with him?" Michelle asked once they'd secured him.

"Severe malnutrition and dehydration, to begin with. Plus I suspect he's dealing with sepsis."

"With what?"

"A blood infection." Circe tested the boy's bonds. "Probably due to the condition of his feet."

"Can he die from that?"

"Without proper treatment, absolutely. I've started IV antibiotics, but there's not much else I can do. The next few hours will determine whether he pulls through or not."

She allowed Michelle to watch for a few more minutes, then shooed her out the door. Tyris stayed with her mother, a silent but attentive observer. Michelle looked back at the boy before she left, wondering whether he had the strength to fight the infection consuming his blood. His drawn features and sickly color didn't give her much hope.

Exiting the sick room, Michelle discovered that the waiting area was crowded with onlookers, at least half the members of the camp having broken regulations to hear the news about the latest arrival.

"How is he?" Calypso asked her at once.

"Alive," Michelle answered. "But just barely."

A murmur passed through the crowd.

"And do we know *who* he is?" Calypso pressed.

Michelle shook her head. "He's unconscious. He couldn't tell us anything."

"Not even where he's from?"

"Nothing." She looked at the faces of the men and women in the room, taken aback that they'd developed such an intense interest in a stranger's past. Not that she wasn't dying to know who the boy was, but the one time she'd inquired about an Argonaut's upbringing, she'd earned nothing but silence and suspicion.

Michelle was spared further inquiries when Jason entered the room, Argus one step behind. The camp members saluted stiffly, probably fearing their leader's reaction to them shirking their assignments. Ignoring the formalities, Jason fixed them with a cold stare. "Don't you people have someplace to be?"

With halting movements but without a murmur of

dissent, the others filed from the room. Michelle was on her way out as well when Jason held up a hand to stop her.

"Wait here." He entered the back room where Circe remained with her daughter and patient.

Michelle took a seat beside Argus, who occupied two of the three folding cane chairs in the waiting area. She pressed her fingers against her temples and tried to massage away the headache she'd become aware of after the excitement had died down. Like the others, she found herself wondering where the boy had come from, what had happened to him. Even more, she found herself automatically connecting his fate to her own. If he regained consciousness and confirmed Jason's worst prediction about the state of the outside world, she'd be doomed to remain with the Argo for the rest of her life. If he brought news of survival beyond the yellow fire, was there another possibility for her future?

A horrifying thought struck her. If the boy's story *did* contradict Jason's, would the leader of the Argo allow that report to get out?

She was about to stand and go to the door in hopes of learning what was taking Jason so long when Argus spoke. "Don't worry. Circe's handled situations like this before."

Michelle smiled weakly at him. "When?"

"A couple of years ago. The twins came to us as runaways. From a sex trafficker, Jason thinks. They were in pretty bad shape, low blood count, PTSD, all the rest of it, but Circe got them fixed up."

Michelle nodded. The frail, stunned silence of Nausikaa and Aristodeme now made sense to her. "Can I ask you something?"

"Sure."

"Why did Calypso want to know where that boy's from?"

Argus shrugged, his shoulder brushing against hers. "Jason has spent the past three weeks monitoring the shortwave, trying to determine who's responsible for the attacks. He's pretty confident it was our own government, but some of the chatter is pointing the finger at foreigners. If a non-U.S. national were to show up near one of the targeted areas, that might help resolve the mystery."

It surprised Michelle to learn that Jason was still searching for proof, so she pressed Argus again. "Why does it matter, though? It's not like we can fight a war against whoever did this."

The big man looked at her strangely, and Michelle realized she'd once again said something wrong, though she couldn't figure out what. Jason had consistently spoken of the Argo in defensive terms, as a place where his supporters could maintain a low profile or, failing that, make a last stand. Had he changed his mind—and was that why he'd been getting so exasperated with her failures in the field? Could he be training his army—herself included—to launch an offensive against the enemy?

"I'm sorry," she said at last, not knowing what else to say.

Tension drained from the older man's face and shoulders. "It's all right. But if you want my advice, I'd be careful what I said around Jason. Especially with this new development. For the time being, we have to assume that anyone we encounter is a potential threat."

Including me? Michelle thought. For all his fatherly concern, she was certain that Argus was going to repeat this entire conversation to Jason, and she didn't want to make it worse than it already was. Yet she couldn't help being surprised at the suspicion that had greeted the newest arrival, so different from the more or less bland indifference she'd been shown by everyone with the exception of Arachne. Was there something about the sick boy she'd missed? Or were people getting more and more edgy as time passed and Jason's dire prognostications failed to come true?

Just then the door opened, and Jason stepped into the waiting area. He glanced back at the sick room before closing the door softly and approaching Argus and Michelle. The brawny lieutenant jumped to his feet, and Michelle, with Argus's warning fresh in her mind, followed a second later.

"We need to talk," Jason said. "All of us."

He led them from the infirmary and made his way across camp to headquarters, his hand hovering behind Michelle's back the whole time. Once inside, he turned to the left-hand wing of the building and switched on the light in a windowless room that looked something like pictures Michelle had seen of the old recording studio at her high school, before the primitive equipment was replaced with up-to-date technology. There was a table with two wooden chairs, a microphone, a reel-to-reel tape player, and a radio with the tubes and circuits exposed, plus a machine that Michelle thought might be for tapping out Morse code. Video monitors ringed the walls, each of them showing a black-and-white image from some part of the camp. Closed-circuit TVs, Michelle realized, and she almost laughed that she'd never suspected the means by which Jason kept such careful watch over his followers. Once everyone had crowded inside—not an easy task with all the machinery and Argus's bulk—Jason removed two small objects from his jacket and held them up, one at a time, for Michelle and his second-in-command to see.

"I found these in the boy's backpack," he said. "These, and nothing else."

The first object was a nondescript jar, a little larger than the ones Michelle's mother used to bottle homemade jam, the glass a dark greenish tint. From what she could tell, the jar was empty, and she had a hard time believing it could be much of a clue. Jason held it to the light and turned it, the video monitors reflecting in miniature across its surface, before he set it on the table as if he too had decided it was meaningless.

The second object made an electric spark shoot through Michelle's body.

It was a cell phone.

She stared hungrily at the flat black rectangle in Jason's hand, while thoughts raced through her mind. If she could get her hands on it for just a moment, if she could make a single call …

She shook herself back to reality. Even if Jason and Argus weren't right there, the phone wouldn't respond to her touch. Quickly, she dropped her eyes, hoping Jason hadn't seen her staring. Argus's warning of just minutes ago repeated in her mind's ear, and she berated herself for not learning her lesson after so many near-catastrophes.

"The battery's dead," Jason said. "But maybe you can encourage it to tell us its secrets, Argus."

The big man took the phone, handling it as if it were a snake that might bite. Jason sank into one of the room's chairs, and Michelle was surprised to see how haggard his face looked. He followed Argus's movements with weary eyes while the older man grabbed the room's second chair and squeezed into a corner where the equipment looked more modern, including a laptop, disc player, and LED screen. Argus selected a USB cable to plug the phone into the computer and then crouched over the keyboard, his shoulders blocking Michelle's view while his thick fingers tapped keys so rapidly she wondered if he'd been a programmer in his past life. He worked for at least an hour, with occasional pauses between flurries of activity, while the phone sat lifeless beside his elbow. The air grew stuffy while they waited, and Jason's silence seemed more than normally dangerous, the calm before a storm. At last, Argus turned to Jason and blew out a huge breath.

"It's blocking me pretty good. I worked around the pass code easily enough, but from there on it's a bitch. Sorry, Diana," he said to Michelle with an apologetic grimace. "Not your garden-variety encryption, that's for sure. Could be defense grade. I can keep trying, but there's no guarantee I'll be able to crack it."

"Can you access anything?" the leader of the Argo asked in a strained voice. "Anything at all?"

"The most recent activity's a recording," Argus said. "It's not protected like the rest, which is curious, to say the least. Why he'd go to such lengths to bury everything else while putting a recording right out there doesn't add up."

"Video?" Jason asked.

Argus nodded.

"Play it back."

Argus turned in his chair and operated on the phone for another minute, keys clacking. The LED screen beside the laptop flickered on, glowing solid white. A second later, the white was replaced by a brief burst of static, and then a color image sprang to life. The picture was shaky, as if the person who'd recorded it was unable to hold the phone still. Jason and Michelle leaned forward to watch.

The screen showed a forest setting, and though Michelle couldn't identify it with any degree of precision, the dusty ground and naked trees told her it was closer to the eruption of the yellow fire than their current location. The shot was taken from high ground, surveying the bare forest below. It seemed as if the person holding the phone had hidden behind bushes, because a tangle of leafless branches partially obscured the view. From that limited vantage, Michelle could see three people running through the woods at a distance of maybe seventy meters from the lens. All of them wore sweat suits like the boy's, black with something red written across the chest, as if they were members of a high school or college cross-country team. With the distance and the phone shaking in its owner's hand and the branches blocking her view, Michelle couldn't make out the school name, or even determine if the students were boys or girls. The only thing that was obvious was that this was no pre-season jog through the woods. The three runners scrambled frantically over the ground, nearly falling a number of times before clawing their way back to their feet and continuing their headlong plunge through the trees.

"They look like they're being chased," Michelle said, remembering her own flight from Caeneus.

"By who?" Argus asked.

As if in answer, a fourth figure entered the frame a good hundred meters behind the original three, its body appearing over the rise of a hill. This fourth person was dressed in the same outfit as the others, and from the speed with which he was moving, Michelle assumed he had fallen behind and was trying to catch up to his teammates.

That was her first thought. Her second was that he was moving *too* fast, closing ground between himself and the first three in mere seconds. It was as if he wasn't touching the forest floor at all—as if, though human in shape, he was cruising *above* the earth at the speed of a hawk.

The rearmost runner of the three stumbled again, and the fourth pounced on him.

It happened so fast and the phone shook so violently, Michelle could hardly process what she was seeing—but all of a sudden there were only *three* people on the screen, the two up ahead and the one who'd been chasing them. The person who'd stumbled hadn't dropped beneath the leaves, or rolled down the incline; he was just *gone*. The only thing that marked the place where he'd been—but it was hard to tell with so much grit having been kicked up from the dead leaves—was a cloud of dust that hung in the air at the point of contact. The phone panned to follow the progress of the other two runners, and Michelle wasn't sure the dust cloud had been there at all.

After the brief pause of the attack, the pursuer picked up speed, until he was running with the unearthly semblance of flight once more. While Michelle watched, he closed ground on the pair, and without warning, a second runner vanished.

"What's happening?" she whispered.

Neither of the two men answered. Argus's eyes were glued to the console. Jason had risen from his chair, his face pale and tight, his eyes gleaming like quicksilver as they mirrored the screen's glow.

The final runner had reached a steep hill and was trying to climb. His desperation was obvious even from this distance: he tore at the ground, clutching for roots and rocks in a way that reminded Michelle of her own descent into the ravine. But he wasn't fast enough. The pursuer leaped impossibly high to reach him, and he succumbed in the same way as the first two, blinking out in a cloud of dust that lingered for a second before dissipating. Then there was only the one, who completed the climb like a spider scuttling up its web after devouring a fly. He stopped when he reached the crest of the hill and stood motionless, his head swiveling back and forth as if he were testing the air for the scent of fresh prey. His eyes seemed to fall on the place where the camera was hidden, and he took a step in that direction. The image blurred as if the hand holding it had moved, and Michelle could make out nothing more.

"They must not find me," a voice said. Then the screen went black.

Argus disconnected the phone and turned the computer off. His massive hands, Michelle was amazed to see, were shaking. When he turned to address Jason, she heard the same quaver in his voice.

"What in the name of all that's holy," the big man asked, "was *that?*"

Jason didn't answer him. His eyes were fixed on the empty screen, but it seemed to Michelle that he was looking through the ghostly reflections on its surface for some deeper truth that hadn't been visible in the video.

"This boy," Argus persisted. "When you found him in the forest, did you notice anything peculiar about him?"

Again, Jason ignored his lieutenant's question.

"Did he say anything to you?" Argus tried once more. "Did he do anything out of the ordinary?"

"Enough, Argus," Jason said, but it sounded less like a command than an entreaty. He turned, glancing vacantly around the room as if he wanted to get out but had forgotten the way. Michelle had never seen him appear so uncertain of himself, and she found his inexplicable loss of confidence almost as frightening as the events they'd viewed on the screen.

"What about what he said in the video?" she asked. She didn't like the pinched sound of her voice, but she figured if Jason could show fear, she was allowed to as well. "He said *they must not find me.* Who are *they?*"

"His unit?" Argus asked, looking up at Jason. "He's clearly a deserter."

Jason stood silent. He closed his eyes and rubbed his forehead as if he were in pain.

"We haven't picked up any troop movements in this area," Argus continued, reaching for a rolled piece of paper. His hand stopped short, and he glanced guiltily at Michelle as if he'd almost given something away. "Whatever it was on that boy's phone moved like nothing we've ever seen. Could all of those people have been deserters, and *that* was what was sent to recover them?"

"Not much of a recovery," Jason murmured.

This time, even Argus couldn't seem to think of anything to say.

Michelle looked between the two men's faces: the lowered brow and lined forehead of Argus, his mouth working silently beneath his bushy beard; the almost boyish countenance of Jason, his lean cheeks appearing as drained and sickly as those of the mysterious visitor whose phone lay tantalizingly close at hand. It occurred to her that, in the short time since she'd joined the Argo, she'd begun to look to Jason for assurance the way the rest of them did. Everyone in camp seemed to be suffering from self-imposed amnesia—as if, when they'd signed aboard Jason's ship, they'd agreed to let themselves drift at the whim of the wind and waves, forgetting the shore they'd departed, mindless of the farther shore that might someday heave into sight. Even someone as big and strong as Argus had forfeited the will to chart his own course. Much as she longed to leave this place, much as she doubted Jason's methods and motives, she too had drawn comfort from the assumption that he alone knew where his vessel was headed. It had never dawned on her that he might be in blind flight from his demons as well.

She found herself breathing again when Jason spoke to his lieutenant in the voice of command she'd grown accustomed to. "I need you to work on that phone. Find out everything you can about this boy—who he knows, where he's been, what organizations he's communicated with. What he knows about weapons."

"Weapons?"

"Weapons," Jason repeated. "But I'm interested in anything you can discover."

"I'll do my best," Argus said, though his voice betrayed his doubts.

"Work all night if you have to. I'll expect an initial report by morning."

Argus slipped the phone in his pocket and rose to disconnect the laptop. Apparently, he'd be working in another cabin, not in Jason's headquarters.

"Before you get started, I want you to alert the others that I'm suspending field exercises," Jason said. "No one but Arachne leaves quarters until further notice. That includes the two of you."

Argus, seemingly grateful for a task he knew he could complete, nodded as he tucked the laptop under his arm. "I'll get the word out."

Jason clapped the big man on the shoulder as he exited the room. Michelle was about to leave as well when the leader of the Argo called out, "Diana."

She stopped. Argus paused for a second before marching down the shadowy hallway, his broad frame filling the narrow space. The door to the outside opened and shut, and she heard him clomping down the stairs. She turned to face Jason.

He stood right in front of her, blocking any thought of escape. Why that thought crossed her mind she didn't know, unless it was because of the video they'd just viewed: the runners fleeing, the figure closing on them, the moment of contact, the disappearance. *Weapons*, Jason had said. What kind of weapon made people vanish at a touch, leaving nothing behind but a cloud of dust?

"Diana," Jason repeated, "I've got a job for you, too."

Michelle waited.

"I can't rely on receiving Argus's report. You heard him: it could be days before he finds anything, or it could be a wild goose chase altogether. I need information *now*." Taking a deep breath as if he realized he'd exposed his anxiety, he continued in a calmer voice. "I want you to talk to this boy. Learn who he is, what he knows. I'm banking on him opening up to someone his own age, which will spare us the time it would take to conduct a proper interrogation."

Having seen what the hunters looked like after their release from the box, Michelle doubted this wounded boy would survive an interrogation at all. "He might not wake up."

"You need to be there if he does. To talk to him, listen to him, draw him out. Peer to peer. You can't let him suspect that you're anything other than a sympathetic friend. Clear?"

Once more, the urgency had crept into his voice. Michelle tried to guess what lay behind his gelid eyes, but the only thing she could see for certain was fear. Whether that was simple fear of the creature from the video or some deeper dread, she couldn't tell, and she couldn't ask, either. He'd given her a job to do, and particularly after his veiled threats at the end of today's war games, there was no way she could show the slightest resistance or reservation.

Jason looked at her anxiously for another second, then relaxed. "That's settled, then. Tell Circe only that I've asked you to relieve her. Have her bring the results of the boy's blood work directly to me. Until further notice, she's off the case."

They exited the building, and stood on the green between the headquarters and infirmary. With her newfound ability to read the sun's position, Michelle noted that the day had progressed past suppertime while they'd been inside. The camp appeared deserted in the lengthening shadows of evening, probably because, after their recent lapse of discipline, everyone was determined to take Jason's new curfew seriously. She would have liked nothing better than to follow their example: to return to the women's quarters, wash the day's sweat and grime from her body in the freezing shower, then collapse into her own bunk and surrender to sleep. Maybe she'd be able to dream away the shiver in her soul at the memory of the video.

But Jason's hand was on her back, not merely hovering there the way it had been on their trip to headquarters. The thought of deceiving Circe didn't sit well with her, but the thought of defying the camp's leader was an impossibility. As if to make sure she didn't doubt that point, he placed both hands on her shoulders and looked her directly in the eye when they reached the infirmary.

"Don't let me down, Diana." He turned and strode back to headquarters.

Michelle watched him go. He reached the front porch and let his gaze sweep over his camp—over her. She knew that, as soon as she entered the building, one of the camp's security cameras would take the place of his eyes, and Jason would be on the other end, watching her every move. She glimpsed the box in the shadowed distance, and she wondered whether Caeneus truly had been trying to gain freedom from Jason's reign. If he had, look what his gamble had gotten him. Was this the only choice the members of the Argo were given—to forsake their past or forfeit their future?

She walked up the steps to the infirmary, holding her head and shoulders erect as long as she felt Jason's eyes on her back, and prepared for her solitary vigil.

Chapter 6

Michelle slipped in and out of dreams all night.

In every one of them, a figure without a face, incongruously dressed in black sweatpants and sweatshirt with a red smear across the chest, chased her as she sprinted through the woods, through Jason's camp, through her own back yard, her own house and bedroom. Her pursuer moved like the wind, swooping and soaring in her wake, and yet somehow she stayed one step ahead of him, never slowing, always sensing his cold breath on her back. Her body felt at the point of collapse, and more than once she thought how easy it would be to stop running, to give up and let the hunter catch her. But her legs refused to listen to her brain, and so she ran on, slowing only enough to glance over her shoulder at the ghostly figure.

Its face emerged from the shadows, and she saw that it was him.

Michelle woke with a jolt. She'd nearly fallen from the chair beside the boy's bed, but she caught herself with a hand on the metal headboard. The room's single window shone silver with moonlight, the shadows of the bed and chair stretching against the far wall. She didn't know what time it was, but it must have been hours since Circe left with Tyris in tow, the doctor grumbling about Jason meddling with her patient and insisting that Michelle fetch her if there was any change in the boy's condition. Michelle hadn't said anything about why Jason had ordered Circe's removal, and despite her grousing, Circe hadn't asked for an explanation. Would it be a different story if Circe discovered that Michelle's orders included specific instructions *not* to notify the camp doctor about her patient's recovery?

She gazed at the bed and found the boy's eyes staring back at her.

They were black as night, but they sparkled in the moonlight. His lashes, like his hair, were thick and just as black, and his cheeks, she was fairly sure even in the dim light, had lost the sickly yellow color that had alarmed her so much when she'd first seen him. His complexion still didn't look healthy; the jaundiced hue had been replaced by extreme pallor, and that, along with the gauntness of his face, accentuated the dark pools of his eyes. Her relief at finding him awake was mingled with the uncanny feeling that she was the one still sleeping and that this was the face from her dream.

She shook her head to chase that thought from her mind and offered him the friendliest smile she could muster. "How are you feeling?"

"I feel ... better." His English was lightly accented but otherwise perfect. "I'm still so tired, though."

"You're getting over a bad infection. Plus you haven't had enough to eat or drink. Do you want anything?" she asked, wondering if she was superseding Circe's medical judgment.

"Just some water, please. If it's not too much trouble."

She rose and went to the sink, finding plastic cups among the supplies in a tall metal cabinet. When she returned to the bed, she remembered that the boy's wrists were strapped to the bedrails, and she had a moment's doubt whether Jason would want her to free him. She decided that if her job was to earn the newcomer's confidence, she couldn't very well leave him tied down like a prisoner—even if that's exactly what he was. She undid the plastic buckles and let the straps dangle over the sides of the mattress. His hands shook so badly when he accepted the water that she had to help him guide the cup to his mouth and tilt his head back to drink.

"Thank you," he said when he was done. Even with her help, he'd spilled water down his chin, so Michelle found a washcloth and gently patted his face and neck dry. A stray memory of doing the same to Rosie when she was sick with the flu rose in her mind, and she found her own hands shaking so much she had to stop.

Michelle returned to her chair, moving it from beside the headboard so it would be easier for him to see her. His eyes followed her with a look of wary gratitude that again reminded her far too much of Rosie.

"Is that better?" she asked, folding her hands in her lap to keep them still.

"Yes, thank you." He held her eyes for a long moment, then tried a smile. It enhanced the childlike appearance of his face, even beneath the long strands of his unkempt beard. "My name is Kareem."

Michelle smiled back. "It's nice to meet you, Kareem. I'm ... Diana." It was the first time she'd said her alias out loud, and her throat caught on the lie.

97

"I'm pleased to meet you, Diana. Can I ask you ... where I am? I don't seem to remember how I got here."

"We call this place the Argo," Michelle said. "It's a ... a camp. For survivors." Deciding it was best not to divulge too much, she changed the subject, trying to cover by infusing extra warmth into her voice and concern into her eyes. "We found you in the woods a couple of miles away, and our doctor wanted you brought to camp so she could take care of you."

"You carried me here?"

"You were too sick to walk."

"I see." He glanced around in the darkness, his eyes bright. "Are there many more ... survivors here?"

"Not too many," Michelle said evasively. She had the uneasy feeling that *he* was trying to interrogate *her*. "There's our commander, Jason, and some others. You're the first new person to come here for a while," she lied.

"Your commander. Can I talk to him?"

"He's not here right now," Michelle said, the acrid taste of yet another lie burning her tongue. "He's been really busy ever since the ... the wars."

"Oh."

He fell silent. Michelle wished she could ask him all the questions she wanted to: whether there were others who'd survived like he had, what the condition of the world was, how far it was to the nearest city. What the thing was that he'd filmed in the woods. But the thought that there might be a camera hidden in one of the room's corners kept all of those questions bottled up in her chest. She hadn't actually seen a camera—not that she'd risked looking—but its possible presence made her even edgier than a confirmed sighting. Half-truths and circumlocutions compounded in her thoughts, so many she was sure she'd slip up and fall into a contradiction. She was already planning ways to dodge questions Kareem hadn't even asked. How did Jason expect her to discover the truth about their visitor if the very basis of this conversation was a lie?

"The wars ... " Kareem said dreamily, as if he'd just been reminded of them. "You said something about the wars. What were they, exactly?"

The question was so unexpected, Michelle forgot to be cautious. "The yellow fire. The ... the bombs, or whatever they were." When he looked at her blankly, she continued, "A little over three weeks ago?"

"Three weeks ... " he repeated, though the way he said it, he might as well have meant three years.

"There was fire in the valley," she said. "And afterwards, the forest looked like it was dying. You must have seen that if you were out in the woods when the fire happened."

"Right," he said. "Well, actually, I was ... inside then. I guess I missed all that."

Michelle cocked her head. "Inside where?"

He didn't answer. His eyes strayed to the rays of moonlight lapping the floor like reflections on a strange sea. Michelle pulled her chair closer to the bed and leaned toward him until he returned his attention to her.

"Kareem," she said. "Do you not remember any of this?"

He stared at the covers that lay across his lap, or maybe at the camouflage top they'd dressed him in. "I'm not ... you see, I'm having trouble remembering the past few weeks." He glanced up with a quick, embarrassed smile. "Could that be from getting sick?"

"I guess so," Michelle said, not sure if that was true. "How much do you remember?"

He searched inward, then shook his head. "Not much, I'm afraid. I remember being out in the woods, but I don't think I saw anything … dying like you said. Or at least, if I did—"

Whatever he was going to say next was cut off by a strangled sound deep in his throat. His eyes blinked rapidly before squeezing shut, and then his whole body convulsed, his back and neck arching and his teeth clamping together as if in intense pain. Michelle sprang to her feet, worried that he was having another seizure. Her hands poised over his body, but she couldn't decide where or if to touch him. Why had Jason insisted she send away the only person in camp who knew how to take care of sick people?

Before she could find a safe place to lay hands on him, his body relaxed, sinking slowly back into the mattress. He drew a long breath, almost a sigh. She had started to relax as well when his eyes flew open, and Michelle saw that they were wide and staring, the eyes of a cornered animal.

"My phone!" he panted. "What happened to my phone?"

With a sick feeling, Michelle told yet another lie. "It must have fallen out of your pocket. It wasn't there when we brought you in."

She thought his eyes clouded with suspicion, but it was hard to tell in the moonlight. Should she have admitted that they'd found his backpack, but lied and told him the phone wasn't in it? Hoping to take his eyes off her, she leaned over the bed to rearrange his pillow, then smoothed the sheets that had become tangled by his spasm.

"Is there someone you'd like me to get in touch with?" she tried. "Someone who should know that you're here?"

He turned his head away. "No. There's no one."

Michelle settled back into the chair and watched him, not knowing what to say next. It was obvious that getting information from Kareem was going to be much harder than Jason had anticipated. She didn't like the way the boy had looked at her just now, as if he saw more about her than she wanted to show. Jason's repeated warnings about the enemies who supposedly surrounded his camp must have been having an effect on her, because she wondered if Kareem was one of them. She was trying to figure out another tack when his eyelids fluttered and he stifled a yawn.

"I'm sorry," he said, his voice calmer and his breathing softer than a moment ago. "I'd like to talk, but I'm just so tired. Is it all right if I sleep?"

"Of course. Do you need any more water?"

"No, thank you. Just sleep."

"That's fine. If you need anything else, I'll be right here."

"That's very kind of you … Diana," he said, and was it her imagination that made her think he said the name in a sarcastic way? Then his eyes closed, and within seconds he appeared to be sound asleep. After what he'd gone through, Michelle couldn't doubt that he was exhausted, and she found it hard to believe that someone in his condition could be onto her ruse so quickly.

She waited another fifteen minutes—she knew because she counted the seconds—before rising and leaning over to check Kareem's breathing. His chest rose and fell regularly, and his mouth had opened partway, each exhalation bearing an unclean odor to her nostrils. After a moment's further hesitation, she walked to the door as quietly as Jason had taught her and slipped out of the room without making a sound. The distance to headquarters was only a few hundred feet, but she ran, not walked, over the moon-silvered grass, gliding silently as a wraith through the net of shadows thrown by the towering trees.

Only when she stood before the pitch-dark building did she stop to ask herself what she was doing. Why had she felt it was vital to report her conversation with Kareem immediately? The details of that conversation had been so fractured, so unenlightening—what was it that made her apprehensive enough to risk barging into Jason's private lodging in the middle of the night? The dream-feeling from before lingered in her mind, and she glanced around her, fearing that some faceless assailant might step out of the shadows. Maybe she was groggy from interrupted sleep and wasn't thinking clearly, or maybe the odd, strained interview with Kareem had thrown her off. Before she made a fool of herself, maybe she should return to her uncomfortable seat by the stranger's bed and hope for a better frame of mind and a more compliant subject at morning's light.

The door to headquarters opened, and she saw Jason's tall, slim frame silhouetted against the light leaking into the hallway from his study. At the sight of him, the sense of urgency she'd felt dissipated into the night air. Of course he'd been watching her and Kareem all along, which meant there was even less reason for her to be here. If he'd been the slightest bit concerned about anything, he'd have come right over, wouldn't he? She hesitated, turned to walk away, but halted in her tracks when his voice floated down to her.

"Diana." It was the soft, unsettling voice she'd heard that

first day in the woods, the voice edged with danger. "What brings you here?"

She was thankful for the dark, which hid her blush. "I'm sorry. I didn't mean to disturb you."

"There's no way to approach this building without disturbing me. I've learned to sleep lightly. One night in the woods, I was nearly joined by a curious coyote who seemed to want to share my pad. I'll have to show you his pelt one of these days."

He beckoned, and she flitted up the stairs as if his hand had summoned her. A minute later, they were seated in his office, the desk lamp casting harsh shadows around the small room, Jason leaning back in the creaking chair while she hunched in the seat across from him. Nothing had changed since her first day in camp, except that the green jar from Kareem's backpack rested with Jason's books on the shelf. The leader of the Argo was wearing his typical uniform of camo pants and black jacket, and the fog of fear that had surrounded him earlier in the day had been replaced by an aura of anticipation, irritation, even anger. He certainly didn't look like a man who'd been awakened from a sound sleep. He looked like a man who expected something, and who might choose to take another pelt if he didn't get it.

"Any luck with our guest?" he asked without preamble.

"Kareem," she said automatically. "Then you weren't watching ... "

"There's a giant from Greek mythology, another Argus, who was supposed to possess a hundred eyes on his body. You probably remember him as the security guard from Camp Half-Blood."

Michelle nodded, wondering what this was all about.

"The god Hermes lulled the giant to sleep with music and cut off his head at the behest of Zeus, who'd been after the mortal woman Argus was guarding," Jason went on. "I've always thought of that myth as a cautionary tale for those who refuse to accept the truth they see right in front of their eyes."

Michelle's mouth felt numb, unable to respond. Fortunately, this was one of those times when Jason wasn't looking for a response.

"You know I've installed my own 'eyes' around camp," he said. "Some of them are machines, but the most reliable ones, I've found, are people loyal to the Argo, people who are dedicated to defending it at all costs. Those eyes have tongues too, which means they have something to lose if they don't speak the truth." He leaned toward her. "So tell me what your *eyes* have seen."

Michelle stiffened at the implied threat, but tried to keep her voice level and dispassionate. "I'm not sure it's anything. He woke up, which is good, but he's pretty weak. And he claims he can't remember what happened to him."

Jason looked at her keenly. "You believe him?"

"I'm not sure. He could be telling the truth, but … "

"But few medical conditions are easier to fake than amnesia," Jason finished for her. "Particularly among strangers, who aren't likely to catch the deceiver in a lie or to challenge him if they do."

"But why?" Michelle asked. "Why would he be pretending?"

Jason shrugged. "Lots of reasons. Caution. Anxiety. Distrust. But it sounds to me"—he raised an eyebrow—"as if you think there's more to it than that."

"There is one thing," she said. "I wouldn't have thought anything about it except—with the amnesia—it seemed strange … "

Jason waited, his eyes flicking over her.

"I think he knows we took his phone. He seemed really upset when he found out it was missing. And it didn't make sense to me that the first thing he'd think about was his phone when he supposedly can't remember anything from the past three weeks."

"Not so hard to believe these days," Jason commented. "Isn't your phone your life?"

The mocking way he said that made Michelle bristle. She hadn't told him what happened to her phone, but he must have figured out that she wouldn't have been wandering the woods all by herself if she'd had a way to contact anyone. Did he really need to remind her that when she'd thrown away her phone, she pretty much *had* thrown away her life?

"I think he's hiding something," she said. "On his phone, or somewhere else. Maybe he needs the phone to track down whatever he's looking for. Which means he's going to try to get the phone back if he can."

"That's not going to be easy for him to do," Jason said casually. "Not with this camp's security measures and the phone in Argus's quarters."

"I don't think that's going to stop him. If he wants it badly enough, he'll try anything."

Jason offered no rejoinder, but his eyes focused on her with all the intensity their piercing blue could command. She felt as if she truly were in the presence of an all-seeing ogre, or maybe in the sights of a high-powered rifle. If she made a single false move, would he pull the trigger? If he did, would she flinch?

Would she run?

Jason rose, his canine eyes seeming to flash a warning in response to her thoughts. "Let's go check it out," he said as he rounded the desk and gestured for her to exit the room before him.

The moon had dipped below the headlands, yielding to the much weaker light of the stars that shone in a cloudless sky. Jason crossed the lawn without faltering, and Michelle stuck close behind him. A wind had picked up, rustling the leaves and raising goosebumps on her arms. Or maybe that was from fear over what would happen when they reached the infirmary. She'd handed Jason all the reason he needed to suspect Kareem of wrongdoing, and she wasn't sure why she'd done so. Because of her dreams? But dreams were just dreams. Had she abandoned her hope that the stranger might help her find a way out of this place, and accepted Jason's conviction that Kareem was linked to the horror they'd seen on his phone?

They reached the infirmary. Jason led the way up the steps, through the waiting area, to the door of the sick room. He gripped the doorknob and opened it as silently as Michelle had when she left.

"Kareem," Jason said in his softest and most dangerous voice, "I wonder if I can have a word with you."

There was no answer. They stepped into the room. It was quiet, not even the sound of Kareem's breathing audible. Michelle could feel a breeze, the source of which she soon located: the room's single window was open. Jason flicked on the light, and the two of them stared at the bed where Kareem's sleeping form should have been.

At the sight of what lay there, Michelle went cold with fear.

"The straps," she said. "I forgot to retie them."

The bed was empty. The impression of a body could be seen in the sheets, but Kareem was gone.

Chapter 7

Jason radioed Argus, who disappeared with his leader into the camp's weapons bunker while Michelle waited miserably aboveground.

Since they'd discovered Kareem's departure, she'd been dreading an explosion that never came. Jason had been brusque and businesslike, his directions to her and Argus delivered in sharp gestures and curt phrases. Her stupidity at not retying the boy's bonds rankled, but she tried to convince herself it wasn't her fault. Jason had left her alone with someone who was apparently supposed to be treated as a prisoner, but he'd never made that a hundred percent clear. He knew how inexperienced she was. What did he expect?

But it was useless to rationalize what she'd done. Despite Jason's warnings, she'd let a possible threat to his camp loose, and she'd given Jason ample justification to eliminate that threat.

Two figures emerged from the dark: Jason first, followed closely by Argus. When they neared, Michelle saw that both men were dressed in full camo gear, their faces smeared with paint. Though Argus had equipped himself with a hunting rifle similar to Caeneus's, Jason carried only his trusty bow. She understood instantly why they'd chosen to arm themselves this way rather than with the high-tech military-style rifles the sentries carried. It wasn't a matter of deadliness; she knew from her field exercises with Jason that these rustic weapons were as deadly in the two men's hands as the most sophisticated of firearms. It was that they wanted Kareem to know exactly what they thought of him.

They were hunting him like a wild animal. And when they found him, they were going to bring him down.

"You'll stay here," Jason said to her. His words were faintly visible as puffs of steam in the chilly night air. "Report what's happened to Circe, and tell her to organize the watch on camp. I've already contacted Arachne, who'll patrol the headlands in case this is part of a coordinated attack."

"Jason, I—"

"You screwed up," he said. "Big time. You underestimated the enemy, and you've put everyone in camp at risk. You won't make that mistake again."

Her head sank. "No."

"But it's not a total loss," Jason continued. "By taking flight, he's announced himself as a hostile. What he doesn't realize is that we know exactly where he is."

"You do?"

He gestured in the direction the Lethe flowed. "I had Circe plant a tracker on him when we brought him to the infirmary. It'll lead us right to him."

"Does everyone in camp—"

"Only people we have reason to doubt," Jason silenced her again. "We'll be back before daybreak. Be sure you've made up your mind by then."

She nodded numbly as they vanished into the night. Though she wanted to protest that her single mistake—no matter how serious—didn't merit such distrust after weeks of following orders, her conscience pricked her, making her wonder if Jason had known all along what she was secretly planning to do. Either way, he would never trust her again, which meant he'd keep an even closer watch on her from now on. She felt as if, with the disappearance of a boy she knew only by name, her own chances for escape had disappeared as well.

Haltingly, she made her way to the women's quarters. Though she wasn't nearly as adept at negotiating the camp's traps as Jason, her feet seemed to anticipate which way to go to avoid the pits and wires she couldn't see in the darkness. When she reached the front door of the building, she paused, taking a deep breath, trying to compose her face to confront Circe. The leader of the women's camp wouldn't be happy to learn that her patient had absconded, and Michelle didn't know Circe well enough to predict whether she'd take her anger out on the one who'd unwittingly helped him escape. She wondered again what Circe's true story was, why she'd left her home and career for Jason's lonely bastion in the forest. That decision might have saved her and her daughter's life on the night of the yellow fire, but did she ever look back at what she'd lost? Did she ever regret her choice?

She must, Michelle decided. You could make that kind of choice freely, or you could make it when all the other options seemed so much worse. But no matter how you made it, there would always be part of you that hated the choice you'd made, and wished you could have it to do all over again.

She entered the barracks, following the snores to Circe's bunk. As always, the doctor slept with her arms twined around Tyris, the two of them seeming like a single multilimbed organism in the room's darkness. Michelle hoped that the five-year-old was a sound sleeper; she didn't want the little girl worrying or, worse, impeding her mother in the work she had to do. She reached out hesitantly, realizing she'd never touched anyone in camp on purpose. Jason laid his hands on her from time to time, and Arachne had pretty much manhandled her the night of her arrival, but for the three plus weeks she'd been here, she'd initiated no human contact at all, except with …

Kareem.

"Circe," she whispered, her hand suspended above the woman's shoulder. "Circe, wake up."

The doctor stopped in mid-snore and lifted her head. Apparently, everyone in Jason's camp had learned to sleep lightly. "What is it?"

"It's … Kareem. The boy we brought in. He … he left."

Instantly, Circe disentangled herself from her daughter and sat up. The little girl whimpered, reaching for her mother, but slept on. Circe stood and headed for the door, Michelle trailing her as if she'd become Tyris's substitute.

"I'm going to wake the men," Circe said when they stepped outside. "You stay here."

"I can help … "

"You'll just slow me down."

"But I'm the one who … "

"We don't have time for this, Diana," Circe said with an edge to her voice. "Now do as I say."

Something about the way she said that, as if Michelle really were her recalcitrant daughter, made the tears she'd been holding inside start to flow. She turned away so Circe wouldn't see, but the older woman was too perceptive for that. "What's wrong?" she asked, no less bluntly than her command.

"I screwed up," Michelle said, hating the fact that Jason's words were the only ones that seemed appropriate. "I didn't mean to let him go, but ... " She wiped the tears with the back of her hand, but they kept coming. "I'm sorry, Circe. It's just that I"—her voice broke, and the trickle of tears became a flood—"I miss home, and I don't know if my mom and dad are still alive, and I'm no good at any of this ... this *surviving*. I want to *live*, not just survive. And I don't even know if there's anything left to live *for*."

The doctor sized her up the way she might assess a patient. Then she reached out and put both hands on Michelle's shoulders. Michelle braced herself—whether for a scolding or a hug she didn't know—but Circe only held her at arm's length, speaking in a calm, unhurried voice despite the urgency of the situation.

"We'll talk later," she said. "For now, I want you to take it easy on yourself. We all make mistakes, Diana. You're, what, eighteen years old?"

"Seventeen. Three weeks ago."

"Seventeen, then. I wish I could tell you the world will seem less scary when you're my age, but it won't. It'll just be a little easier to get through each day without wanting to curl up and hide."

Michelle nodded, and to her surprise, Circe reached out to wipe a tear from her cheek. If the doctor had offered to fold her in her arms, stroke her butchered hair, sing to her the way she did to Tyris, Michelle wouldn't have objected. But she didn't. She'd no sooner withdrawn her finger than she was making her way down the stairs, her voice a thin trail of steam on the night air.

"I'll be back soon," she said. "Now try and get some sleep."

Michelle watched as the woman's small figure dwindled into the darkness. When Circe disappeared completely, Michelle drew a deep breath, willing the tears that had mostly stopped to dry completely. A bulb blinked on in the men's barracks, etching a rectangle of light on the lawn. She could go back inside now. Circe and the other grown-ups would take care of everything.

She threw a long, searching glance at Jason's headquarters, the largest of the black shapes among the trees. As she did, the light from the men's barracks showed her the shadow that ducked behind the building.

The human shadow.

It was unmistakable, and the instant she saw it, Michelle knew who it was. No one else would be skulking around Jason's sanctum in the middle of the night. No one else would be so brazen as to break into the commander's quarters so he could get his hands on the object that seemed to have burned itself into the newcomer's mind.

A thrill shot through her, mingled with dread. Jason and Argus had set out at a brisk pace, aiming straight for the tracker that Kareem must have deposited along the Lethe before he circled back to camp. She couldn't catch up to them, and by the time they discovered his trick and returned, Kareem would be long gone. She knew that the best thing to do if she wanted to get back into Jason's good graces was to alert Circe and let the doctor deal with her wayward patient. But now that the prospect of Kareem's capture was real, now that a single word from her would make it happen literally in front of her face, she suffered a fresh pang of doubt. Would the posse that was assembling at this very moment take the chance of apprehending the fugitive, or would they shoot on sight? What if they tried to arrest him and he resisted? She didn't question Jason's belief that Kareem was a danger to camp: he'd deceived her with his stories of memory loss, he was wily enough to mislead Jason, and who knew what he was up to now? But if he died, all of the possibilities he represented—knowledge of the outside world, reunion with her family, a life beyond the Argo—died with him.

A new plan formed in her mind, one that made her heart pound with excitement and fear. *She* would be the one to apprehend him. Under the threat of her bow, he'd have to answer her questions. And then, when she'd gotten all the information she could from him, she'd hand him in, earning Jason's thanks and his restored trust while keeping alive her own hope for the future.

I can do this, she said to herself. *I can be the hunter for once, not the hunted.*

As quietly as she could manage, she slipped into the women's quarters and tiptoed to the locker at the foot of her bunk, where the twins had stored her gear when she returned to camp. No one woke as she eased the locker open and grasped her quiver and bow. She glanced at Tyris before cracking the door open to peer outside, and was thankful the little girl was turned toward the wall so there was no chance of seeing her sleeping face.

The light had gone out in the men's barracks. Straining her eyes against the darkness, she made out five shadowy figures across the lawn, one of them much smaller than the others: Circe. Michelle waited until they fanned out to take positions on the outskirts of camp, then she ducked all the way outside and quietly closed the door behind her. Circe had vanished with the others rather than returning to the women's quarters; Michelle guessed she wouldn't return until the renegade was captured or killed. With any luck, before that happened, Michelle would have had her own private interview with Kareem and would be marching him to headquarters with an arrow aimed at his back.

Marshaling all of Jason's tips for moving noiselessly, she crept up to the central building and flattened herself against the wall. She'd seen Kareem sneak around the left wing, where the communications center was located. Maybe he wasn't only looking for his phone; maybe he was also planning to use the shortwave to send out a message. It struck Michelle that this boy might be even more dangerous than she—and possibly Jason—guessed. Was he a spy? A lone wolf like the Argo's leader had talked about? Or just a survivor like her, who'd gotten caught up in events beyond his control?

It didn't matter. Whoever he was and whatever he was planning, all she knew for sure was that she couldn't let him get inside headquarters, where he might be able to spring a trap on her. She'd have to intercept him out here, and then take him someplace where she could conduct the interrogation *her* way.

With her shoulder blades pressed against the logs and her feet inching across the grass, Michelle stole around the right-hand wing of the building until she reached the spot where it intersected the oak tree. Her eyes, accustomed to the dark by now, could discern the building's other wing jutting out from the tree to her left, but there was no sign of Kareem. Holding her breath, she slunk right up to the tree and leaned out to peek at the juncture where the communications center connected to the trunk. When she did, she almost gave herself away with a gasp.

Kareem was there, not five feet away, facing the building with his back to her. His hands rested on his hips as he surveyed the blank wall, his eyes probably scanning for a window to climb through or, maybe, for a way to get onto the roof. He took a couple of steps toward the building, but even with him this close, Michelle couldn't hear the sound of his feet pressing against the grass. Her eyes dropped to the ground where she saw that he'd outfitted himself with a pair of boots, probably extras he'd found in the infirmary. He didn't move like a novice unaccustomed to the clunky footwear. He moved like Jason, like someone who'd tracked others—or been tracked—many times before.

Michelle took a cautious step toward him just as he laid his hand on the wall.

A siren, loud and jarring, made her jump. At the same moment, spotlights flared on from the oak tree's branches, and Michelle realized what Jason had meant when he said no one could sneak up on his command center undetected. Kareem flung himself away from the building, his eyes turning wildly, and that's when he saw Michelle. A look of utter terror distorted his features before he spun and set off at a sprint across the campground.

Michelle swore under her breath as she followed him. The siren's blare had alerted others in the camp, and she could hear slamming doors and rushing feet. The alarm sounded loud enough to reach Jason and Argus wherever they were, but her immediate danger, she knew, was that

116

someone in camp might glimpse her fleeing figure and shoot without recognizing her. The spotlights were blinding; it would be nearly impossible to make out faces from any distance. Kareem, twenty strides ahead of her, had become little more than a shadow among the trees, and with the siren's racket, she couldn't use her hearing to track her prey the way Jason had instructed her in the woods. That Kareem *was* her prey she no longer doubted. His guilt was obvious, though what he'd been doing before they found him in the woods and what he was planning to do now remained a mystery. If she could catch him, she'd have no qualms about trading his freedom for hers.

Michelle kept her eyes on the boy's darting shape as the two plunged deeper into the trees and the siren's scream diminished. She realized that the noise hadn't been as loud as she thought, just loud enough to wake the camp in the silence of the woods. If Kareem had headed anywhere except the narrow pass to the headlands, he'd have been boxed in and easy for her to hunt down. But somehow, with the unaccountable instinct that had led him to search Jason's headquarters first among all of the camp's buildings, he aimed straight for the opening in the cliff face, then disappeared into the shadowed recess. Michelle's heart sank, and she considered halting her pursuit. At the top of the pass, Arachne waited. With her lethal skills and the element of surprise on her side, there was no chance Kareem could avoid getting tangled in her web.

A rifle's crack made her flinch. From the base of the cliff, she heard Arachne's faint voice—but instead of a victory cry, it was a string of vulgarity like nothing Michelle had encountered in any high school hallway. She vaulted onto the trail and climbed, conscious but heedless of the jutting rocks she could barely see as she followed the twisting course upward. When she exited the trailhead, she missed a step in astonishment.

Here on the ridgetop, the last light of the setting moon showed her that Arachne was down, her rifle nowhere to be seen, her forehead bleeding from an ugly gash. In itself, that might not have been enough to stop the sentry—but then Michelle saw that the woman's left ankle was twisted unnaturally, possibly broken. She reconstructed what must have happened: Kareem bursting from the pass, miraculously evading Arachne's shot and disarming her, then knocking her down with her own weapon and racing away as she fell. Which meant not only that Michelle's quarry was a far deadlier close-quarters fighter than she'd imagined, but that he was armed with the sentry's rifle. She could continue her chase, but she'd be taking her life in her hands.

Jason's warning echoed in her mind. *Out here, it's kill or be killed.* She'd never fully believed him until now.

She leaped over the prostrate Arachne, who retained enough fighting spirit to grab at Michelle's heels as she sailed past. Then she was sprinting into the woods at the top of the ridge, with the sentry's enraged curses ringing in her ears.

"Traitor!" Arachne screamed. "You're dead if you show your face here again! Do you hear me? You're dead, you little piece of ... "

Michelle concentrated on the woods in front of her, shutting out Arachne's cries as best she could. There were no other sounds of pursuit, but there was also no sign of Kareem, who'd easily be able to lose her in the dense darkness of the forest. She trained all her senses ahead for any hint of him, any blur of movement or crunch of boot heel on fallen leaf. That he might be lying in wait for her she was all too aware, but she didn't let that stop her. She'd make a poor target, moving fast in the dark. If he shot, if he pounced, at least she'd know where he was.

A cry came from up ahead, followed by a splash of water. Michelle allowed herself a small smile. However well trained he might be, he'd fallen into the stream in his haste. She immediately changed course and angled in his direction, using the trees and the darkness for cover and hoping his own footsteps would bury the sound of hers.

She saw his shadow no more than twenty-five meters away, heard his pounding feet, tasted his fear in the air. With his back to her, she couldn't tell if he was carrying Arachne's rifle or not, but she could tell that she was gaining on him. If he hadn't been recovering from an illness—he couldn't have faked *that*, could he?—he might have been able to outrun her. But she was in possibly the best shape of her life thanks to Jason's training regimen, and her strides were fueled by a combination of anger, hope, and fear. With every step, the gap between them closed, until she knew he must be able to hear her descending on him like the creature from his own video.

At the last second, Kareem threw a panicked look over his shoulder, only to find that she wasn't where he thought she was. She came at him from the side, and would have tackled him if he hadn't saved her the trouble by tripping and skidding to the turf. His hands were empty—he must have traded Arachne's rifle for speed—but when he tried to push himself to his feet, Michelle unstrapped her bow and swung it like a baseball bat, sweeping his legs out from under him. By the time he'd flipped onto his back and made an effort to crab-crawl away from her, she had an arrow fitted to the string and pointed at his chest. The night was immeasurably dark beneath the trees, but her eyes had sharpened so much during her run she could clearly see the terror in his.

"Please—" he began, before she cut him off.

"You're going to say, *don't shoot.*" A feeling of power flowed through her, and she was both shocked and exhilarated to discover that she wasn't the least bit out of breath. "Give me one good reason I should listen to you this time."

His hands were in the air, the way they'd been the day before. But his next words surprised her.

"You need my help!" he said. "Please, I can show you something that you—that all of you—need to see. Something that might save you."

"And your way of saving us is by running away in the middle of the night?" She shook her head. "I'm not buying it anymore, Kareem. If that's even your name."

"It is," he said. "I swear, it is. I'm sorry I ran, Diana. I was … I was scared. I didn't know what to do. I thought you might be … "

She waited for him to finish, but he didn't. "Might be what?"

"One of them," he said quietly.

His voice shook. His words made so little sense to her, she was silent for a minute before spitting another question at him.

"What about the other things you told me? You say you can't remember the past three weeks, yet somehow you know this vital information that will *save* us. How can you know something without remembering it?"

He closed his eyes as if trying to remember, but then he shook his head. "It doesn't make sense to me either. I *know* these things, but I don't know *how* I know them."

"So you don't remember *anything* from the past three weeks?"

"I swear I don't."

"Not where you were living?" she pressed. "Not what happened to the ... to the world when the yellow fire came?" Her throat tightened, but she squeezed the words out. "Not whether anyone else is alive?"

"I'm sorry, Diana," he said, and he genuinely did sound sorry. But his sympathy only made her angrier.

"This is such a load of crap," she said, and was taken aback to hear a murderous undertone that might have come from Jason's throat. "The longer you're out here making up stories, the more time you have to plan your getaway. You know what, Kareem? I was going to bring you in and let Jason deal with you. Maybe it would be better if I just shot you right now."

He threw himself at her feet, and she flinched away, the fingers of her right hand burning with the impulse to let the arrow fly. But he wasn't trying to attack. He lay stretched on the ground before her, his black eyes beseeching, his hands clasped. As if she were Artemis, Goddess of the Hunt, and he was Actaeon in the moment before she transformed him into a stag for his own dogs to tear to pieces.

"*Please*," he said. "I'll walk in front so you can shoot me if I try to run, and if you're not convinced by what I have to show you, you can kill me then. But you have to see what I've seen. If you kill me now, you'll never know until *they* come."

The way he said *they* made her shiver. "Who are you talking about?"

"I don't know their name," he whispered. "But I know they have the power to destroy us all."

Without shifting the arrow an inch from its target, Michelle took a step closer to the fallen boy. Her eyes narrowed as she looked into his.

"You mean the thing you saw in the forest," she said. "The thing you recorded on your phone."

His face darkened. "So you *did* take my phone."

"We're not talking about me. What *was* that thing?"

He was silent. She took another step closer, and his eyes widened, fear visible in their dark depths. Fear of her, or of something else?

"Why would you think," she asked slowly, "that I was one of *them*?"

He held her gaze. His eyes glistened as if with tears. "You won't believe me unless I show you."

She stood motionless for a long time, feeling like a marble sculpture except for the ache in her shoulder from the bowstring. *Be sure you've made up your mind by then*, was the last thing Jason had said to her. When he said it, she'd thought she would have the rest of the night, alone in her bunk, to come to her decision. She hadn't known it would be made right here, with the thread of a life in her hands and a straining arrowhead ready to snip that thread in two.

And yet, now that the moment of decision had come, she realized it had already been made. Her impulsive flight from camp meant there was no way Jason would listen to her even if she marched Kareem back under guard. He and Argus would have found Arachne by now, and the injured sentry would have told them her own version of events: that Kareem ambushed her so he and Michelle could escape together, that the two of them were in cahoots, that if the newcomers dared return to camp, it was nothing but another trick. Jason already distrusted her for letting Kareem go. Whose word would he believe—hers or his chief sentry's? The commander and his favorite assassin might eventually get the full truth, but only by cutting it out of her and Kareem at the point of a knife. She'd never have another opportunity to discover what had happened to her family. She would die with that question tormenting her to the very end.

She lowered the bow. Her fingers were so slick with sweat, it was a miracle she hadn't released the arrow by accident.

"On your feet," she said gruffly. "I swear, if this is some kind of trick, I'll gut you and leave your body for the coyotes to fight over. And if you try to lead me into a trap, I'll kill your friends, too."

Kareem didn't move at once, as if he couldn't believe she'd decided not to shoot. Then, shakily, he stood, wiping leaf litter from his hands. Michelle gestured with the bow, and he took his position several paces in front of her. A deep breath emerged from him as a cloud of steam before he began walking, with Michelle right behind.

"Where are you taking me?" she asked.

He didn't turn his head, but his voice was clear in the silent forest.

"To the city," he said. "They come from the city."

Chapter 8

They headed east, into the rising sun.

This deep in the forest, Michelle couldn't see the daytime star break the horizon, but she became conscious of the woods gradually brightening around her, the shapes of rocks and trees growing more distinct, the sky filling with a pale glow. She was on the verge of ordering Kareem to walk faster when he picked up the pace on his own. He must have felt as exposed as she did.

They followed the banks of the Lethe, drinking their fill while the stream flowed clear and strong. He seemed sure of his direction, but not of anything else; when she asked him which city they were heading for, he pleaded ignorance. She tried out names, hoping they'd spark his memory, but nothing seemed to click. From the route they were taking, she assumed their destination was near the site where she'd watched the yellow fire, but she'd seen no evidence of a city there, and she had a hard time believing they'd find anything now. She kept the arrow nocked to her bowstring, and stayed a safe enough distance behind him that he couldn't disarm her. At the same time, she kept her eyes and ears peeled for any sign of danger: movement among the trees, the whisper of voices, the tread of another human foot. She knew what an awful risk she was taking by allowing him to lead her into unknown territory, and she told herself she had to be prepared to carry out her threat if she sensed the slightest intention on his part to deceive.

At first, they traveled over ground that was familiar to her from her training sessions: thickly wooded hills that possessed the abundant underbrush, varied tree species, and evidence of natural burns Jason had taught her to associate with forest health. The trees' foliage was lavishly green, the duff on the forest floor smelled rich and earthy, and the occasional rustle in the branches or the undergrowth revealed that some small mammals, probably rabbits and squirrels, had survived. The absence of birdcalls troubled her; it seemed as if the dale where the Argo lay was the only place that birds still sang. The impending loss of their water source once the Lethe ran dry was a concern too, as she'd violated one of Jason's ironclad rules when she'd left the women's quarters without a full canteen. In fact, now that she thought about it, she was horribly equipped, with nothing to start a fire, cut branches for a shelter, or strain the mud she'd be obligated to dig up if no cleaner body of water presented itself. She hadn't even brought a bite to eat. She could hunt for a meal, but Jason's nifty shortcut with the deer's blood wouldn't work if she had nothing to fry it in. She'd been so concerned with capturing Kareem, so convinced that her encounter with him would be brief, bloody, and final, she'd brought only what she needed to menace his life, not preserve her own.

They'd been walking for a little over an hour when she noticed the thinning of the canopy, which let in more and more of the morning light until she was forced to admit that the trees around her were dying once again. When she looked up, she saw skeletal branches mingled among those that remained verdant with leaves, as if winter were bidding to reverse the tide of spring. Not long afterward, other signs of the forest's sickening reached her: the ground crackled where she and her guide stepped on dry leaves, the sounds of hidden wildlife grew less frequent before ceasing altogether, and the robust smell of new growth was replaced by the dry, ashy patina of death. She'd been drawing deeper breaths as the morning wore on, which she'd attributed to fatigue, but she was forced to admit at last that the real culprit was the air she was pulling into her lungs. Everywhere she looked, the sunlight revealed a smoky ambience she hadn't seen since the morning she left her car. An anxious feeling gathered in her chest at the thought that the residue from three weeks past hadn't dissipated by now; in fact, as far as she could tell, it had thickened. The condition of the forest had worsened along with it: she and Kareem had walked for only a couple of hours, and yet they'd already met with devastation as bad as what she'd seen in the woods immediately overlooking the valley of the yellow fire.

Michelle called a halt, the first words she'd spoken since she'd asked Kareem the name of their destination. While she leaned her bow against a tree and squatted to scoop a handful of powder from the ground, he sat and rested his legs. The morning light showed that his skin remained unhealthily pale, the tracery of blue veins visible beneath his cheeks. She wondered how he'd managed to walk this far; unless Circe's diagnosis was wrong, he should have been dead on his feet by now. The fear that had gnawed at her since their journey began reared its head once more: was he truly leading her to the city, or was he planning to lose her in the woods? She watched him sidelong while her hands were occupied, but he didn't budge.

A quick scan of the contents in her palm proved her instincts right. This was the same fine, scaly residue she'd seen much farther east on the first day. To her mind, that could mean only one thing: the assault that had stricken this region had caused damage that was not only irreversible but progressive. In less than a month, it had spread inexorably westward, gobbling the deep woods for miles. Jason maintained that the fire she'd witnessed was only one of many that had burned throughout the region, if not the nation. If that was true and all of these strange fires were spreading death like widening ripples in a pond, how long would it take before no safe place was left?

She stood and squinted at the sun, which had crested the naked treetops by now. Visible particles hung in the air, forming a dusty corona around the yellow globe. Even more disturbing, the sky itself seemed the wrong color, the blue dotted with brown like a kindergarten sketch that had started to freckle and fade after years boxed in an attic trunk. The day wasn't cloudy; there were no signs that a storm was brewing. It looked, instead, as if the sky was starting to die. That led to another, equally worrisome thought: there'd been no rain the entire time she'd lived in Jason's camp, no April showers as there should have been. The weather had remained constant for the past three weeks, the sun shining in a virtually cloudless sky, turning the afternoons as balmy as mid-summer. Could it be coincidence, or could the disaster that had affected everything at ground level have caused the same damage to the atmosphere? She closed her eyes for a second to block out a vision that rose without conscious thought: long strips of sky peeling away, falling to earth, exposing the bare white bones of the heavens.

"Is something wrong, Diana?"

Michelle jumped and found Kareem standing right next to her, peering into her face. She realized she'd been too preoccupied with the eerie sky to pay attention to him for the last few minutes; he could easily have run away or armed himself with her own weapon if he'd wanted to. Instead, he was just standing there, looking at her with what appeared to be honest concern. It could be an act, of course; he'd done a brilliant job of hoodwinking her last night in the infirmary, pretending to be much weaker and more disoriented than he was. But the fact that he hadn't taken advantage of her carelessness earned him the benefit of the doubt, as did the look of sincerity in his dark eyes. She decided it was time for a confession.

"My name's not Diana," she said. "Everyone in camp goes by code names. My real name's Michelle."

The tension in his face departed. "I like Michelle better."

Hearing him say that made her realize how much she'd missed the sound of her name. "And you're Kareem? For real? That's not an alias or anything?"

As quickly as it had gone, the anxious look returned to his brow. "I told you I can't remember much from the past few weeks. I should have told you I can't remember much about my life at all."

"Not even your name?"

"That I remember. But whether it's my real name or an alias like you said, I couldn't tell you."

"How is that possible?" Michelle asked, distrust creeping into her voice once again. "Did you hit your head? Did you have some kind of … I don't know, surgery or something? People don't just lose their memory."

He lifted a corner of his lip. "That's the problem with losing your memory. You can't remember how you lost it."

"It's not funny, Kareem," she said. "You're asking me to believe you, but you're not giving me a lot to go on."

"I remember *most* things," he said defensively. "Basic things, like what a phone is for and why the sun comes up in the morning. I was able to read the labels on the IV bags your doctor gave me, and I can understand everything that's said to me. But the details of my own life are very fuzzy, or maybe *fractured* is a better word. I can't make the pieces fit together."

"Tell me what you *can* remember."

He faced away from her, toward the east. He drew a deep breath, as if he were trying to catch a scent on the air. When he spoke again, his voice had a faraway sound, the voice of a sleeper talking from the depths of a troubled dream.

"I remember the city. The city—but not the sunlight or the streets or the trees. Somewhere else, a place full of light, and darkness. There were others with me—others like me. We were all together, and we were afraid. Something terrible had happened to us. We were hiding at first, and then we were running. But we couldn't run fast enough. The ones who pursued us were much faster."

He turned back to her, and his eyes revealed a depth of confusion and pain Michelle couldn't believe was counterfeited. Whether his tale was true or not, she no longer doubted that *he* accepted it as true. She took her bow in hand, and in one fluid motion, spun toward him, sighted, and let an arrow fly. He ducked pointlessly, then turned his head to look at where the arrow had embedded itself high up in the knothole of a desiccated tree. When he faced her again, his complexion was even paler than before.

"That was a warning," she said. "If I hadn't tried to miss, I wouldn't have."

While he watched, she strapped the weapon onto her back. His face remained wary, but he didn't shy away at her approach.

"I want to trust you, Kareem," she said. "I haven't been able to trust anyone for … for a long time. But you've done everything possible to make me distrust you, and it's going to take a while for you to win my trust back."

He nodded.

"You know how to get to the city? You weren't just saying that?"

"I know. But I swear I don't know *how* I know."

"That's all right. For now, I'm going to believe you. That doesn't mean I won't be watching. It just means I won't be quite as quick to shoot."

He nodded again, a smile tugging at the corners of his mouth.

"But you have to listen to me," she continued. "The commander of the camp—Jason—he was planning to kill you when you got away. For all I know, he was planning to kill you even before that. He's scared of you, though I'm not sure why. And then you went and attacked his favorite sentry, which didn't earn you any points either."

"She tried to shoot me."

"Regardless. He's hunting us right now—not just you, but *us*—and he's got his lieutenant with him. If Arachne's back on her feet, she's joined the party. We can't fight all three of them. The best we can hope for is that they don't find us. Ever."

He took that in, chewing his lip in silence.

"You understand what this means, right?" Michelle asked. "We're on our own out here. For as long as this trip lasts, it's just you and me. We *have* to be able to trust each other, or we're never going to make it."

"I understand," he said. "And I'll do whatever it takes to win your trust."

"I'll do the same," she said. "So I have another confession to make: I'm not one of Jason's soldiers. I joined his camp only three weeks ago. Because of the … the wars. That's why he doesn't trust me either. And it's why I'm willing to take this chance to get away from him once and for all."

He nodded, as if he'd already suspected she was a rookie from something she'd said or done, maybe from her negligence in the infirmary.

"Now it's your turn," she said. "Tell me more about these things that live in the city. I need to know *everything* you know about them."

"It won't be very helpful. You know I can't remember much."

"Anything is better than nothing."

"Okay," he said with a heavy breath. "To start with, they don't *live* in the city. I'm not sure they live at all. They *dwell* in a place until they've drained it. These woods"—he gestured at the cadaverous trees—"might have died because of them."

"You mean they drain the water from things?" she asked, remembering her dehydration the morning after the yellow fire.

He shook his head. "Not water. Life. I can't explain it."

She waited for him to say more, but he shifted his eyes to the side in a way that made her wonder if he was already reneging on his promise. "All right," she said. "So these creatures got out of the city ... "

"I think so. And then they were free to go ... wherever they wanted to. I was worried that they had invaded your—Jason's—camp, which is why I ran."

"But we'd have known if they were in camp. Jason would have seen—"

"No," he said. "He wouldn't have."

His certainty stopped her cold. She wanted to explain that nothing entered or left the Argo without Jason knowing about it, but she decided to try another tack.

"This should be easier," she said. "What do they look like?"

She thought he'd answer at once, but instead, his face froze, as if he were on the verge of another seizure. A look of dreamy intensity flashed across his dark eyes, and for a second she was reminded of old myths she'd read in school, the ones about prophets paralyzed by the truth they foresaw but were powerless to change. He raised his hand to his forehead, as if to summon or expunge the vision. It was a long time before he lowered his hand and returned to the world of the present.

"I know this makes even less sense than the rest of it," he said. "But I can't remember what they look like. I can remember myself running from them, checking behind me to see how close they were—but then there's nothing. It's like there's a ... a blankness in my mind whenever I try to recall their faces. Like they've cast some spell over me, and all I can see is … "

"Is what?"

His eyes took on a look of infinite sadness. "My own face."

The similarity of what he was describing to her dreams of the previous night chilled her. She wished she could believe he was simply crazy, suffering from what her Psych teacher called a "dissociative state"—but that wouldn't explain what she'd seen on his phone. Unless she was crazy too—and she was beginning to feel like she was—there was *something* out there, something with the power to make living people disappear at the touch of its hand. And, maybe even worse, to make itself vanish from the minds of those who'd escaped it.

"That's all you can tell me?" she asked.

"I'm sorry, Michelle."

"Don't worry about it." She tried to keep her voice breezy, but it grated without her permission. "Jason's sure to be on our trail by now. You okay to keep going?"

He nodded.

"Then let's go. We can talk more as we walk."

Even as she said it, she doubted there would be any more talk this morning. When she envisioned the long, desolate trail that lay before them, a wave of utter loneliness crashed down on her, so strong it was as if no time at all had passed since the day she'd lost her way and been separated from everything she knew and loved. She desperately wished that instead of tramping across the dying land with this boy she barely knew and had to struggle to trust, she was home right now—that everything that had happened to her since the day she woke up to find the shiny new Mustang parked in the driveway had been nothing but a terrible nightmare, and that when she woke up for real, she'd find Rosie sitting at the end of her bed the way she had years ago, holding out her hands for her big sister to paint her nails with her favorite purple polish. She realized that no matter how strong she'd tried to be, no matter how many lessons in wilderness survival she'd learned from Jason or tips on surviving the ravages of her own heart she might have gleaned from Circe, she was still bewildered, hurting, and scared, and she needed someone to share all the feelings bottled up inside of her. A companion. A protector. A friend.

She turned from him and was about to take a step when she felt his hand on her arm. His touch wasn't threatening or painful; if anything, it seemed he was trying to steady himself. She sought his eyes, and found that the dreaminess had vanished, replaced by determination. At that moment, *she* was the prophet, because she knew what he was going to say the second before he said it.

"We're heading to the city," he affirmed. "It's possible we'll still find them there. If we don't, we'll track them to wherever they've gone. If we're careful, maybe they won't find us. And if they do—well, then maybe we can fight."

She looked at him with a rush of gratitude. Whatever lay ahead, it clearly terrified him—but he was willing to risk it with her. On an impulse, she reached out and squeezed his hand.

"Thank you," she said.

He ducked his eyes. "I'm the one who should be thanking you. You saved my life. Twice."

"Except the second time, I saved you from myself," she said teasingly.

He looked at her without smiling. "I want you to trust me. So you need to promise me something before we leave."

Her gift of prophecy departed as swiftly as it had come. "What?"

He pointed to the bow strapped on her back, pantomimed pulling back the string and releasing. At first, she didn't know what he meant, but then she realized he was asking her to arm herself. She did, and when she'd fitted an arrow to the string, he nodded in satisfaction.

"When we get to the city," he said, "don't trust *anyone*."

Chapter 9

They walked in silence, saving their breath.

Michelle wished she could say it was a comfortable silence, relieved of the tension and suspicion she'd felt since last night. But Kareem's final, ambiguous warning had raised fresh alarms, while the thought of Jason's team following in their tracks, calling on powers of detection she could neither match nor outmaneuver, kept her on edge. Their surroundings did nothing to put her at ease: the woodlands continued to wane the farther east they traveled, until by late morning they were walking through a zone of leafless trees whose branches etched stark outlines against the gleaming sky. Having grown accustomed to the canopy she'd lived under for the past three weeks, Michelle found the open vault unnerving, especially now that the advancing sunlight distinctly revealed brown veins creeping through the sky's natural blue. She kept an eye out for movement in the scanty brush, not only alert for enemies but hoping for a meal. Eventually, though, she had to concede that the woodlands were not going to experience a miraculous revival. She held the bow ready nonetheless, remembering her final training session with Jason and vowing that if he were to appear, she would do exactly as he had ordered.

The day grew steadily warmer, portending another cloud-free, sweaty afternoon. At the same time, the Lethe diminished to the point of uselessness. They'd taken their last drink at noontime an hour ago, Michelle using her barely watertight quiver—the only receptacle she had—to preserve some of the precious water. After that point, Kareem veered from the banks of the clotted stream, seeming absolutely sure of himself as he took a southerly direction that brought them onto higher ground without having to negotiate the ravine in which she'd met Caeneus. They crossed barren woodlands where nothing was left of the fallen leaves but a fine powder, and where the remains of birds and beasts had rotted past the point of attracting flies—if, that is, insect life hadn't succumbed to the forest's blight along with everything else. Within another couple of hours, they'd reached a long downhill slope on which even the mummified trees thinned practically to nothing. Michelle had hoped they might climb the ridge where she'd left her car, but Kareem's new route didn't pass that way, and she couldn't very well ask him to deviate from his course for sentimental reasons even she couldn't explain.

For the past hour, as they trudged downhill, she'd caught glimpses through the diminishing tree trunks of something that looked like an ocean of brown receding to a distant horizon. Finally, the trees gave out altogether, and she saw that what lay in the basin was a broad plain that shimmered with heat distortion in the sun. The occasional stump dotted the expanse, but other than that, it looked like pictures she'd viewed in her Environmental Studies class of western deserts cracked and lined by drought. They stopped once they reached the bottom of the hill, and Michelle searched fruitlessly across the sun-bleached plain for an end to the waste. She'd told herself she was prepared to face whatever lay ahead, but the sight of this desolation made her heart curl into a ball in the corner of her chest. So far as she could judge, they were nowhere near the valley of the yellow fire, but the damage here was even more total than it had been there. With destruction on such an unimaginable scale staring her in the face, what hope was there that her home had magically been left untouched?

Kareem stood a few paces ahead, shading his eyes against the glare. She held her sorrow in check long enough to speak. "How far is it to the other side?"

"It's grown," he said in the dreamy voice that told her he was reciting things he barely remembered but nonetheless knew. "We have to cross it to get to the city."

"Can they ... " She swallowed, trying to collect moisture in her throat, but all she got was a mouthful of dust. "How can those things live in a place like this?"

"I told you, they don't *live*. They take life, but they don't have anything to do with it."

A shudder passed through her as if she were feeling a blast of Arctic cold rather than the heat of the relentless sun. She craned her neck to gauge the time of day; it was late afternoon, and though she didn't know exactly when they'd started their trek, they must have been walking for something like twelve hours. "Maybe we should take a little break."

Kareem eyed her closely. "We don't want to give Jason time to catch up, right?"

"Of course not." Carefully, making sure not to spill any of the water, she removed the quiver from her back and scooped out a handful to drink. She offered it to Kareem, saying nothing of her dismay to find how much had already leaked. "Let's get moving."

The first step they took onto the plain was as bad as she'd feared.

The impact of her foot sent a chalky cloud flying into the air, momentarily blinding her and filling her lungs with powder. At the same time, her boot sank above the laces, the dust so deep and loose it was like sand. There was a solid surface a few inches down, but if she'd told someone from another country that grass and trees had grown here less than a month ago, they'd have thought she was playing a cruel joke on them. Even for her, the geography was so foreign she couldn't have said if she was close to home or hiking across the surface of the moon. With every step, the thought recurred that she might be walking on the ashes of people, even of people she'd known. That thought made the pressure in her chest swell to the point where she felt sure she was going to release it in a cry, but she reined it in and pressed ahead.

There was no wind on the plain, no movement except the wormlike ripples of heat in the distance. No matter how carefully they tried to plant their feet, the clouds of dust they kicked up produced a miniature sandstorm around them, the fine particles flying into Michelle's eyes, clinging to her cropped hair, catching in her nose and mouth. After a half-mile of squinting against the billowing dust and spitting precious fluid to clear her mouth of grit, Michelle called a halt and, with the tip of an arrow as her only cutting tool, sliced strips of cloth from the cuffs of her pant legs and Kareem's. These she wrapped around their faces above and below the eyes, leaving only a thin gap for visibility. Breathing through the thick material wasn't pleasant, but it was preferable to gagging on the remains of whatever or whoever had lost their lives here. She wished she could make a fuller covering for their heads, but she'd run out of places to tear their uniforms without exposing skin to the sun and sand.

They made better progress after that point, partly because of the face shields, partly because they developed a rhythm for keeping their balance on the shifting sand. But being out on the open plain, with little water and no breeze to cool them down, was torture in itself. Sweat flowed into Michelle's eyes, obscuring her vision as much as the sand, and it wasn't long before she felt the stinging tightness on the nape of her neck that told her she was going to have a bad sunburn. Her parched throat spasmed every time she drew a breath, while her muscles felt weak and achy from lack of rest and fluid. The sandy dust seemed to concentrate the sun's rays, making the ground temperature even higher than the surrounding air. Michelle could feel the heat through the thick soles of her boots, and by the time the sun started its downward course, she felt as if she were crossing a parking lot barefoot during summer vacation. Beneath the grains of sand that clung to his eyelashes, Kareem stared straight ahead with a determined expression, but considering his illness and the condition his feet had been in just a day before, she had to believe the scorching plain was even worse for him.

With the red orb hovering over the dunes at their back, she had another decision to make. The desert would cool down somewhat at nightfall—in fact, if what she'd heard about deserts was true, it might get dangerously cold. But could they risk continuing their march at night? She'd seen no signs of pursuit during the day, nothing moving on the plain except heat mirages. Still, she felt totally exposed in this wide open place, where the security of knowing she'd be able to see Jason approaching was more than counterbalanced by the uncanny sense of eyes lying in wait everywhere: ahead, behind, all around, even up above, as if something were about to swoop down on them like a bird of prey. Would nighttime cover their tracks, clouding hostile eyes with sleep? Or would the desert darkness blind their own eyes, making it all the more likely they'd walk right into Jason's trap?

As if in answer to her question, she and Kareem had no sooner descended a slight slope in the plain than they found themselves wallowing in sand up to their hips. Michelle, by luck somewhat less deeply snared than her companion, struggled free of the pit and held out her bow for him to haul himself to more solid ground. At that point, she decided it was too dangerous to advance any farther. They were exhausted and dehydrated, she couldn't see far enough ahead to know if the city was anywhere near, and the chance of falling into quicksand seemed an even greater risk than the possibility of encountering Jason. Much as she hated to admit it, what they needed now was rest. They could take shifts on watch through the night, and hope they had put enough ground between them and Jason to complete their journey at the first appearance of dawn.

Kareem didn't say anything when she told him her plan, but his eyes looked haunted. For the hundredth time, she chastised herself for not packing any supplies—food, water, a tarp to sleep under. Trying not to dwell on what she couldn't change, she approached her partner, who had stripped off his headgear and lay sprawled on the sand disconsolately searching the cloudless sky. The departing sun's rays lit his features the color of blood.

"Kareem," she said, pulling down her own scarf, "I need to check your feet."

His attention drifted to her. "My feet?"

"Take your boots off," she said. "Keep your feet up so they don't touch the sand. I have to see if they're okay."

He looked genuinely puzzled. "There's nothing wrong with my feet."

"There was a day ago. And they'll get worse if we keep up like this. I might need to wrap them. Now let me take a look."

"But—" he began, before quieting at the glare she threw his way. Obediently, he sat up, unlaced his boots, and pulled them off. He rested back on his palms and lifted his feet into the air.

Michelle set aside her bow and kneeled in front of him, carefully taking his heels in her hands. With a delicate finger, she traced each sole, wondering how on earth she'd be able to treat them if their condition had worsened. Then her finger stopped, and she choked a single word.

"How—"

Her eyes jerked to his, but there was nothing in his expression that suggested he knew why she was so surprised.

"That's impossible," she said. "It's only been ... it's only a little more than a day."

"What's the matter?"

"Your feet," she said, her voice and her grip rougher than she intended. "They're ... "

"They feel fine."

"But they shouldn't!" she exclaimed. "They were all cut up and bleeding—they were a mess. And your blood was ...

142

Circe said you had a blood infection. We thought you were dying. And now ... "

She curled his right foot toward him to present the evidence. His flesh was warmed by the surface they'd walked on, but the bleeding cuts that Circe had cleaned and covered with gauze were gone. Not just healed, which would have left ugly scars—*gone*. They'd vanished as completely as if they were part of the dreams she'd fallen into overnight—dreams of him chasing her, silent and relentless as a wraith, so fleet and tireless his soles had no need to touch the earth at all.

Michelle let go and crouched on the burning sand, eyeing him as warily as she would have watched an unfamiliar dog that blocked her front walk. She remembered Jason focusing on Kareem's feet when they first found him—touching the bleeding flesh with his knife, then bringing a bright spot of blood to his lips. It had seemed grotesque then, this strange obsession he had with the blood of anyone who came near his camp, herself included. Now she wondered if there was something he'd known all along, something he feared had been released when the bombs fell: an infection, a plague, one that gave its carriers the power to fight off wounds that would have killed anyone else.

Kareem had retied his laces and stood, his sun-lengthened shadow spilling over her to drape the dunes to the east. She stayed on the ground for a long moment, then slowly regained her feet. The bow and arrow she'd laid down to inspect his nonexistent injuries were back in her hands. He gazed at her with a look of sorrow, not fear.

"Michelle ... "

"You told me not to trust anyone. Does that mean I shouldn't trust you, either?"

"In the city," he corrected. "I said not to trust anyone in the *city*."

"But why is that different? If I can trust you out here, why can't I trust you there?"

"Things might change there," he said quietly.

"But *what?*" she insisted. "Are you planning to meet someone? Are you worried that you'll have to make a choice between me and them? What are you not telling me?"

He took a heavy breath. "If I could show you ... "

"No!" she said. "I can't wait for that anymore. Tell me now, or ... " The bow was held firmly in her hands, the arrow nocked. "Please, Kareem. Don't make me do this."

"You don't have to," he said, with the combination of persuasiveness and force a person might use to talk someone off a ledge. "Put the bow down, Michelle. You just need to trust me a little while longer."

"Until we reach the city? Is that what you were planning to do from the start?"

He said nothing, only looked at her sadly.

"Who are you, Kareem?" she asked, then spoke three more words, so softly she might have been talking to herself. "*What* are you?"

He glanced away, toward the east, but offered no answer.

Michelle drew the bowstring back until she felt the tension straining against her sunburned neck and shoulder. Releasing it would be so easy. She could hardly believe she'd trusted him, after everything Jason had warned her about, everything Kareem had done. There must have been something he wanted from her all along, something he'd sensed last night in the infirmary he could get from her if he took advantage of her vulnerability and confusion, and she'd been so desperate to discover the truth, so desperate for someone she could trust, she'd failed to see that the one who promised her the truth was the greatest threat of all.

"I'm going to count to three," she said.

He stared at her, his eyes shadowed.

"One ... "

He took a step, holding out a hand. "Michelle, wait!"

"Two ... "

That was as far as she got.

The ground between them erupted, throwing a shower of dust into the air and obscuring her view of him and the landscape. Through the swirling cloud, she saw two figures standing where there'd been no one before, hunched shadows that faced her menacingly. The thought flashed through her mind that Jason and Argus had tunneled beneath the sand and lain in wait while she and Kareem argued. But when the cloud settled, she saw that these weren't people she knew.

She wasn't sure they were people at all.

They had the shape of men, though they were bent over so far their hands nearly touched the ground. Dust caked them like a second skin, exposing little but their eyes and teeth. Sparse, filthy hair hung to their shoulders. When the two took a step toward her, the dust seemed to flake from their frames—but then Michelle realized it wasn't dust but strips of peeling skin, as if they were shedding the outer layer of themselves as they moved. Their feet had burned to toeless nubs against the superheated sand, making their steps unsteady, teetering. As they closed on her, she saw that patches of skin on their faces and hands had melted completely away, forming deep pockets like bite marks gouged from their flesh.

Michelle's mind shrieked into action, and she leaped back, avoiding the creatures' clutching hands. The two kept coming, groping for her as if they were wearing blindfolds in Rosie's favorite childhood game of pin the tail on the donkey. From this close, Michelle felt a wave of cold radiating from them, smelled a stink like spoiled meat. She could see that their eyes were glazed with dust, their irises and pupils lost beneath the filmy coating. Or maybe they had no eyes, and all she was seeing were the empty sockets beneath their ragged brows.

One of the creatures lunged, its hand curled into a feral claw. Before its fingers could close on her arm, Kareem threw himself at its legs, and its right shin disintegrated in a torrent of dust. Unbalanced, the monster pitched forward, catching itself against the ground with an outstretched hand. Upon contact, the hand and forearm crumbled to dust as well, leaving nothing but a stump. It made one more convulsive attempt to pull free of Kareem's arms, but the motion seemed to tear it in two, its torso toppling to the ground. When Michelle glanced at its face, she was horrified to see a hole like a smashed sand castle where its features should have been.

The other creature was still coming at her. She raised her bow and shot from no more than ten feet away.

The arrow punctured its chest, and it flinched as the missile tore through its body. But it didn't break apart like the other one, and it didn't stop. After a moment's swaying as if to regain its balance, the thing took another lurching step.

Where the arrow protruded from its chest, there was no blood.

146

Michelle fired again, her second arrow penetrating the monster's forehead with enough force that it should have splattered the thing's brains on the sand. Instead, the arrow merely caused the head to snap back before the creature took another step, the feathered fletching planted like a macabre headdress above its vacant eyes.

Michelle emptied her quiver at the thing, each missile staggering it just long enough for her to reload and fire again. Once, an arrow aimed at its heart tore through the sinews of its left arm, leaving the limb dangling by a thread from its shoulder. Another time, the arrow point embedded itself in the creature's open mouth, the red feathers waggling like tongues. The monster showed no pain, uttered no sound, bled no blood. It stalked her with the blind instinct of an underground predator drawn by the motion of its prey. If not for the arrows, it would surely have caught her.

It seemed to know when she'd exhausted her ammunition.

The monstrous thing in the shape of a man paused for a moment, what was left of its face twitching strangely. A shudder ran through it from chin to stomach, and the flesh of its chest peeled back, revealing a depthless cavity in which the shafts of arrows protruded like broken ribs. Michelle glanced behind it for Kareem, but couldn't find him. She heard his voice, crying weakly as if he'd been dragged beneath the sand.

"Michelle, run!"

Dropping her bow, she obeyed.

Maybe she could have escaped the monster on solid ground. Here, there was only shifting sand, which skidded under her feet, clutched at her ankles, tried to pull her into its belly. She felt more than heard the footfalls behind her, and knew she couldn't outrace it. She didn't stop to wonder how it moved so fast with its feet worn away practically to nothing and its body riddled with arrows. She only knew that, like the thing she'd seen on Kareem's phone, this phantom would never relent, never tire, until it had caught her and made her its own.

She leaped down a short hillside, landing awkwardly, her ankle twisting. With a yelp, she tumbled on her face in the hot sand. Before she could get her hands beneath her, she felt the thing grip her wounded ankle.

She screamed.

It wasn't the ankle injury that tore the sound from her throat. It was pain such as she'd never felt before—all-consuming, gut-wrenching pain. At the creature's touch, her body went rigid, every muscle straining against a razor-sharp agony as if its hand had opened her up with a scalpel, reached inside her body, and scooped pieces of her away. As the pain increased, she lost the ability to focus on what was happening to her, couldn't remember where she was, what she'd been doing just a moment before, how she'd found herself in this empty place. Faces flashed through her mind, but she had no names to attach to them, no memory of their time together, no sense of who she ... who she ...

She couldn't remember who *she* was.

With an effort that felt as if it would tear her apart, she wrenched her leg from the creature's grasp. Instantly, air rushed into her lungs, the pain subsided, and her mind cleared of the fog that had descended over it. She kicked with all her strength, smashing the monster's head with such force that her boot tore straight through the hollow where its face should have been. Then she was on her feet again, her twisted ankle throbbing as she limped away. She glanced back and saw that the thing was right behind her, its head cloven in two but the ravenous mouth that had formed from the rest of its body looming over her like a dark wave.

She knew she couldn't outrun it any longer. She spun to face it. The mouth stretched wide in a leer.

A stream of fire struck the creature from the side, and its body ignited as if it were soaked in kerosene. The first sound it had made in all this time emerged from somewhere within the body cavity, a thin wail or moan that was barely audible above the crackle of the flames. The monster thrashed violently against its fiery cocoon, but couldn't free itself. Michelle watched the hideous form soften and flow into slag, then cinders, then nothing. The last traces of it burned away in acrid smoke that stank of decaying flesh, until the only reminder of its presence was a scorched black circle on the desert sand.

Michelle fell to her knees, gasping for breath. The memory of being in the beast's grasp returned to her, and her gut twisted with what she could only describe as soul-sickness. She leaned over and retched onto the ground, her empty stomach spitting nothing but bile. In the back of her mind, she knew that she would never fully recover from the creature's touch, that it had taken something from her she could never get back. It was a loss she couldn't explain, as terrible in its own way as the loss of her family and her home. The thing without a face had excised some treasure from deep inside her, and she knew that from now on, nothing she did or was would ever be the same.

She was lying on the ground, curled around this new pain, when an iron hand gripped her arm.

"I gave you a chance," a voice murmured in her ear, just before she felt a sharp pinch in the crook of her elbow. "You failed me."

Michelle tried to look at the one who'd spoken, tried to resist whatever it was that he had injected into her veins, but her strength was gone. Two blurry shapes rose in front of her, and she felt herself being lifted from the desert sand. Her vision shuttered to a pinpoint of light, and everything fell away.

Chapter 10

She woke in darkness.

The first thing to assault her senses was the smell of piss and excrement, far worse than any locker room she'd ever set foot in, worse even than the camp latrine. Her eyes stung with tears, and she tried to take shallow breaths against the stink. As consciousness sharpened, she became aware of the various pains that attacked her body: her head throbbed, her throat felt dry and raw, and an unnatural lethargy spread through her limbs. She perceived that she was sitting with her back against a hard wall, but when she struggled to stand, something constricted her. It took her muddy mind a minute to determine what the problem was, but then the clanking of metal and the bite of cold iron at her wrists told her that she was chained in place. Another minute of pulling against the shackles convinced her that she couldn't fight her way free.

"Poetic justice," the unmistakable voice of Jason spoke from the darkness. "After all that running, to find yourself right back where you started."

She couldn't see him, but she could sense his presence, hear his quiet breathing. She'd finally put two and two together and figured out where she was: the box. Why he'd joined her, how he could stand the stench of this airless room where he'd confined other members of his camp, was beyond her. Unless confinement wasn't the only form of torture he practiced here.

She heard a shifting sound, and guessed that he had moved closer. Her muscles tightened defensively as she strained into the dark, thinking she might see his piercing blue eyes, but there was only his silky voice when he spoke again.

"I've talked to Arachne," he said. "She told me everything I need to know about the night you left camp, and the tracker I planted on you enabled us to figure out where you were headed. The only thing I don't know yet is *why*."

She remembered the hand he'd placed on her back when he walked her to the infirmary. Was *that* when he'd attached a tracker to her uniform? She opened her mouth to respond, but the reek of the box entered with her first breath, and she swallowed convulsively. Her words came out through clenched teeth. "You told me I wasn't tracked."

"I told you we track those we have reason to doubt," Jason answered. "I had my doubts about you from day one— a lone teenage girl wandering my woods far from the nearest habitation, refusing to tell me anything about her past. I've been keeping a close eye on you since then, trying to uncover your true history. But it wasn't until I saw how interested you were in this Kareem that my suspicions were fully aroused. What better way to sniff out the truth than to put the two of you together and see what plan you'd devise once you were reunited?"

She considered a retort, but forced it down. It no longer surprised her that Jason had distrusted her from the beginning, though it did rattle her to realize how focused he'd been on exposing her. Was everything—the field training, the lectures, the times he'd asked for her assistance—nothing but a lie? For that matter, was everyone in camp—not only Arachne but Argus, Circe, even Tyris—helping him test her, feeding her a range of stimuli to measure her responses? "What are you going to do to me?"

"That's up to you," he said. "It's always been up to you. Throw your lot in with those who mean the Argo harm, and you'll go down with them. Show me that you're willing to give up your friend to protect the community I've built, and your fate will write itself in a totally different way."

He took a step closer to her, so close she could feel his breath tickle her cheek. She flattened herself against the wall, but something slimy and cold made her jerk away.

A blue light flickered on, its brightness unbearable after hours without sight. Michelle squinted against the glare until it resolved itself into a glowing rectangle gripped in Jason's hand. The light was strong enough to outline his features, illuminate his eyes. He held it before her so she had no choice but to look straight into it.

Kareem's phone.

"Argus cracked the code last night, while you were sleeping," Jason said, his face betraying not the hint of a smile at the euphemism. "He's given me the information I need to draw the broad outlines of the conspiracy, but not to fill in the boy's part. Seems this isn't his personal phone, but one he was provided—or took—from a nearby base of operations. Given where we found you the morning after the attacks and where you were headed yesterday, I have reason to believe you're familiar with that base. So why don't you start by telling me what you were planning to do once you got there?"

Michelle shook her head, which made the light dance dizzily in front of her. "I wasn't planning to do anything. I don't even know what base you're talking about."

"You'll have to excuse my skepticism." Jason swiped the phone, which dimmed then brightened again. "You don't want to tell me about this?"

He shoved the screen toward her. It was solid black except for a string of red letters in a rounded, computerized script.

SKLDI

"Is that ... code?" Michelle guessed.

"You tell me."

"I don't know. I've never seen it before."

"But I have," Jason said. "Before I founded the Argo, before I swore I'd never let anyone threaten my camp. Anyone—or anything." Behind the obsidian screen, his eyes glowed as if with their own light. "So I'm going to ask you one more time. What were you and the boy planning to do once you reached the city?"

Michelle tried to review the past day with Kareem. It was hard to recall the details, her mind clumsy with exhaustion and whatever drug Jason had given her. The events since she'd left camp returned to her in broken images, elusive, incomplete. It was, she thought, similar to what Kareem had said about his own memory. The day she'd spent with him had the quality of a half-forgotten dream, coiled within her like a snake that lay camouflaged against the dusty ground, revealing itself fully only when it struck ...

With a gasp, she remembered the thing from the desert. "That creature. The one you killed. What was it?"

"Something I thought had been destroyed long ago," he

said. "Something I only learned had survived on the day your friend showed up at my camp." Again he swiped the screen, then held it before her eyes. "Maybe this will jog your memory."

The letters had disappeared, replaced by the video she'd watched in the communications center with Jason and Argus. This time, the image had been zoomed in and slowed down, advancing frame by frame. She watched the pursuer close in on its first victim, watched the moment of contact, watched the fallen figure disappear, just like before. Except ...

"Wait," she said.

Jason's face shone with eagerness in the phone's light. "Yes?"

"Show me one more time. I want to make sure."

He replayed the footage. With the close-ups and frame advance, she could clearly differentiate between the two figures, despite their identical uniforms. The one who was trying to get away was small, slim, possibly a child, while the pursuer was much larger, broad-shouldered, an adult or nearly so. Yet at the moment of contact, what happened wasn't as simple as she'd first thought, with the victim disappearing in the blink of an eye. Instead, one series of frames showed the pursuer pouncing on the other's body, and the next showed something Michelle wouldn't have believed if not for what she'd undergone yesterday: the pursuer's torso opening wide, the two bodies joining briefly together, a cloud of dust spreading from the point of contact—and then only the *smaller* body remaining. It had *replaced* the larger one, and it was in this new body that the creature resumed its pursuit.

"It ... took him," Michelle said.

"That's right," Jason said. "Now, maybe you'd like to tell

155

me what you know about the base you and your friend were headed for."

Michelle didn't answer, but her mind raced with this new, terrible insight. Kareem had told her not to trust anyone in the city; he'd warned her that if the mysterious assailants had infiltrated Jason's camp, no one would know. The faceless thing that had attacked her in the desert—when it touched her, she momentarily lost her sense of self, felt as if it had robbed her of something that had belonged to her all her life. Even now, her recall of the attack remained murky. Whatever these monsters were, they didn't simply kill their victims. They *became* their victims, claiming the bodies of those they consumed.

"You knew about this?" she said to Jason. "You knew about these things—and you didn't tell anyone?"

"This isn't about what *I* know," he said. "This is about you, and your friend. It's about how I'm supposed to defend my camp against creatures that can mimic the people I count on for defense."

Michelle was surprised by the laugh that rose from her throat. "Isn't that your problem?"

"I can easily make it yours," he said, and she heard a knife slide from its sheath, saw the blade glint in the light of the phone. "If you don't tell me exactly what you and the boy were planning to do in the city, I can make it very much your problem."

She watched the knife wave hypnotically before her eyes. Without blinking, she let each word out as carefully as if the blade were pressed against her throat.

"Jason," she said, "it's not what you think. Kareem and I aren't working together. And he's not in league with those …

those things. If he was, why would they have attacked us in the desert?"

Jason leaned forward, the light from the screen wrapping his face like the strands of a glowing web. He made no reply, but his blade inched closer to her eyes.

"He must have been attacked by one of them," Michelle continued. "He was trying to guide me to them, to show me what they're capable of so we could warn you. But he's ... when they attack, they take away parts of you. Even if you live. It's not his fault. He can't remember what they are. Or who *he* is."

The knife moved again, and Michelle flinched. But Jason had only shifted the weapon in his hand so he could once again hold out the phone.

"If he's been looking through this device, he knows plenty," he said. "The files Argus opened are full of information about those monsters, including their vulnerability to fire. You owe your life to that—to that, and to the fact that the Argo is equipped with flamethrowers. If the boy has access to this information, he must be working with the ones who brought them to our world."

"But ... " Something he'd just said made no sense, and it took her a few seconds to realize what it was. "If Argus only opened the files after you got back last night, how did you know to bring a flamethrower with you?"

Without warning, Jason spun and paced away from her. The light of the phone in his hand showed her the dirt floor of the box, the cement walls of the subterranean prison. He covered the tight distance from wall to wall, then returned, the phone stabbed in her face as if it were his blade.

"I've answered your questions," he said. "Now you're

going to answer mine."

"I can't give you the answers you want."

"Three days in the box are typically enough to break anyone. And I've got techniques for speeding the process along."

The screen went dark, plunging them into the eternal night that reigned in the cell. She felt his hand on her chin, forcing her head up, exposing her neck. A shard of steel, cold and hard as ice, pressed against her throat. She held perfectly still, not even daring to swallow. If he chose to kill her, she knew he could do it easily. She doubted, though, that he *would* do it easily. He'd do it in a way that caused her the greatest possible pain, and no matter how much she screamed that she didn't know the answers to his questions, he'd cut as many screams as he could from her until she could scream no more.

"I could kill you without losing a minute's sleep," he murmured in her ear. "But I think you might be more valuable to me alive."

His fingers slipped from her face, and she heard him move away. The light stayed off, his voice coming out of the darkness in a tight, clipped cadence, as if he were holding himself back from committing violence.

"The boy got away from us in the desert. We scoured the area, but there was no sign of him. My guess is that he made straight for the city. I'm not about to put anyone in my camp at risk by having them follow."

"You want me to go back," she said.

There was a pause where Jason might have nodded. "I'll accompany you as far as the outskirts. If I suspect for a second that you're planning to double-cross me, I'll finish you right then and there." The tip of his knife returned to the cleft of her throat. "You've seen what I can do to a deer. Any large mammal can be skinned the same way."

Sickness crept into Michelle's gut as her mind conjured images she was powerless to dispel. "What am I supposed to do when I get there?"

"You'll be carrying a weapon to cripple the enemy. If you do as you're told, it should put an end to the threat for good."

"Won't they know what I'm there for?"

"The weapon is small. You should be able to plant it without their knowledge." He sheathed the knife with a *snick* of metal against leather. "If you complete the job, I'll guarantee your safety from that point on. You can leave this place behind and never look back. But if you refuse ... "

"You'll kill me."

"You, or others," he said. "I've been thinking a five-year-old girl and a couple of brainless mutes aren't much use to me."

Michelle's heart froze. "You wouldn't."

"You have no idea what I would do. I'd gladly sacrifice a handful if it meant stopping an invasion with the power to destroy us all."

Michelle found her eyes filled with tears—whether for herself, for Kareem, or for the most helpless members of Jason's camp, she didn't know. She did know enough about the Argo's leader to doubt she'd be let free after satisfying his demands. She tried to trace the events that had brought her to this point, tried to see what she'd done to deserve such a fate. The car, the phone, the deer—was this punishment for that? It didn't make sense. Maybe she should have run from

Jason as she'd run from Caeneus, taking the chance that she wouldn't end up with an arrow in her back. Or maybe, after submitting to join the Argo, she should have become like the others, forcing herself to forget her home, handing her life to Jason to do with as he pleased. That wouldn't have made her happy, but it might have spared her the pain of clinging to a past that was almost certainly dead and gone.

"I guess I don't have a choice," she said.

"You've always had a choice," he answered. "You can reject my terms, and die along with the others. Or you can agree to those terms and deal with the results of that decision. I don't choose for you. I only show you the choices that are yours to make."

She closed her eyes and leaned her head against the cold cement. The darkness was total even with her eyes open, but somehow, she felt as if she were alone this way, as if Jason and the camp he commanded had vanished along with all her hopes and dreams. Yet his words refused to disappear; they echoed deep in her mind, louder and more insistent with each reverberation, and she knew that what he said was true. His lessons might be harsh, but their logic was something she'd come to accept.

She opened her eyes. "Turn on the light."

"I don't take orders from you."

"You want to know my decision, don't you? You want to look me in the eye when I tell you."

He didn't comply at once, but at last the screen flickered on. She blinked and saw him standing before her with arms crossed, no expression in his ghostly eyes.

"I'll go," she said. "I'll do what you ask, and I won't try to trick you. Even if I don't come back, I'll do it. If I can help

160

destroy those ... those monsters, it'll be worth it."

He nodded.

"But I'm not doing it for you," she said. "I'm doing it for the world I knew, the people I loved."

He smiled derisively. "The noble huntress Diana."

"You can make fun of me all you want," she said. "You've never known anything except cruelty and hatred your entire life, so I'm not surprised you don't know what it means to fight for what you love. But if you're going to send me out there to die, there's one thing you need to get straight."

His smile faded. "And what is that?"

"My name isn't Diana, you son of a bitch," she said. "It's Michelle."

Chapter 11

She stood on the crest of a dune overlooking the city. Or what was left of it. Though Michelle had never seen this place and didn't know its name, she was stunned by how completely its architecture had been demolished, the network of streets and buildings and bridges blurred beyond recognition. The tallest structures, office towers and churches and parking garages, had slid to the ground, leaving only an occasional house or store to rise above the flattened topography. But these lone survivors had been stricken as well: walls had come down, roofs had been sheared off, back yards had been transformed into junk piles of pulverized brick, glass, and wood. There were no trees standing, no visible reminders of the parks and green spaces that might once have dotted the urban grid; everything was choked by debris. Here and there, half-covered shapes poked from beneath the wreckage: the hoods of trucks and buses, the crumpled rectangles of road signs, the rounded crown of a collapsed water tower whose printed name had been effaced by its fall. The landscape reminded Michelle of pictures she'd seen of Hiroshima, a city whose life had been buried beneath the ash of the structures that had once supported it.

Gazing at this anonymous, shattered metropolis, a silent

cry rose in her chest, one she'd been holding back since the night of the yellow fire. For all this time, she'd harbored the hope that the devastation beyond the Argo wasn't as bad as Jason portrayed it, that the fire she'd seen burning the woodlands had left civilization intact. The desert she and Kareem had tried to cross had shown her how tenuous that hope was, how much a child's fantasy. But she'd clung to it all the same, and it was only now that she was forced to admit the truth.

The search for her family was over. They were gone, or at least lost to her forever. What purpose she would find to carry her through the days that followed, assuming she lived to see any days after this one, she had no idea.

She shifted uncomfortably beneath her burden, trying to focus on the immediate task to prevent herself from breaking down in front of the armed man who accompanied her. Whereas she and Kareem had crossed the desert with nothing but her bow and the clothes they were wearing, she and Jason were outfitted like an army of two heading off to defend the final front. Strapped to their backs were Vietnam-era M9 flamethrowers, the same kind he and Argus had used against the monster in the desert. When Jason first hoisted hers on, she thought there was no way she'd be able to use it; the thing weighed fifty pounds at least, and even after an hour of aiming at tree trunks, she doubted she could point the unwieldy mechanism at a smaller target. Added to the weapon's weight were a protective helmet, goggles, gas mask, and gloves, all of which trapped sweat and stank of oil and rubber. To compensate for lost body fluid, they were loaded down with as much water as two people could carry. Though Jason had warned her during their early field exercises that the problem with this most essential of supplies was its high weight-to-volume ratio, she was surprised by how much the canteens clipped to her belt weighed her down. By contrast, their food stores were light, protein bars and a few strips of turkey jerky. That in itself told her all she needed to know about the likely outcome of this mission. Jason wouldn't let the two of them starve on their journey across the desert, but once she performed her duty in the city, he didn't care if she had to dig beneath the rubble in hopes of finding a scrap to fill her empty belly.

It was probably pointless to worry about a slow, lingering death. Even if she lived long enough to do what he'd brought her here for, Jason's own weaponry made it pretty clear what awaited her afterward. He carried not only a matching flamethrower but one of the camp's ubiquitous military rifles—obviously intended not for creatures that couldn't bleed but for his flesh-and-blood partner if she tried to attack or escape. He also bore an ammunition belt, a fire starter, a compass, a set of walkie-talkies, a pair of binoculars on a cord around his neck, and a bulletproof vest, not to mention a clutch of hand grenades. He carried all the extra baggage with ease, reminding Michelle of how dangerously strong he was beneath the lean, wiry build.

There was only one thing that gave her any hope for her future, and even that was probably wishful thinking. It had happened just before they set out for the city. She'd been staggering toward the headlands with Jason, wondering how she was going to climb the trail and then walk across the desert in this outfit, when a voice sounded behind them. Turning her whole body was difficult, so she turned her head to see Circe hustling across the green, with Tyris her ever-present shadow.

"Jason," the doctor said when she caught up to them. "Argus didn't tell me you'd lifted the ban on field exercises."

Michelle was struck by the note of sarcasm in Circe's voice. Jason heard it, too.

"This has nothing to do with you, Circe," he said. "I'd suggest you get back to work."

"Taking care of people *is* my work, as you know very well," Circe answered. "And it seems to me this girl could use some taking care of."

Beneath the sweat and stink of her heavy gear, Michelle felt her heart lighten the slightest bit. She'd emerged from the box that afternoon famished, weak, and woozy from the injection Jason had given her. When she caught sight of her reflection in the flamethrower's fuel tank, she was astonished at how pale she'd become. The other women had shied from her as if she were some noxious insect, and Circe had been no different. Arachne was out of the infirmary by now, stalking the camp with her ankle in an air boot, and Michelle assumed that Circe accepted the sentry's story and saw Michelle as a traitor and a sneak, one who'd played on the doctor's sympathy to facilitate her and her companion's flight.

Now, though, the older woman took a step toward Michelle, reaching for the flamethrower as if to help her out of it. "Let me get some fluids in her," she said to Jason. "She's in no condition to travel."

"Back off, Circe," Jason said, stepping between them. "If you know what's good for your daughter."

Circe squeezed Tyris to her. "You wouldn't—"

"Take your pick," Jason said. "Maybe you can nurse *her*

165

back to health."

Michelle looked back and forth between them—the tall, ice-eyed leader, his hand resting on his rifle, and the short, fiftyish woman, who held Tyris in a grip so tight the little girl, usually compliant, had begun to squirm and whine. The doctor held her ground until Michelle broke the stalemate.

"It's all right, Circe," she said. "I'll be okay."

Circe opened her mouth as if to speak, but then turned her head away, pulling Tyris into an even tighter embrace. When Jason took a step toward them, the doctor backed off, and he smiled smugly before herding Michelle toward the trailhead.

"I'll deal with you later," he said to Circe over his shoulder. Michelle took a look back and saw the mother still clinging to her struggling child, a haunted look on her face. Setting Tyris free, she hustled back to the women's quarters, the little girl skipping by her side.

"She forgets her place," Jason muttered as they started up the trail. "Make sure you don't forget yours."

Michelle's heart pounded, and not only from the climb. She didn't completely understand what had just happened, but it was obvious that Circe had some ongoing dispute with Jason, possibly having to do with how the camp leader treated Tyris. Whatever the conflict was, might Circe be willing to help Michelle if she was able to return to the Argo? Or would the prospect of Circe's mutiny make it more likely that Jason would ensure that Michelle *didn't* return?

She arrived, sweating and trembling, at the top of the pass. The thought occurred to her that Jason was trying to kill her *before* they arrived at the city—or before they even started out.

"Wait here," he said, and vanished into the woods a short distance away. She couldn't have run if she'd wanted to, but the new sentry who'd taken Arachne's place made sure to emphasize her helplessness, standing well out of range of her flamethrower while his rifle never deviated from its target on her chest.

A minute later, she heard the roar of a motor. A vehicle emerged from the woods with Jason at the wheel. It was nothing like any car she'd seen—more like a moon buggy, all spindly metal and oversized wheels. She guessed it wasn't the only high-tech toy the leader of the Argo kept hidden for his personal use.

"You didn't think we were going to walk all the way there, did you?" he asked with a laugh as he came to a bouncing stop. He hopped out of the driver's seat wearing only his black jacket and camouflage uniform, and helped her wiggle free of the flamethrower, storing it atop his own in the ATV's rear compartment. Before he slammed and latched the storage unit, she caught sight of one item Jason hadn't been carrying on the way up: a black metal box, about twelve inches square, that lay partially covered by a tarp. She didn't get a good enough look to know what it was, and Jason didn't volunteer any information as the two of them settled into their seats.

The journey that had taken almost a day by foot took only until evening in the ATV, with exhaustion traded for tooth-jarring bumps and jolts. They'd driven deep into the desert, plumes of sand spitting out behind the vehicle's rear wheels, when Jason came to a stop and told Michelle to get out. Not a word had been exchanged during their journey. Now he directed her to help him unload the supplies and lowered the flamethrower onto her shoulders after he'd secured his own. The black box remained in storage while Jason used his binoculars to scan their surroundings—a waste of time, so far as she could tell, since the creatures evidently possessed the ability to blend with the desert sand.

Jason must have been satisfied that the way was clear. He reached into the compartment and lifted the box, which seemed almost weightless judging by how easily it rose in his hands. Michelle tried again to determine what it was, but he'd wrapped the tarp around it.

"We'll walk from here," he said. "Don't want to alert them to our presence."

She looked toward the east, but saw no sign of a city on the horizon. "How far is it?"

"About a mile. Won't be hard."

"I don't see anything."

"There's a drop. You'll see it soon enough."

She nodded but said nothing. She took a plodding step and had to struggle to lift her boot to take another. With the extra weight, she felt as if she were floundering in quicksand. Jason, not surprisingly, made no offer to lighten her load.

"You'll get used to it," was all he said.

Step by painful step, they made their way across the desert. Jason walked behind her, cradling the box as if it were a swaddled newborn. Even this late in the day, the sun beat down on them like a demonic force, made worse by the fumes and extra weight of the flamethrower. The mile took over an hour to complete. If it was a mile. To Michelle, sweating and struggling through the sand, it felt like a marathon.

At the peak of the final dune, Jason halted her and set

the box down. His hands were surprisingly gentle as he rested the covered object on the burning sand. He made no mention of the smashed city that lay below, not even deigning to glance at it while Michelle stood trembling on the brink.

"This is as far as I go," he said. "Your job is to transport this device to a specified location. I'll be guiding you all the way." He reached over to clip a walkie-talkie to her belt, then took a moment to set up his binoculars on a retractable tripod. "If you have to communicate with me, I'll be right here. You shouldn't need to, though."

She might have argued about his definition of *need*, but she knew there was no point. "How does that thing work?"

"It's a pulse weapon," he said, not bothering to explain what that meant. "When you reach the designated spot, you'll prime it and leave it there. You'll then have two hours to return before it detonates."

"And how do I prime it?"

He knelt to unwrap the device. "Take a look."

Michelle joined him while he folded the tarp back with exaggerated care, as if he were opening a longed-for birthday present. Inside sat the inky black box, which opened on a hinged lid to reveal an equally black canister nestled securely inside. His hands careful despite the slight quiver she perceived in them, Jason drew the canister from its resting place and displayed it to her. A smooth metallic shape roughly twice the size of the jar he'd found in Kareem's backpack, the canister was totally unreflective, remaining flat black even in the light of the setting sun. It lacked tail fins or nose cone or any of the features that might have convinced her it was a weapon. Only on closer inspection did she notice the string of blood red letters etched across its black curve.

S K L D I

Her eyes snapped to Jason's, where she discovered him watching her. "You got this from *them*?"

"It came into my possession," he answered noncommittally. "Along with instructions for its use. It's designed to deliver the same explosive force as the weapons that were deployed in the initial attack."

"But then … " She had little faith he'd answer, but she had to ask. "Do you mean this is one of the same bombs they used before?"

He shrugged. "Or similar."

"And *you're* planning to use it?"

"One of history's enduring lessons," he said, "is the wisdom of turning the enemy's strength against them."

The last thing she was in the mood for was a history lecture. "But what if—"

"No more questions," he said, waving her away. "Just do as you're told, and I'll hold myself responsible for the outcome."

Michelle returned her gaze to the ugly black thing, appalled to think that *this* was what she'd been ordered to transport into the city. The weapons that had been used before had destroyed everything *except* the monsters. What reason was there to believe that another of those weapons would work now?

She glanced at Jason. His hand was on the skinning knife at his belt, his coiled energy apparent in the set of his shoulders. Clearly, he was intent on getting this evil thing into the city—which meant that if she didn't do it, he'd kill her and find someone else who would. The twins? Tyris? Refusing him now wouldn't save them. She would have to do what he ordered, and hope that she lived through the experience.

"Show me how it works," she said.

His hand left the knife, his body relaxing noticeably. "All you need to do is press and release the trigger," he said, pointing to a square depression beneath the red letters. "Just don't do it until I give you the order. Remember, you have only two hours to clear out after it's set."

"Anything else?"

He stood and carefully passed her the device, which weighed as little in her hands as it had seemed in his.

"I shouldn't have to tell you this," he said, "but don't try to make contact with your friend. If you deviate from my directions, you'll pay for it when you get back."

"If I get back," she asked, "how will you know it's me?"

She thought that might throw him, but he simply unsheathed his knife and ran a finger along the edge.

"They don't bleed," he said. "You do." He made a show of returning the knife to its sheath and switching on their walkie-talkies. "Now get moving."

Michelle stepped to the edge of the dune, pausing to glance back at the red ball of the sun as it hovered above the western horizon. She'd be entering the city as darkness fell. She tried to meet Jason's eyes, but he ducked behind his binoculars and gestured at the city, as if he were a tour guide showing her some natural wonder rather than a killer sending her into a monster-infested war zone. Refusing to rise to his bait, she directed her attention to the hillside ahead of her, where the barely human shadows the two of them cast lay long upon the dune. With the device held tightly against her chest, she took her first step down the hill toward the city.

She slipped on that first step, but somehow kept her balance despite the extra weight and her inability to use her hands. With each succeeding step, she became more confident of her footing, as she found the equilibrium between the burden at her back and the slope at her feet. There were other things she couldn't feel confident about, starting with how she was supposed to operate the flamethrower with the cylinder held in both hands. For the time being, she concentrated on staying upright, avoiding the debris that blocked her way as she approached the jagged line where the smeared outskirts of the city blended into the pure sand of the desert. Now that she'd set her feet on this path, what was the use of worrying about complications she couldn't do a thing about?

She reached the bottom of the dune and looked ahead into the ruined city. From ground level, it appeared even more chaotic than it had from the elevation; distance had softened what turned out to be a treacherous jungle of steel and concrete. The few rays of sunlight that straggled down to the valley floor weren't enough to penetrate the canyons and crevices that had been formed by the city's collapse. Anything could be hiding in those dark spaces, and she'd never know until she was right on top of them. For that matter, the monsters could be out in the open, camouflaged as debris and dust, waiting for her clumsy approach. Maybe she should drop the device, shed the flamethrower, and run back up the hill. Except Jason was waiting for her there.

The crackle of the walkie-talkie made her jump. "Base to Diana," his slightly distorted voice came through. "Do you read? Over."

Shifting the cylinder in her hands, she managed to press

172

the talk button on the two-way radio. "Michelle here. Over."

"Is everything okay? I can barely hear you. Over."

"That's because I can't put the thing to my mouth."

"Not a problem. I'll be doing most of the talking anyway."

She bit back a response.

"Your destination is a good mile ahead," he continued. "I'll be tracking you so I can orient you via landmarks, but it's likely I'll lose sight of you before you get there. If you're not seeing what I'm telling you you should be seeing, then I need to hear from you."

Michelle let out a breath. She considered putting the device down to wipe away the sweat that streamed into her eyes, but she was afraid to lose her grip on it for even a second. She peered into the ruins, wondering what landmarks were left for him to orient her by. "Why is it so important I go to this particular location?"

"It's where the device will be most effective."

"And you know this how?"

"I've learned what I need to," he said with typical evasiveness. "And I'm telling you the site is a mile away."

"Then you should have come with me instead of hiding up there."

There was silence on the line for a long moment. She glanced behind her, but couldn't see his silhouette against the crimson sky. Finally, his voice crackled through again. "I want you to head toward the largest building on your left. The one with the flagpole. Do you see it?"

She turned to the left and found a long, low building that had been cracked in its approximate center, leaving a concavity between two more or less upright mounds of brick.

Her eyes searched for a flagpole, and eventually she located what he must have been talking about, though the metal pole had been reduced to a mere stump like a burned-out candle. She wondered what the absent flag had once flown over, a post office or government building? Right now, the place looked like nothing more than another humpbacked dune in the flow of this desert city.

"I see it," she said.

"Good. Head toward the left corner. You're going to have to make your way around it. When you get there, I'll tell you where to go next."

She tramped toward the building, kicking up dust. Small obstacles rose in her way, chunks of stone that might have fallen from nearby structures, buckled slabs that had once belonged to street or sidewalk. She moved slowly, negotiating a careful path around the hazards, cupping the device protectively. Her biggest source of worry were the holes punched through the concrete, each one leading to a dark cavern with no discernible bottom. The broken pavement shifted under her feet enough to make her nervous that it would give way beneath her. She tried to distribute her weight evenly as she'd learned during her training, but that was impossible with the clunky flamethrower. She rounded the building's left-hand corner—or really, it was too pulverized to call it a corner—and stopped short at the sight that lay before her.

Dust and debris covered the blacktop, but she'd seen enough places like this for it to be unmistakable. The twisted remains of a chain-link fence, the fragments of fallen backboards, the angular framework of brightly colored metal poles now bent like straws and coated with chalky dust: an elementary school playground. Her heart rose to her throat when she remembered long-ago games of kickball, more recent trips behind the wheel of her mom's car to drop Rosie off at school. Trembling, she rested a hand against what was left of the fence and stood there as if the barely visible white lines curling across the blacktop were a fairy circle she couldn't cross.

"Diana?" Jason's voice crackled over the line. "Are you there yet?"

She ignored him. Letting the fence go, she stumbled to the center of the playground before her legs gave out and she landed, her knees hitting the blacktop painfully amidst the matchstick swings and tilted merry-go-round. She knew this couldn't be her old school, Rosie's current school; she didn't know where she was, but she certainly couldn't be there. But that was just the problem. She felt utterly lost, having no idea where on earth she could be, with nothing holding her to the shifting present or sliding past. Clutching Jason's killing device to her chest, she bent over and keened her grief to the ghostly city.

"Rosie," she wailed, while tears made miniature ripples in the dust. "Oh God, no, please, no … "

She heard Jason's voice over the radio, but it was a thousand miles away and she couldn't answer. "Diana. Is everything okay? What's going on? Diana."

A final sob escaped her. "I'm here."

"Good. Thought I'd lost you."

You did. "What do you need me to do?"

"Head across the open space until you see a gap between buildings. Then go straight through."

She held the black cylinder in the crook of her arm and

stood with an effort, the flamethrower threatening to drag her down. Mechanically, she wiped dust from her knees. The remaining march across the blacktop felt unreal, as if she were floating a few inches above the cracked pavement. When she stopped at the playground's edge, she could just make out the phantom trail where her feet had stirred the dust. She voiced a silent prayer and blew a final kiss before resuming the course Jason had set.

"I miss you," she whispered, and then left without looking back.

The walk dragged on for an hour or more after that, as daylight faded and the shapes around her turned to shadows she saw only out of the corner of her eye. Within half that time, Jason lost sight of her as he'd predicted, the maze of the city throwing walls between them that were reinforced by the gathering dark. That slowed her even further, as he was constantly checking in for a description of her surroundings, telling her to retrace her steps or change her course. The deeper she dived toward her goal, the more dangerous the going became, as if the outskirts of town had been the mere splashes of surf that wash up on shore after a towering wave rears its head far out to sea. The solid ground gave way to huge pits spanned by precarious walkways; the surrounding rubble thickened like impassable underbrush in the depths of the forest. Despite what her unreliable eyes and jumpy mind kept telling her, she was the only thing moving through the dead city so far. But if what she guessed from Jason's fragmentary answers was right, he was steering her not only toward the epicenter of the attacks that had leveled this metropolis, but directly to the nightmarish creatures' point of origin.

She'd doubled back at his insistence three times in the past ten minutes, each time finding it harder to return to her starting point, when his voice came to her again. "Stop. What do you see?"

She stared ahead. The world had faded to black and white, the mounds of rubble giving off a pale radiance in contrast to the impenetrable pits and caverns. "It's a hole. Maybe a tunnel?"

"Are there pipes going into it?"

She took a step closer, and saw a bundle of thick metal tubes snaking along the ground before plummeting into darkness. "Yes."

"Perfect. You've reached the utility tunnel I was looking for. Ordinarily you wouldn't be able to access it, but there's enough surface damage to expose the lines. This will be your ingress point."

Michelle had barely been listening to his excited voice, but the final two words brought her up short. "Wait. You want me to go *in* there?"

He let out an exasperated breath. "The creatures are subterranean. They burrowed under you in the desert, right?"

"So?"

"So the bombs that damaged the surface must have left their dwelling intact. Which is how they escaped, and why the device needs to be placed belowground."

She breathed evenly to calm herself. His half-answers hinting at knowledge of this place and its creatures, along with his possession of the SKLDI device, made her positive he meant to deceive her. But even if there'd been a way to turn back before, she was too lost to think of that now. "What am I supposed to use for light?"

"Your helmet has an LED lamp. Switch it on."

She kicked herself for forgetting the headlamp, which he'd showed her when they suited up at the Argo. She couldn't help thinking he'd deliberately chosen not to remind her of it so he could enjoy the spectacle of her stumbling through the city in the dark. She flipped the switch and watched the dusty beam light up the mouth of the tunnel. "What now?"

"Take the device inside. I'll tell you when to prime it. Then get the hell out of there if you want to save your skin."

She cringed at his choice of words, the image of the desert creatures' peeling flesh forcing itself into her mind. She chased the thought away and, taking a deep breath, plunged into the tunnel.

It was barely tall enough for her to stand straight, barely wide enough for her to fit through with all her gear. Metal pipes and bundles of insulated wires coated the walls and ceiling, but where concrete showed through, she could tell that the tunnel was much less battered than the terrain she'd covered to this point. Still, the underground city hadn't been completely spared: some of the pipes were broken or hanging loose, and some parts of the floor had cracked and shifted so badly she had to keep her headlamp pointed at the ground to avoid tripping. When she aimed the beam straight ahead, all she saw was a fifteen-foot cone of light fading into Stygian blackness. If one of the creatures came at her from out of the depths, she doubted she'd have time to drop the device and activate the flamethrower. Even if she did, the heat in this enclosed space would likely cook her along with her target.

Jason's voice crackled over the line, so loud she was sure it would attract anything for miles. "How's it coming?"

"Fine," she whispered back. "How much farther?"

"Hard to say. To identify the site of maximum impact, it's going to take … "

His voice faded, either because of a problem with the walkie-talkies or because he was as uncertain as she was. "Jason?"

There was a pause, then his voice returned in mid-sentence. " … need to penetrate to a deeper level. Are there any service ladders going down?"

She turned a slow circle, scanning the walls. "Not that I can see."

"Keep looking. There should be … "

Again, his voice trailed into static. Michelle waited for him to resume, but this time there was only silence on the line.

"Jason?" She unlatched the walkie-talkie and held it to her mouth. "Jason, do you read? This is Michelle. Do you read? Over."

" … Diana?"

"Yes, it's me," she said, too desperate to object to the hated code name. "I'm losing you. Please repeat what you just said. Over."

Again, there was silence.

"Jason?" Nothing. "Jason!" she screamed, her voice echoing in the tunnel.

The radio emitted a steady hum that was even worse than total silence.

Her fingers shook as she reattached the useless walkie-talkie to her belt. The helmet lamp's single polka dot of light swung across the walls, showing her nothing but an undifferentiated tangle of pipes and wires. Paranoia

179

whispered in her ear that this was his plan all along, to lead her into this terrifying place and then abandon her. But then why the elaborate pantomime with the SKLDI device? Whatever this thing she held in her arms truly was, Jason must have believed it would work. If so, wasn't her best bet to prime it right here, then use the two hours that were left to her in an attempt to free herself from the labyrinth of the city?

She angled her headlamp downward to inspect the device. Her hands shook so badly, it seemed as if the trigger had disappeared into the smooth skin of the canister. Then she found it, and her finger jumped to press it the way Jason had shown her.

Except ...

Her finger paused over the button. The sound of her breathing was a roar in her ears. She brought the lamp as close as she could to the letters printed on the canister, and then she knew.

The trigger had already been depressed. Where it should have been, there was nothing but a square black hole like a missing tooth.

Michelle dropped the thing, its hollow clatter rebounding up the tunnel and back. When had the trigger been pressed? She'd been extra careful not to touch it on her trek through the city, which meant that Jason must have primed it before they parted. But that was close to two hours ago. If he was telling the truth about the deadly device, she might have only minutes—only seconds—before it went off.

His deception became crystal clear. If they hadn't lost radio contact, he'd have kept her wandering through the tunnel until the very moment of detonation. And then she'd have died along with the monsters his bomb was meant to destroy.

Michelle raced back up the tunnel, colliding with walls and exposed pipes, barely feeling the pain. When she realized she was still carting the cumbersome flamethrower, she unlatched it with frantic hands and let it thud to the floor, the canteens and gloves following immediately afterward. It had seemed only minutes that she'd been in this underground trap, but now she wondered if it could have been much longer than that. No matter how fast she ran, the exit was nowhere in sight, the beam of her headlamp revealing nothing but endless pipes slithering into darkness. The irrational thought flashed through her mind that Jason had led her into a subterranean funhouse, where hidden mirrors turned what had seemed a perfectly straight corridor into a maze. Should she turn back? Had she missed the opening that led to the surface? Her own heartbeat assailed her ears, but she imagined it as Jason's laughter, ridiculing her pathetic belief that she could escape his retribution.

A shadow rose in the path of her lamp, and she scrambled for the flamethrower, forgetting that she'd dropped it somewhere back in the tunnel. A hand clenched her arm, its nails digging into her skin.

"You shouldn't have come back," a voice said.

Chapter 12

In the light of the lamp, she saw the speaker's face. She barely recognized it as Kareem's.

In the short time since she'd last seen him, his beard had grown longer and wilder, his cheeks more hollow. His skin was blackened with dust, and his eyes had regained the bloodshot look from when she and Jason first found him. For whatever reason, he'd exchanged his camo uniform for another of the black sweatshirt and pant combos, though it was covered with chalky dust that made it look almost white. He glared at her from beneath thick eyebrows.

"Why did you come back?" he demanded. "It's dangerous."

Urgency to escape the tunnel tangled her tongue. She blurted out, "Jason made me bring back a weapon."

He leaned close. His breath stank. "What kind of weapon?"

"A bomb, I think." She tried to remember, but her brain seemed to be back in the darkness of the tunnel. "A ... a pulse device. That's what he called it."

His grip tightened on her arm. "Where is it?"

"There," she said, gesturing with a toss of her head. When he started toward the circle of light, she scrambled for his arm. "It's triggered."

"What?"

"It was Jason. I don't know when he trig—"

Kareem didn't wait for her to finish. With the surprising strength and speed he'd shown the night he tried to escape from camp, he reversed course and pulled her along behind him, her feet numbly following.

It was only seconds before they burst into the softer darkness of nighttime. Michelle tried to determine if they'd exited where she'd entered, but in the riot of broken streets and collapsed buildings, the light from her headlamp did more to confuse than to reveal. Kareem showed no hesitation. With her hand clenched in his, he headed straight up a steep mound of debris, nimbly leaping across unbalanced stones, dodging and ducking to avoid lethal spears of wood and metal rebar. Michelle found herself copying his movements without thought, as if his hand were transmitting secret signals deep into her muscles. They were like a single being, a strange urban mountain goat whose four feet felt completely at home on precarious ledges and unstable piles of scree. While her heart raced and the thought of the ticking time bomb they'd left behind screamed a silent warning, her body performed aerial maneuvers that would have terrified her had she taken a moment to contemplate the vortex below.

They scaled the Alpine rubble until they reached a sharp peak. Without stopping, Kareem plunged down the steep incline, Michelle's body—and most of her stomach—following a step behind. Hand in hand, they careened down the slope so fast that even if her lamp hadn't confused the terrain ahead, everything around her would have been nothing but a blur. She felt as if she were back in the dream that seemed to come over her whenever she was near him, a dream of speed and wind and freedom that was terrifying and exhilarating all at once, like riding a roller coaster in pitch darkness. Or no—that didn't do justice to it. She felt as if she'd sprouted wings and was no longer tethered to the earth, each effortless wingbeat lifting her higher and higher while everything else—her past, her sorrow, her fears—dwindled to nothing on the ground far below.

Eventually, like all dreams, it had to come to an end. They skidded to a stop at the bottom of the slag heap, Kareem letting her hand go to dig in the rubble underfoot. After a minute of kicking aside stones and clearing dust, he gripped an exposed handle and flung open a door that lay flush against the ground. A second later, he scrambled into the opening and disappeared halfway down. Before he vanished completely, he reached for her hand, and she craned her neck to see into the hole. Her lamp revealed a dark vault where Kareem hung from a ladder affixed to the wall. Now that they'd stopped moving, she hesitated, unsure about trusting herself to the dark again. But the urgent beckoning of his hand and the memory of what waited in the tunnel behind them had the effect his mere touch had had moments before, and she grabbed the top rung of the ladder to lower herself into the darkness after him.

It was only a short climb before her feet touched bottom. The lamplight swung across the cement-block walls of a room that was no more spacious than the prison cell in the Argo. But this place was dry and comfortable—cooler than outside, but not cold—with an odorless atmosphere totally different from the reek of Jason's torture chamber. At the other end, a door stood partway open—not enough to see what lay beyond, but enough to convince Michelle that, unlike Jason's box, there was more than one way out.

"You can turn off the light," Kareem said, his voice echoing. Michelle did as he asked, and once the harsh lamplight was extinguished, she realized that the room had lights of its own: glowing blue squares embedded in the floor and ceiling like the emergency lights on an airplane. They provided enough illumination to see, though not quite enough to read the expression in his eyes.

"What is this place?" she asked.

The enigmatic look deepened. "I think it's where I came from."

He walked the three steps to the door and pulled it all the way open. More of the blue lights sprang to life on the other side, revealing a cement corridor every bit as sterile as the outer room. Michelle followed him into the corridor, but when he made a move to shut the door behind them, she held out a hand to stop him.

"If it's okay with you," she said, "I'd rather not be closed in."

He said nothing, but he swung the door as wide as it would go and wedged a fragment of brick beneath it to keep it open. Then he started down the corridor with Michelle a step behind.

The air hummed softly from the blue lights. The corridor continued in a long, straight line, with no doors visible along the walls or up ahead. Michelle tested her voice, heard its echo.

"There are tunnels beneath the Argo," she said. "Jason's camp."

He nodded without glancing back at her. "I get the feeling Jason didn't build the ones out there."

That answer surprised her, but she didn't pursue it. "And we're safe? If the device goes off?"

He stopped, and this time he did turn back. "I don't know."

"Then why'd you bring me here?"

"To show you," he said simply, before resuming his walk.

Michelle kept pace behind him. A thousand questions crowded her mind, questions about the tunnels and the Argo and the creatures and the city. And about Kareem—how he'd escaped the desert, where he'd been living since then, what he'd found to eat and drink. Who he was. But she kept all those questions to herself. She had a feeling he wouldn't answer them, and an even stronger feeling that when they got to where they were going, he wouldn't need to.

They walked for at least a half hour, the corridor never deviating from its course. With each step, she kept expecting to hear the distant explosion of Jason's device, followed by the shaking of the floor or collapse of the ceiling as the place imploded around them. But the only sounds were the unvarying hum of the lights and the soft pad of their footsteps. At last, she sighted a door up ahead, cracked partway open like the previous one. As they drew near, she saw something written on the doorframe, and as soon as she saw it, she realized it was what she'd been expecting to see.

S K L D I

"Do you know what it means?" she asked Kareem.

He paused with his hand on the door. "I keep thinking I should, but … " He shook his head as if he were trying to clear it of a bad dream. "Come with me."

He pushed the door the rest of the way open. Michelle noticed that there was no knob or handle, nothing that looked like a locking mechanism. Once she was through, he bent to place something on the floor so the door wouldn't fully close. Michelle glanced down and saw that he'd propped a glass jar there, the same dark green color as the one Jason had taken from his backpack but larger, about half the size of the jug from an office water cooler. Unlike the smaller jar, this one wasn't quite empty, but the translucent glass made it difficult for Michelle to make out its contents.

She turned her attention to the room they'd entered. Where the corridor had been lit only with the blue lights, this room was brightly illuminated by cold white fluorescent tubes. The ceiling was much higher than outside, and the room was correspondingly wider, roughly classroom-size with a second door at the far end. In fact, it did look something like a high school science lab, with white walls, a tiled floor, and a cluster of brushed metal tables behind neat rows of metal chair-desks. There was even a ceiling-mounted projector and a whiteboard at the end nearest to the door they'd entered. But instead of the periodic table or posters of famous scientists on the walls, there were metal shelves stretching from floor to ceiling filled with hundreds of identical objects.

The green jars.

These ones weren't empty. Inside each jar, distorted by the glass in a way that made them seem bigger than they probably were, a doll-size figure gazed blankly back at

Michelle, each puckered mouth fixed in an astonished O that matched her own expression. When she removed her helmet and drew closer to the shelves, what she saw made her shiver. The things in the jars weren't human; their arms and legs were too spindly, their lopsided heads disproportionately large, their cavernous eye sockets empty. But they were human enough to make her gut squirm with reluctant recognition. Being surrounded by their frozen faces felt like being onstage—or maybe on trial—on an alien planet. Yet Michelle knew immediately that the creatures in the jars were the ones on display. Their bodies were suspended in a clear gel like frogs waiting for dissection, their chests marked vertically by a razor-thin line as if from a scalpel. Whoever had sealed them in these containers was evidently gone, but in the past, she could imagine this room as a theater in which their creators congregated to study the captive monsters.

"I decided to call them Skaldi," Kareem broke the stillness. "I have no idea what they're actually called. But I thought giving them a name might make them more real."

Michelle leaned toward the nearest shelf, peering through the glass. Was it just the light, or did she see one of the creatures wiggling its fingers? "What are they?"

"They're *them*," he said. "The ones that dwell here. The ones that almost killed you in the desert."

Michelle shot him a look. "How do you know that?"

"I don't," he said, coming over to join her by the jars. "But it's the only thing that makes sense. I think these ones must be … babies. When they mature, they become like the other ones. The ones that eat souls."

Michelle shuddered, remembering the thing's icy hand on her ankle. She turned back to the shelf, and this time, she was almost sure she saw movement among the jars. There were so many angular reflections traded across the shiny green surfaces, it was possible for her to convince herself they were *all* moving, reaching out with stick-thin arms to clutch at the host bodies they saw, distorted in their turn, on the other side.

Unconsciously, she flinched away. "So you think some of them escaped?"

"I don't know what happened," he said. "This place feels incredibly familiar, but I can't remember the details. I can guess, though, that some of the Skaldi might have been released when the city was bombed. And then they ... I don't know, I suppose they grew." He waved a hand in front of one of the jars, and either his reflection on the glass or the thing inside waved back. "I can also imagine that, once they got out, the ones who created them were the first to lose their lives. Let me show you something," he said, leading her to a supply closet against the far wall. He swung the door open. "Look familiar?"

Michelle peered inside. Hanging from a rod within the closet was a row of outfits she recognized instantly: black sweatshirts, matching black sweatpants. The one Kareem had on was covered with city dust, but it was the identical uniform, right down to the red letters stitched across the chest that she'd missed seeing through the chalky coating. He was marked with those five letters, the unknown code that held the secret to this place.

S K L D I

She turned from the wardrobe, and sought his eyes. In the room's bright light, his exhaustion was unmistakable, but his expression remained impossible to read. "Then you think

189

you're ... one of them?"

At that, he gave a short laugh. It produced a strange tinkling echo in the glass-filled room. "If you're worried that I'm going to attack you, don't. Based on what I've seen of these things, they don't waste time on conversation once they get their victims alone."

He slammed the cabinet closed. As with his laugh, the glass jars caught the sound of metal clashing and turned it into a ringing like wind chimes.

"I wish I could tell you who I am," he said. "I'm pretty sure I'm not one of these things, but it's possible I'm one of the ones who created them. If Jason were here, I suppose we could ask him."

"Jason?" Michelle asked. "He knows about SKLDI—or suspects, anyway. Do you think he had something to do with it? With the ... with the Skaldi?"

"I don't know," he admitted. "But you say his camp out in the woods has tunnels like this one. And when I was there, it felt familiar—like I'd lived there before. So he must be connected to this place somehow."

She remembered how strange she'd found it that Kareem seemed to know which building was Jason's headquarters, which way to go to reach the exit from camp. "Jason's trying to destroy the Skaldi, though. That's what he sent me here to do."

"So he says. But don't you think it's the tiniest bit suspicious that he knows so much about this place? And that he got his hands on one of the pulse bombs? Seems to me your friend is keeping a lot of secrets."

"He's not my friend," Michelle said. "He sent me here to die."

"Then he knew what he was doing," Kareem said with surprising savagery. "Because that's exactly what's going to happen when that bomb goes off."

He scowled at Michelle as if she were the one who'd caused all of this: the room, the Skaldi, his own forgotten past. Then he threw his hands up in defeat, before sinking to the floor and hanging his head between his knees. He remained motionless for so long, Michelle wondered if fatigue had finally caught up with him. When she lowered herself to the floor at his side, his dark eyes flashed at hers.

"I came here after Jason captured you in the desert," he said. "I don't know how I found my way, but it was like I was ... led. I've been walking around inside for the past day, trying to put the pieces together, but the answer's just beyond me—like a word I can't remember no matter how hard I try. I'm almost positive I was here before, in this room. And not only here, but other rooms throughout this compound. Whether that means I used to work here or was part of whatever experiment they were running, I don't know. I guess it doesn't matter now."

He looked so broken, so vulnerable, she reached out and laid a hand on top of his. Other than a slight tightening of his fist, he made no response. "Have you eaten anything in all that time?"

"There was some food in one of the rooms."

"Can you show me?"

"I ate it all," he said, looking guilty.

"Not for food," she said, though the truth was, she could have used something right now, even if it was only turkey jerky. "Just to show me around."

"Sure, why not," he said. "Maybe you'll see something I

191

missed."

Using a table leg for balance, he stood. All of his extraordinary strength seemed to have deserted him at once; he wobbled on his feet, shuffling forward like an old man. As they approached the rear doorway, he stumbled and nearly fell. She reacted instinctively, catching him beneath the arms. Maybe he could have walked the rest of the way on his own, maybe he couldn't. But he didn't show any inclination to let go once she was holding him, and so they exited the room like that, with his arm draped over her shoulders and his feet dragging across the tiles.

He led her down a new hallway, or she half-carried him. Each door off the blue-lit corridor was frozen partway open, each room brightening with fluorescent light as they entered. One of the rooms looked like an auditorium, except the circular stage was in the center of a ring of seats that rose steeply around it. Another was overflowing with exercise equipment, stationary bikes and treadmills and Ellipticals. A third had clearly been a cafeteria, though Kareem must have found his meal elsewhere; the room smelled like disinfectant, not food, and the huge shiny ovens that stood behind the glass-and-steel counter were cold to the touch. The impression that this compound had been designed to resemble a school increased with each room they entered. But if so, it was a school that had been abandoned by teachers and students alike, leaving only the bottled monsters as mute evidence of what had been studied here. There were no nameplates on the doors or desks, no file cabinets, no textbooks or charts or maps, not even any scribbles on the facility's numerous whiteboards. Michelle got hopeful when Kareem led her into a computer lab, but the screens remained blank no matter how much they fiddled with the mouse or checked the cables. The only word they encountered in all their investigations wasn't even a word, and it maddened her to see the red letters everywhere—on doors, on exercise machines, on closets, on the housing of the computer monitors—but not be able to decipher them.

S K L D I

Skaldi? she thought. Was that the name of the creatures who'd been bred here, or of the ones who'd bred them?

Their tour came to an end with that question unanswered. The corridor terminated in a knob-less door that was sealed shut, and they had no choice but to double back. How long they'd been wandering the facility, Michelle couldn't guess. She had no doubt, however, that they'd far exceeded the two hour ultimatum Jason had given her. That either meant the pulse bomb was dead like most everything else in this city, or it had already detonated but hadn't affected them this far from the blast site. She couldn't believe the latter was true. Clearly enough, Jason had led her to a spot where he was convinced his bomb would wipe out not only the creatures but the facility in which they'd been born.

Why, she asked herself, *was he so eager to do that?* Was he trying to destroy a threat to his colony, or to cover up a massive crime he'd had a hand in committing?

Michelle led Kareem to one of the chairs in the room with the green jars. His arm hadn't left her shoulder for more than a few seconds during their walk, and though his filthy clothes and reeking breath bothered her, she hadn't tried to push him away. Now, seeing how badly he limped as she helped him into the chair, she wondered if there was any way to revive him. There were clean uniforms in the supply closet, and they'd found a bathroom with shower stalls during their investigation of the facility. Come to think of it, it was a little surprising he hadn't tried to clean himself up when he first found his way to this place. Maybe he'd been too tired, or too busy exploring the rooms and corridor, struggling with the fragments of his memory. It struck her that if they'd headed in the opposite direction after they exited the utility tunnel, they might have had time to retrace her path and escape the city before the bomb went off. Instead, he'd brought her here, convinced that they were both going to die, because he wanted to—what? Tell her his story? Show her where that story began? Or be with another human being when it came to an end?

She could have been furious with him for making that decision for her, but she found that, looking at his frail, weary face, all she could feel was a rush of sympathy. They'd both been betrayed: by Jason, the makers of the bombs, the builders of this place. They'd both lost their connection to the past, and if not for each other, they'd both be completely alone. Maybe, she thought, they were *meant* to find each other. And maybe, together, they could find a way to start over again.

"Kareem," she said. "Do you feel strong enough to walk?"

He looked up at her. "Why?"

"We're getting out of here," she said. "I don't want to sit and wait for the creatures to come back."

"They won't. They're all gone."

"You can't be sure of that. If we can get out of the city, we can go someplace they've never been. Maybe we'll find other people, other survivors. Good people, not people like

Jason." Her chest felt fragile when she thought of Rosie and her parents, but she tried to smile at him. "It's worth a shot, right?"

It took a minute, but finally, he returned her smile. Gripping the back of the chair, he stood. "When do we leave?"

Michelle went to the supply closet and took out a uniform that looked about his size. "Why don't you clean up and put this on first? We'll leave when it's light outside. Get a fresh start."

That made him laugh—the first genuine laugh, she realized, she'd heard from him. The first real laugh she'd heard from anyone in a long, long time. His laughter grew stronger, and Michelle allowed herself to believe that meant he was growing stronger, too. She joined her voice with his, her throat feeling at first as if she were fighting the impulse to cry, but then opening up to let out a surprisingly joyful sound. The room rang with it. The glass jars hummed their approval.

"I'll be right back," he said, still laughing as he let himself out the rear door.

Michelle continued laughing to herself while she looked around the lab. She made a slow, patient search of the room, checking the shelves she could reach and peeking beneath tables and chairs to see if there was anything they could use on their journey, but her search was unsuccessful. She decided that when Kareem returned, they would make one final raid of the cafeteria, in case any food was left in the cupboards. She retrieved her helmet from the table where she'd set it, thinking it would be good to have an extra light when they left. They might return to the utility tunnel to search for her flamethrower, reluctant as she was to cart it any farther. They'd need to be cautious when they exited the city, not only because of the threat of Skaldi but on the off chance that Jason was waiting where she'd left him. The more she thought about escape, the more excited she became. The world had changed—so much she could hardly bear it. But she had changed too, hadn't she? Enough, she hoped, to face whatever lay ahead.

She laughed again, loud and long. The jars rattled appreciatively in answer.

When her laugh fell silent, they continued to rattle.

Michelle looked up in alarm. The jars were not only rattling but moving, clinking against each other as they shifted and jumped on the shelves. The floor had started shaking too, and the vibrations were growing stronger. One of the jars fell to the floor and shattered, spraying viscous liquid along with its tiny inhabitant onto the clean white tiles. Another jar fell, and another, and soon they were raining all around her, the sound of breaking glass drowning out the rattling from the jars that remained. Behind those sounds there rose another, one Michelle had heard before: a deep, rumbling hum, the roar of a giant the size of the city. The floor trembled like a trampoline, while the ceiling lights danced and flickered. Some of the fluorescent tubes burst or blinked out. The room and all of its contents were being shaken like a snow globe in the hand of a spoiled child.

Michelle rushed toward the rear door where Kareem had exited. Before she got there, a deafening concussion deep underground rocked the room, and she was thrown from her feet, the helmet bouncing from her grasp. A sound like an avalanche came from behind the wall with the whiteboard, as if rocks and soil were tumbling deeper into the bowels of the earth. With a groan, the entire room tilted from the horizontal, and Michelle slid down the incline as pieces of furniture, the remains of jars, and the humanoid figures bounced along with her. She clutched for purchase on the slick tiles, but couldn't hold on. She saw the wall rushing toward her and braced for the impact.

She came to a jarring stop in the corner, the thump of her body accompanied by the crash of shattered glass. Dark shapes hurtled toward her. She threw her hands in front of her just in time to receive the stinging blows of metal furniture against her forearms. She'd landed in a pool of green glass and sticky fluid, with the bodies of the Skaldi-creatures puddled around her like so many limp squid. The room had stopped shaking, but it had tipped at an angle of at least twenty degrees, and she'd been deposited against the wall farthest from the rear door. The shelves had collapsed in front of the other door, blocking any chance of escape—though based on the sound she'd heard, there was probably nothing but a yawning pit there anyway. When she tried to clutch the tiles, glass cut her fingers and palms. A bank of the overhead lights had died, but in the checkerboard glow of the fluorescent tubes that survived, she saw a pool of red liquid spreading in widening ripples beneath her. Something other than her lacerated hands must be spilling blood from her body, an injury she could neither see nor feel.

She lifted her head and called out as loudly as she could. "Kareem!"

Silence.

"Kareem!" she called again, then waited for his response. Panic rose in her when it didn't come.

He could have been killed when the bomb detonated, she

thought. The blast must have been unthinkably powerful to destroy this well-protected bunker, far from where she'd left the device. She opened her mouth to call out once more, but the sound of tinkling glass made her turn her head.

Not fifteen feet from where she lay, one of the humanoid figures was curled against the wall, its flesh speckled with glass and spots of her own blood.

Slowly, as if awakening from a deep sleep, it shook its ungainly head and opened its toothless mouth wide.

Chapter 13

Michelle stared in horrified fascination as the Skaldi came to life.

The tiny figure stretched its skeletal arms, flexing fingers tipped with miniscule claws. Veins just beneath its corpse-gray skin created unsightly purple bumps and bruises. The most disturbing thing, though, was the mouth: as it opened, the delicate line running down the creature's throat and chest opened too, making it seem as if its flesh had been perforated from chin to stomach in preparation for a skinning. When the lips of the scar peeled back, waving like miniature fingers, a stench of rotting bodies bathed Michelle's nose, and she couldn't help gagging.

That was enough to direct the creature's attention toward her. Its eyeless face tilted upward, and it tried with weak arms to push itself from the floor. It seemed impervious to the glass shards that lay everywhere; if the sharp pieces cut its skin at all, it didn't bleed. But like its intended victim, it couldn't manage the slope of the room, and it vented its frustration with a wail that seemed to issue from the cavity carved out of its gullet.

The tipping of the room had thrown most of the furniture in a pile farther down the wall from where Michelle lay. Several chairs, though, had come to a stop between her and the immature Skaldi, forming a cage of metal legs. With whatever inhuman brain rested inside its skull, the creature quickly developed the idea of using the chair legs to drag itself toward her. A hissing noise escaped from its mouth as it inched closer, now ten feet away, now seven, now five. It was smaller than a newborn, but Michelle had no doubt that if it reached her, it would devour her just the same.

No more than three feet away, the Skaldi gripped one of the chairs to pull itself upright. The scar on its chest opened fully, the smell making Michelle want to vomit. Even worse than the stink was the sight of the creature's insides, a smooth gray emptiness that looked like wet modeling clay.

It lunged for her, but she was ready for it.

She gripped the nearest chair and thrust it between herself and the miniature horror. The Skaldi collided with the chair and screeched, whether in pain or anger she had no idea. Its claws scratched against metal, the sound shivering down Michelle's spine. The creature banged the chair with its fists, tried to climb over the top; when that didn't work, it gripped the leg closest to it and struggled to free the shield from Michelle's hands. But it was too small and weak to fight its way past the barrier, and so all it could do was flail against the chair and moan in defeat.

Taking advantage of its helplessness, Michelle pulled the chair back and swung it with all her strength.

It hit the Skaldi with a rubbery smack, and the small body sailed away down the tilted floor before landing amidst the tables and chairs piled in the shadowy corner. The violent movement made Michelle double over with pain. She wondered if she'd ruptured an organ when she hit the wall.

Now that she had the chair planted in front of her, she gritted her teeth and pulled herself to her feet. The chair slid back against the wall, but held. She spared a glance at the creature, whose unmoving legs were visible atop the pile. It was either dead or stunned.

Seating herself, she rolled up her uniform top and discovered the source of the blood and pain: a sliver of green glass the size of a kitchen knife protruded from her abdomen, making her look like a voodoo doll someone had stuck a pin in. She didn't know how deeply embedded it was or whether pulling it out was the right thing to do, but the sight of it made her sick, so she grabbed it and yanked it free. A fresh jolt of pain tore through her midsection and a new slash of blood appeared on her palm, but removing the glass relieved the stabbing agony in her stomach. With the fragment gone, blood soaked through her uniform. She pressed her burning fist against it, hoping the wound was nothing worse than a deep cut. With her eyes fixed on the door that seemed impossibly far away up the steep slope of the half-darkened room, she balanced against the chair with her other hand and tried to stand.

A mistake.

As soon as her weight shifted, the chair skidded out from under her and she found herself pitching headfirst against the back wall, then tumbling down the glass-strewn slope toward the tables and chairs where the Skaldi lay. The crash was like a bowling ball scattering pins, except pins don't cause bowling balls excruciating pain. Her vision flashed brightly, each pulse of light a razor-sharp ninja star jabbing her forehead. She'd have welcomed unconsciousness to escape the torment, but then she noticed that she wasn't the only thing moving in the pile of tangled furniture, and her eyes gaped wide.

The room's half-light made the entire pile seem alive. Concentrating hard to focus her spinning vision, she saw Skaldi swarming over the metal legs and tabletops like pale spiders, too many of them to count. Their bodies were crisscrossed with cuts from all the shattered glass. One or two were missing limbs. But there was no blood. The creature that had tried to attack her was easily distinguishable because the blow from the chair had torn its head from its neck. Yet even that injury didn't stop it from creeping toward her, the lower portion of its mouth splitting its chest in two.

There must be no brain inside these things at all, Michelle thought. *Only the lure of heat and breath and blood.*

The lure of their prey.

Of her.

Feebly, with the last shreds of reason that remained to her, Michelle tried to pull the closest chair free from the pile to use as a shield or a weapon. It was no use. The chair was trapped too tightly, and her grip on consciousness was ebbing along with her strength. She watched the monsters inching closer, and had the horrifying pre-vision of becoming one of them, her body rising from the floor like a ghoul to seek out its next meal. It wouldn't find anyone to consume, she realized with her last conscious thought. There was no one left in the city except her and …

"Michelle!"

A voice cut through the fog, and she raised her head to see Kareem's face at the rear door above her. The next thing she knew, he'd leaped into the room and was barreling down the incline toward her and the Skaldi. He hit the pile of furniture feet-first, upsetting the monsters' precarious balance and sending them flying in all directions. Either by skill or pure luck, he'd missed colliding with her, but the Skaldi lay dazed and mangled against the back wall. Some wailed as they struggled under objects too heavy for them to lift. Others had been crushed beneath tables and didn't move at all. Yet enough of the creatures were able to free themselves to swarm toward this new target.

Kareem met them with a chair he'd pulled from the pile. With his feet planted on the sloping floor and his back braced against the wall, he stood between Michelle and the attackers, fending them off by flattening them against the glass-covered tiles or sending them careening across the room. They were fragile in this newborn state, their limbs ripping from their torsos as if they really were clay dolls in the hands of children, their heads exploding in jelly-like goo when the chair came down on them. But they were also blindly, fanatically persistent. No matter how many times he knocked them down, no matter how crippled their bodies became, they wouldn't cease their efforts to reach the two living beings in the room. Headless monsters dragged half-bodies across the floor; severed arms and legs twitched convulsively as if they could still sense their prey. The longer this advance guard forced Kareem to fight, the more opportunity there was for the reserves to liberate themselves and join the attack. None of the creatures had escaped some form of damage, but there were so many of them—twenty, fifty, a hundred—Michelle couldn't believe that Kareem would be able to hold them all off. Even now, his arms were tiring, his strokes becoming weaker and more uncoordinated. She saw blood pooling at his feet, watched it dripping from the exposed skin of his

JOSHUA DAVID BELLIN

hands and neck where he'd been cut by glass. It was a miracle he was standing at all.

As if in response to her fears, the next swing he took caused him to stumble, the chair flying free as he caught himself with a hand. Instantly, the creatures that hadn't been completely decimated by the fight thronged toward him, their mouths gaping hungrily. The combined odor of rot from so many bodies hit Michelle like a physical wave: she gasped, fought against it as if she were drowning in deep water. Consciousness stuttered again, and she almost welcomed the plunge into the suffocating depths.

Kareem's feet slipped out from under him, and he fell against the back wall. The nearest creatures were within inches of his bloodied, battered face when Michelle broke the surface of her swoon and threw herself at his assailants.

She had no weapon to fight them with, so she fought them with her hands. She swept them aside before they could touch their prey; she clutched their limbs and snapped them like whips against the wall. The burning wound in her gut dizzied her, but she didn't let up. Every time she made contact with their skin—if it was skin—she felt a momentary lapse in awareness like the sensation of nodding behind the wheel of a car. The only difference was that she was pretty sure that whatever thoughts or memories or pieces of her soul the Skaldi were stripping away were gone for good. The part of her that was conscious of herself wondered how much you could lose before you had nothing left, before you weren't *you* anymore. But that part of her was buried in a whirlwind of swinging fists and faceless banshees. The core of her being was small, and getting smaller by the minute.

At last, when her arms felt like twin weights dangling

from her shoulders and her mind was a mist-wrapped coast with only a pinprick of light shining through the gloom, the parade of creatures stopped. She blinked, hardly believing she'd won, only gradually realizing that she'd cleared a large enough space around her and Kareem that she could take the time to kneel and check on his condition.

He was breathing, but his face was covered with blood and his eyes were closed. *He heals fast*, she reminded herself, hoping it was still true.

Looking around the room, she saw that a small number of the Skaldi remained alive, or at least intact. They were bashed beyond recognition and unable to stand, but they were beginning to crawl from shadowed corners toward her and Kareem. In minutes, maybe less, she'd have to resume a fight she didn't think she had the strength for. If only there was another way ...

She never knew if the thought came from her brain or if her body acted on its own. All she knew was that her leaden arms started grabbing and stacking chairs on their backs up the slope of the floor, bracing the first one's legs in the corner of the room and balancing the next above it, then using that platform to drag another chair farther up the incline. Each level took longer to build than the previous one, as she had to slide all the way down to retrieve a new piece of furniture, then drag the metal object all the way back to the top, wrapping her legs around the structure and using a single hand to pull herself up. She didn't have time to make sure everything was perfectly balanced; she would have to trust it to stay in place while it supported not only her weight but Kareem's. She knew that, once it was completed, the scaffold would provide footing for the Skaldi as well as for her and her partner. But she didn't slow, didn't allow herself the luxury of doubt. Her hands burned and bled, the wound in her stomach leaked blood into her already sopping uniform, but moment by moment, level by level, she constructed the only chance they had to escape.

When it was finished, when it reached from the bottom corner to within five feet of the rear door, she clambered down one final time and shook Kareem to wake him. He moaned, a sound uncannily like that of the Skaldi, but his eyes didn't open. She shook him again, more roughly than she wanted, and this time his eyelids fluttered before closing. Michelle glanced over her shoulder, saw that the nearest Skaldi were only feet away. Ducking her head under Kareem's body and using her shoulders to balance him, she gripped the first rung of her homemade ladder and pulled.

He was much heavier than she expected, probably because he was all dead weight. Her arms trembled with the strain as she inched up the slanted tiles, with Kareem draped against her shoulders like a sandbag she was trying to wrestle into place. He was far too heavy to lift from the floor, so she remained lying on her side, gripping the legs of the chairs and pulling herself with her burden up the incline like a rope climber in gym class. Glass shards cut into her, but the majority of the pieces must have settled to the bottom of the slope, because after a few feet she didn't feel them pricking her skin anymore. Or maybe she was past feeling, past pain. She heard the metal chairs grinding as she dragged herself and Kareem up the makeshift structure, and she was convinced that at any moment the entire thing was going to collapse. Her numb hands clenched slick metal, her biceps flexed, and she gained another precious few inches of ground. She could barely see through blood and sweat, but the black square she had to believe was the doorway drew incrementally closer with every beat of her heart, until it was finally within her grasp.

She reached for it, and felt a clawed hand bite into her ankle.

Black night flooded her vision. Searing pain tore her apart. She would have screamed, but she couldn't remember how to scream. She was a fish flopping on the hook, a marionette dangling at the end of a string. She closed her eyes and fell into a pit without bottom, without escape.

Then the hand was ripped from her ankle and consciousness returned, a great gulp of it so overwhelming after its momentary absence she had to struggle to breathe. She opened her eyes to see Kareem's battle-scarred face hovering in the black square above her, his hand reaching down to take hers. His other hand held a strip of wet gray flesh, the remains of the Skaldi that had grabbed her ankle. Dropping the monster in a sodden heap, he reached for her with both hands and grasped her wrists. Light and hope rekindled in her breast as he drew her through the doorway.

She fell against him, and they both tumbled a short distance before landing hard on the cement floor. All the lights had died outside the room, leaving the corridor pitch black. The tilt of their bodies told her that the hallway wasn't level, but whether it was as bad as the room, she didn't have the presence of mind to determine. Kareem's warmth vanished for a second, and she heard metal clattering and echoing in the room they'd just left. A chorus of howls erupted from the Skaldi. Then he was back, helping her to her knees. "Can you stand?"

She tried to answer, but her tongue thickened. "I … "

"It's all right. I've got you."

She was lifted from the ground, and instinctively wrapped her arms around his neck. Dreamily, she inhaled the scent of soap and fresh clothes, and realized he must have had time to shower and change before the bomb detonated. He started off down the corridor, moving slowly and cautiously, sometimes leaning one way, sometimes another. She rested her head against his chest, felt his solidity and warmth, savored the scent of clean skin and fabric. The moans of the creatures they'd left behind faded into silence, and then there was only the soft, steady sound of his footsteps and the beating of his heart.

Consciousness flickered. She had no idea how long they'd been walking, how he could find his way in the dark. She felt herself sliding into sleep when his voice thrummed against her ear. "Oh no."

She raised her head. "What is it?"

"Nothing. Just took a wrong turn."

She heard the quaver in his voice, but found herself too exhausted to protest. Her brain told her to ask another question, to free herself from his protective grasp and figure out for herself what the problem was, but her body sank deeper into his arms and her eyes closed. The last thing she heard was a scratching sound as of stone grating against stone.

Her eyes opened to bright light. She blinked, wondering how long she'd been asleep. As her vision adjusted, she saw that she was lying on one of the bottom bunks in a room with ten identical bunk beds, five on each side with a narrow corridor down the middle. Footlockers rested at the base of each bunk, and there was a single mirror on the wall made out of a piece of buffed tin. The room's features were so similar to the barracks in Jason's camp her heart misgave her, but then she realized that the walls were cinder block, not wood. Kareem stood by the half-open door, leaning out into the hallway. He turned at the sound of her movement and closed the door, throwing the bolt before coming over to her.

He sat beside her on the bunk. He'd not only washed but shaved, and his thick black hair shone in the light. His face was covered with nicks and cuts, but all of them appeared superficial, and none was bleeding any longer. She tried to lift herself onto an elbow, but shooting pain in her middle made her wince. Kareem's eyebrows contracted.

"You're hurt," he said.

"I got cut."

"Can I ... ?" His hands drew near her uniform top. When she didn't object, he undid two of the bottom buttons and carefully folded back the blood-soaked cloth. He leaned close to look, his face hidden under his glossy hair.

"How bad is it?" she asked.

"The bleeding's mostly stopped," he reported. "I think I should wrap it, though."

He rose, rummaged in a footlocker, and returned with tape and gauze. His eyes showed his reluctance as he approached her. She nodded, let him undo the rest of the buttons and slip the uniform top off, leaving her upper body in nothing but the one and only sports bra she'd worn since joining the Argo. She could see the wound in her stomach, to the left of her belly button, a four-inch gash with dried blood crusted around the edges. He frowned and set his supplies aside. She was about to ask him what he was waiting for when his fingers reached delicately into the cut and pinched something. She gasped at pain that felt like a blade sliding from her skin, then stared at the splinter of bloody green glass he held between his thumb and forefinger. Breathing heavily, she lay back and closed her eyes while he patted the wound gently with a cloth, packed it with gauze, and wrapped tape across her stomach. Then he helped her back into the uniform top and buttoned it carefully, all the way to the top.

When he was done and the pain in her abdomen registered only as a dull ache, she opened her eyes again. "Where are we?"

"The first room I could find with a locking door. I tried to get us back to the surface, but the corridor was blocked. Some of the tunnels must have collapsed when the bomb exploded."

"Are the Skaldi gone?"

He shook his head. "But they'll have to rebuild that contraption themselves if they want to get out of the lab. You'll have plenty of time to rest."

She'd started to drift off again, but something about his words brought her back. "How long are we staying here?"

He lowered his eyes. Michelle felt coldness creeping up her back like the Skaldi's freezing touch. "Kareem?"

He looked at her, guilt and anguish overtaking his haggard features.

"I'm sorry," he said, his voice breaking. "I couldn't remember the way to go. Half the tunnels were closed off—I tried to break through the debris, but there was too much of it, and I was afraid of getting lost … "

He buried his head in his hands. Michelle reached out and touched his shoulder until he turned to face her. His eyes were red and teary. She tried to smile for him.

"It's all right," she said. "It's not your fault."

Then she sank back in the bunk and closed her eyes, waiting for them to come.

Chapter 14

The first thing she heard was the moaning.

It seeped into the bedroom from the corridor outside, a tortured sound like the wailing of the damned. Michelle couldn't believe the feeble creatures they'd escaped in the lab could produce such a din.

Kareem must have been thinking the same thing. He rose and went to the door, pulling back a slot that enabled him to spy into the corridor. A second later, he gasped and slammed the aperture closed. Michelle's body felt like one giant bruise, but she stood stiffly and limped over to join him. Kareem threw another grief-stricken look at her before stepping aside so she could see for herself.

The corridor was dark, though not the pitch dark of the hallway outside the lab. In the faint blue glow of the running light or two that remained, she detected a wriggling, undulating movement like maggots swarming a dead animal. Expecting the miniature creatures from the lab, it took her eyes a minute to make sense of what she was seeing. Twenty or more beings as large as herself or Kareem, with skeletal arms and legs, crept across the floor and climbed over each other in a hunched position, as if the weight of their newly grown bodies had outstripped the capacity of their muscles and bones. From each creature's neck sprouted a blunt knob shaped something like a head, except it had no eyes, no features whatsoever. All it had was a gash that started where its mouth should have been and extended downward the length of its torso, ending at the waist. The gash was too dark to see inside, but the rest of the body was the same sickly color of the Skaldi in the lab, with bundles of bloodless veins running over the dead gray tissue as if their skin had been stripped away.

Michelle closed the slide and backed from the door. Though she couldn't smell the Skaldi's stink through the metal barrier, her stomach lurched with the memory of their corpse-rot. She made her way to the bed and sat, trembling.

"It's them," she said. "How could they have changed so much?"

Kareem sat beside her. "I think this is what happens when they mature."

"But it's only been ... How long was I asleep?"

"About an hour," he said. Then, with a grimace as if he were being forced to swallow something that had died weeks ago, he continued. "The fluid in the jars must keep them from growing. Without it, they get big fast."

The moaning outside had increased in intensity, as if the creatures sensed their prey just beyond the door. It rose to a crescendo, so loud it seemed to come from inside the room. The unearthly sound was accompanied by the dull echo of something striking the door, first one thump, then two, then a succession without pause. The floor shook with the impact, the bed tremoring in response. Kareem stood and walked shakily to the door, but no sooner had he pulled back the slide than he jerked away and snapped it shut.

"They're trying to get in," he said. "They're throwing their heads against the door, one after another. I don't think they can break it down, but it doesn't look like they're going to stop trying."

He returned to the bed while the battering of the creatures' bodies continued, the blows coming faster and faster until it was obvious that more than one of them was attacking the barrier simultaneously. The heavy door rattled in its frame. From her position across the room, it seemed to Michelle that she could see where their heads collided with the metal, as if they were denting the door or making it bulge inward. That might only have been her eyes playing tricks on her, the same way her other senses were convincing her that the creatures were already in the room, their moans penetrating her ears and their stench flooding her nostrils while their icy claws pulled her into black nothingness.

The pounding on the door and the moaning of the creatures rose to a fever pitch. Michelle covered her ears with her hands, tucking her body into a tight ball despite the pain in her stomach. At some point, she became aware that Kareem was huddled in the same defensive posture only inches away. She reached out impulsively to pull him close, as if feeling his warmth against her could help her maintain her grip on sanity. His arms found the back of her head, and he drew her into him as she gripped him even tighter, their bodies wrapped around each other in a quivering cocoon. He trembled, gasped. She realized he was sobbing, a second before she realized she was, too. Hot tears coursed down her cheeks and stung her dry lips, and she could no longer tell if the salt she tasted came from her eyes or from his.

"Stop it!" she screamed at the mindless creatures outside.

"Just stop it!"

He held her even closer. His own voice joined hers, crying out in a language she didn't know, didn't need to know. His desperation was as plain as hers.

"Oh, God, please stop," she whispered, while Kareem clutched her to him. In his panic, he pressed her face so tightly against his chest she could barely breathe, but she didn't ask him to let go. Instead, she pulled herself even harder into his embrace, preferring the stifling pain over the wailing of the wild things beyond the door.

"Please," she begged, and had no idea whom she was imploring. "Please stop."

Kareem responded in his own language, broken oaths and whispers that probably made no more sense to him than they did to her.

The creatures pounded against the door. Their shrieks drowned their victims' cries. It went on forever. It would never end.

Then it did.

The shaking ceased. The room fell silent, except for Michelle and Kareem's shuddering breaths. The moaning that had nearly driven her mad echoed in her ears, but this time, she knew that it was an illusion. She and Kareem pulled away at the same time, each of them looking into the other's wet, shining eyes. She wanted to smile at him, but succeeded only in letting loose another flood of hopeless tears. A laugh that was more like a sob rose from her throat. She had a moment to study the thickness of his lashes, the way the tears clung to them like long-forgotten dew on summer grass.

Then they were back in each other's arms, and his mouth came together with hers.

His lips were hot and moist and salty with tears, but she could feel how full they were, how they softened to welcome her touch while at the same time enveloping hers with an urgency that was almost frightening. She and Mark had never kissed like this—deeply, hungrily, as if they were dying for a taste of each other. It wasn't exactly romantic—there was too much spit and clicking teeth for that—but it was definitely exciting. For whatever reason, maybe because he was a boy, she'd expected Kareem to be vastly more experienced than she was, but the clumsy way he kissed made her realize he was as much of a novice as she. Maybe even more; had he ever been free to walk the world beyond this prison, or had he been caged inside it all his life?

Almost before she knew it, the two of them had lain down on the bed, arms wrapped around each other, lips locked together. She didn't know what to do with her hands, so she settled on sinking them into his thick hair, which he seemed to like, or she assumed so from the contented sigh he made. His own hands were on her back, massaging through her uniform top. In a flash of inspiration, she let go of his hair so her hands could snake beneath his sweatshirt and clutch his bare skin just above his shoulder blades. He seemed to like that even more; he didn't even object when her uncut nails accidentally clawed him. To her complete surprise, Michelle discovered that the closer she got to him, the less self-conscious she felt. It was as if her body had talked itself into being sexy and taken over from there. When they'd started kissing, she hadn't been thinking of anything except the need to be near someone, but now …

At the thought, a bright flame of desire blossomed in her chest, and her hands raked down his sides to tug at the waistband of his sweatpants. Only then did he pull back, lifting his face from hers.

"Are you sure?"

"I need … " The only thing she was unsure of was how to finish that sentence. *To remember, to forget, to live, to love …* "I need you now."

She smiled at him, and he smiled back, though his eyes still looked red and wet. Making sure not to put any weight on her covered wound, he pulled her shirt over her head, then reached behind her and fumbled with her bra, finally figuring out how to unclasp it. The heat of his hands on her naked flesh made her skin tingle and hum. Her pants were next to go, Kareem pulling them down to her ankles before she kicked them free. Self-consciousness descended on her once more when she realized she had nothing on except her underpants, but the look on his face as he surveyed her body—a look she could only describe as *awe*—helped her to relax. She shivered, and reached up to caress his cheek with her fingertips.

"You're so beautiful," he said softly.

The image that had been playing in her head since she glimpsed herself in the tank of the flamethrower returned. She was pale except where she was sunburned, with a body whittled down to muscle and sinew; her ribs showed. Her shorn hair had only just grown long enough to soften again. "I'm not," she said.

"You are." He leaned down to kiss her, and for the first time since they'd started, it was a gentle kiss, as if he knew that the wrong thing could break her. She felt something she'd never felt before, a warming, melting eagerness in the pit of her being, and the knowledge of what his hands were doing no longer frightened her. When he lowered himself fully against her, her hips arched upward as if drawn by the magnetic pull of his body. He responded by pressing against her thighs, and she knew she could wait no longer. With his mouth covering hers and her need so strong she thought it might consume her, she pulled him to her and lost herself in the mystery of this strange boy's love.

When she returned to herself, when his physical touch had departed but the ghost of his presence lingered, she kissed him once more on the lips, deeply but tenderly, then rested her head on his chest and listened to his thundering heartbeat. In minutes, his breathing slowed and leveled. She saw that his eyes had closed, exhaustion finally overcoming him.

The gravity of what they'd done came to her powerfully, but it came without guilt or remorse. Who was there to justify herself to, what was left for her to feel guilty about? She couldn't say why the longing to merge her body with his had swept over her just then. Maybe she'd done nothing but trade one form of oblivion for another. At the same time, she felt that joining herself with him had been right. Whatever followed from here, she would carry this moment with her to the end, and be thankful that they'd found each other when their need was greatest.

She rose, covering his nakedness with the sheet and her own with the discarded bra and uniform bottoms. She noticed a sprinkling of blood on the sheet, which she thought was from her stomach wound until she realized where it really came from. The room felt cold now that she'd left his fiery touch; her thighs and groin ached, but at least her heart no longer did. Digging through the locker at the foot of the bed, she found an extra sweatshirt and slipped that on. Then she padded to the door and leaned her ear cautiously against the cold metal.

Everything was quiet outside. She risked a peek through the slot, and found the hallway dark and empty. Her heart lifted for a moment, but anxiety quickly quelled her mood. The Skaldi in the lab had shown themselves capable of using tools to get at her, but whether they could work together to devise a scheme was another question. While Kareem slept, she decided she might as well look around the room. Maybe she'd find something to fight them off if they came back. Maybe being locked in the barracks wasn't as much of a death sentence as Kareem believed.

She walked the central aisle and then the perimeter of the room, checking methodically behind and beneath beds for anything that might be kept hidden—a secret exit, a stash of weapons. As with her inspection of the lab, her search came up empty. Next, she dropped to her knees to explore the footlocker where she'd found the sweatshirt. She came across a second black and red outfit, a pair of boots, and a series of laminated cards with nonsensical patterns of black dots on them. There was a medical kit at the bottom. At first she assumed it was the one Kareem had used to patch her up, but when she opened it, she found that it contained a rack of glass vials the size of eyedroppers, each vial capped with a rubber plug. She took one of the vials out and held it up to the light, but there was nothing inside. She'd stacked all of the items on the floor and was staring at the empty locker, about to move on to the next one in the room, when she noticed what looked like a scrap of paper tucked in a bottom corner. She picked at it, only to discover that it was the edge of a larger sheet that had been slipped under the felt lining. Heart pounding, she pried the lining loose with a fingernail, revealing what lay beneath.

At first, she was disappointed by her find. It was an eight by ten photograph, in black and white, but not old; instead, it looked professionally done. It showed a group of adults— four men and two women—standing in a row behind eight children, all of them elementary school age except one, who looked like a teenager. Everyone was dressed casually, in T-shirts and shorts, and each of the children had an adult's hand on his shoulder, which enhanced the impression that this was a school trip or family gathering. The setting was similarly unexceptional: a forested area, nothing like this elaborate underground fortress where the Skaldi had been bred. Michelle gave a start when she realized that the man at the right-hand edge of the picture, who wore his black hair and beard in long braids, was easily seven feet tall; though he stood slightly stooped with one of his hands clutching a metal forearm crutch, he nonetheless towered above the other adults. It was only when she scanned the faces of the children that her heart started pounding again.

The teenager was Jason.

Or at least, the boy looked enough like a younger version of Jason for her to persuade herself it was him. His face had the same eerily bright eyes and cocksure grin of the man who would come to rule the Argo, while his slim legs and forearms showed the beginnings of the wiry muscles that would achieve full expression in the adult Jason. It was hard to tell his height, because he stood directly in front of the giant man, compared to whom even the other adults looked like children. One of the man's huge hands rested on the teenage boy's shoulder, a gesture that might have appeared fatherly but that Michelle couldn't help finding disturbingly proprietary.

She turned her attention to the other children, and received an even greater shock. The child to Jason's right was no more than ten years old, but his dark eyes, thick black hair, and full lips were unmistakably those of the boy who had kissed her so passionately not an hour ago. The thought that she was gazing at her lover's younger self provoked a mixed feeling of intimacy and wistfulness, and she reached out with a fingertip to trace the features of the boy who would one day be hers. The discovery that he and Jason had known each other—had even, it seemed, been part of the same school group—made her reverie dissolve in a miasma of vague dread. She flipped the photograph over and saw that someone had written a note: *Pre-Trial Phase, Strategic Kenos Living Defense Initiative.* There was a date, too, from eleven years before the present time, when Jason would have been about sixteen, Kareem about eight.

Strategic Kenos Living Defense Initiative, Michelle repeated the words in her head.

S K L D I. Skaldi.

She studied the picture again. All of the children were boys, years younger than Kareem. All, except for the one she was now certain had to be Jason, were dark-eyed and had thick black hair. The only one of the children who was smiling was Jason, though all of the grown-ups were. Smiling like people who shared a secret, and who were holding that secret in their hands.

A rustling in the bed made Michelle lift her eyes to find Kareem propped on an elbow, the covers bunched loosely around him. His dark gaze was disorienting after staring at the eyes of the boy in the photo for so long. She returned to the bed, clutching the picture in both hands, and sat beside him. He reached out to pull her into a kiss. She sensed that all it would take was the slightest sign on her part for them to end up in each other's arms again—and if she was being completely honest, she had to admit that the promise of giving herself to him was tempting. But the photo raised questions she needed to have answered. She broke the kiss and held the picture out to him, watching as his eyes traced their own reflection in the still image.

"That's you and Jason, isn't it?" she asked, trying to keep any hint of accusation out of her voice.

He bit his lip, reached for the photo, and perused it for long moments, his eyes flicking back and forth. She watched him closely, so she saw when his brow contracted as if with intense pain. He laid the photo face down on the sheets and looked at her, and her heart melted when she saw in his eyes the little boy in the picture.

"I remember the tall man," he said. "Though I never knew his name. Jason was … I don't think he called himself Jason back then. I doubt I'd have recognized him even if I'd seen him at his camp."

"Do you know who he was?"

"He was … " Kareem squeezed his eyes closed. She saw them moving beneath his lids, the way your eyes move when you're watching your own dream. "He was an assistant, I think. He stayed with us, kept an eye on us. He wasn't cruel or anything, but he never let us out of his sight. He was the one who would let the tall man in when he … when he came to the room at night."

Michelle gripped his hand. "Did the tall man ... "

Kareem shook his head. "It wasn't like that. He would come get some of us, and Jason would watch the rest of us while the tall man took the ones he'd chosen to ... " His face screwed tight with the intensity of his concentration. "The tall man would take us to one of the other rooms, and then when we were done, he would lead us back. The doors must have been keyed to his palm print or something—they would always open for him, but not for us. One day Jason left us alone for the whole afternoon, and we tried to open the door, but we couldn't. He must have locked it from the outside. We couldn't get out."

He fell silent. Michelle massaged his hand, waiting, encouraging him to go on.

"Then the next day," Kareem resumed after a while, "Jason—or whatever his real name was—wasn't in the room when we woke up. The tall man let himself in that night, and we kept waiting for Jason to return, but he never did. I thought he'd died. And I thought ... this sounds terrible, but I was glad. Because I was the oldest, and I thought that maybe, without him hanging around all the time, I could find a way out. For me and"—he indicated the photo with a flick of his head—"for the rest of them. But I couldn't. Even without Jason, the door stayed locked all the time."

"Do you remember who the others were?"

Kareem reached for the picture and stared at it for a long time.

"They were ... my brothers," he said. "But I can't remember their names."

"Your brothers? You mean literally?"

"I don't think so. More like we thought of each other

that way. Especially after Jason left. We were all in the same room, and the older ones took care of the really little ones. They would get scared, because … " He rubbed his forehead, his eyes closed tight. "Because … "

She touched his cheek. He dropped the photo and gripped her hand in both of his, as if she were the only thing keeping him from being swept away by a raging current. When he opened his eyes and spoke again, he stared vacantly into the distance, his voice carrying the faraway sound she'd first heard in the woods.

"Not long after Jason disappeared, the tall man started taking small groups of us out of our room and bringing us to the lab. That's the one place we'd never been before. The other grown-ups would be there already, and they would put us in the chairs, and then … " A shudder ran through him, and his eyes met hers. "My God. They … they *fed* us."

"Fed you?"

"To the Skaldi. They restrained us, and let the immature ones attack."

Michelle's mind swooped with horror. She clutched his hand, which felt clammy and cold. "But you … how did you survive?"

"It wasn't for long. They'd expose us, let the Skaldi touch us, then ward them off. With a thing like a cattle prod. It must have burned them." His breathing had quickened. Michelle pressed her hand against his cheek, trying to soothe him. "Each time the Skaldi touched us, it stripped away a little more of who we were. Our memory, our selves. The younger ones, they couldn't take it. They'd wake up screaming, and sometimes … "

His body shook, then stiffened, the way it had when they

first found him. Michelle pulled him to her, having no idea what to do, only hoping the warmth of her body, the softness of her touch, would keep him anchored to this world. He thrashed against her, too weak to break free. It was as if he were shivering from intense cold. When his rigid muscles finally relaxed, she held him close and rocked him, stroking his hair, hushing him as she would a child.

His voice rose faintly, tremulous with memory. "We'd find the little ones stretched out in their bunks, staring at the ceiling, with nothing in their eyes. As if they'd been completely burned out from the inside. Then their bed would be empty, and the next day or the next week, another would replace them. I tried … when we found the doors open one day, I tried to protect them. But we got separated in the woods. I hid with the phone we'd stolen, because I wanted to have a record of it in case the Skaldi hunted me down too. Or in case I couldn't remember what had happened to us."

Michelle said nothing, just held him as his words came out in broken snatches.

"They were … testing us against the Skaldi, seeing how much we could take before we succumbed to them. They must have known … no, they must have *wanted* those things to get out. They must have been using us to develop an antidote, a cure, something for when they released the Skaldi. But the wars came before they were ready, and the Skaldi escaped on their own." He lifted grieving eyes to hers. "All the others died, Michelle. Either here, or in the woods. And every time one of them died, it felt like a part of me died, too."

He lowered his head to her breast and cried, wracking sobs that seemed as if they might tear him apart. She held him close, mingling her tears with his. He had wanted to remember, had been desperate not to lose the last traces of himself the way the younger children had. Now that he'd remembered, he knew something she'd already learned: memory could be either a blessing or a curse. It wasn't all that different from forgetting. It had the power to comfort, as well as to kill.

She found his lips and kissed him again, a long, lingering kiss into which she poured everything her words couldn't say. When he failed to respond, she continued to probe his lips with hers, promising him silently that no matter what he'd lost, she was his, for as much time as remained. He heard her message at last and answered with a wordless pledge of his own, their kiss deepening as they rested back on the bed. They made love again, but it was completely different this time—slower, less awkward and urgent, with hours to discover each other's bodies and years to live in a single day. It was, she thought while the glow of his touch suffused her, as if this were her wedding night, and he the man she'd sworn herself to until the end of time. She knew that was a lie. But it was a lie that felt more honest than the truth, and it was what she needed to face the fate that lay ahead.

"I want you to promise me something," she whispered while they lay beneath the sheets, his arm around her and her head on his chest.

"Anything."

"I don't want to die as one of them. As a monster without a soul. If it's close, if there's no way out, I want you to promise me you'll let me die as myself."

He lifted his head to look at her. "You mean ... ?"

"Yes. Will you do that for me?"

He was silent, his fingers stroking the soft new growth of her hair, his breath warm and steady on her cheek. When she looked up at his face, tears sparkled in his eyes.

"I'll do it," he said. "If you promise you'll do the same for me."

She lifted herself to look squarely into his eyes. With a finger, she brushed tears from their corners, then leaned down to kiss him as gently as she'd ever kissed anyone in her life. "I promise," she said.

"Thank you," he said with a great sigh of relief, as if he'd been worrying about the same thing all along.

She cuddled closer to him, listening to his heart.

"We should come up with a secret," she said. "Something no one knows but us."

He cocked his head and half-smiled. "Because ... ?"

"Because then we'll know if the other's been ... " She couldn't bring herself to say the words. "Then we'll know it's time."

He turned his face from her, but not before she saw his jaw quivering. He breathed slowly, deeply—once, twice. Then he turned back, and she watched a tear slide down his cheek and nestle in the corner of his lip before his tongue flicked it away.

"I'm not sure that would work," he said. "When they take over, don't they gain the person's memories?"

"We don't know that," she said. "Let's just try, okay?"

He opened his mouth as if to object, but then he nodded. "What kind of secret?"

She had to think about it. She wasn't sure why this felt so important, even more important than its ostensible purpose. The idea had come to her, just as the need to be with him had come to her, and she trusted it in the same way. Even if the stratagem didn't work as planned, she felt as though sharing something that Jason and Arachne and the people who had built this place didn't know was as much a consecration as the love they'd made. And when she thought of it that way, she knew what the secret had to be.

"I want a code name," she said. "To cancel the one Jason made me take. But a private name. One we'll never say out loud unless we absolutely have to."

"A name."

"Yes. I want you to give me a name."

He smiled, and maybe the smile was a little indulgent, as if her wish were something a child would ask for. Something with magic. But that, she decided, was exactly what it was, and why it felt so right.

"Okay," he said, and put his free hand behind his head as he stared at the bunk above them. "How about Shelly?"

"You've got to be kidding me."

"Missy?"

She punched him playfully. "Or Miss Hell. That would be more appropriate."

"No," he said, and touched her cheek. "You're the last piece of heaven left in this entire world."

She couldn't believe such a corny line could make her heart shimmer. "Any other ideas?"

"Hmmm … " He closed his eyes, and his lips moved soundlessly, as if he were trying something out. Michelle waited, striving for patience. Even though the creatures hadn't made themselves heard for hours, even though she and Kareem had been lying there languidly, in no apparent rush to rise or disentangle themselves from each other, she felt as if they had so little time. Her tongue itched to speed him along, but just as her lips parted to speak, he opened his eyes.

His beautiful, beautiful eyes. They stared at her with such love and longing and sadness, she felt her tears begin to flow again. He reached up to catch the first tear on his fingertip before it had a chance to fall.

"Chelle," he said.

Chapter 15

They were lying in each other's arms when the noises resumed outside.

Michelle had fallen half-asleep, and she woke to the faint sound of moans in the corridor. Kareem's arms circled her, but his eyes were closed, his breathing peaceful. She didn't want to wake him, but she didn't want the first thing he heard upon waking to be the Skaldi's ghostly wails, either. *Let it be my voice he hears*, she said to herself. *Let it be the voice of his lover, his Chelle.*

"Kareem," she whispered. "Wake up. They're here."

His eyelids fluttered. She kissed each one softly, and they opened all the way. When he saw her, he smiled. As if the two of them were the only ones left in the world, as if the creatures just beyond the doorway didn't matter anymore.

"Stay here," she said, giving him one more quick kiss before she rose and padded to the entrance. Her foot clinked against the rack of glass vials she'd left on the floor, sending them spiraling across the tiles. She ignored them as she reached the door and pulled back the viewing slot.

The Skaldi had returned to the corridor, their numbers, so far as she could tell, the same as before. But their behavior was entirely different: they had stopped moving and were crouched in neat rows, as if they were circus animals commanded to perform some trick. Their moaning was constant but restrained, a low mutter like wind in autumn branches. Though their grotesque appearance sickened her, she could almost believe that they had no intention of attacking, that whatever arcane power drove them had been drained from them during the night.

Kareem stood behind her, his naked body pressed against hers. He took one look into the corridor then drew the slide closed. "They're so calm."

"Do you think we could get past them?"

He bit his lip. "It could be a trap. To get us to come out."

"Can they make a plan like that?"

"I wouldn't have thought they could," he said. "When the tall man used to bring us to the lab, the Skaldi acted like they did last night. They'd throw themselves at us in a frenzy. That was the immature ones, though. Maybe, when they grow, their brains develop."

"I don't think they have brains." She glanced into the corridor once more. The Skaldi hadn't moved. "It might be worth the risk."

He put his arms around her, drew her close. "Or ... "

She nestled against him. "Or what?"

"Or," he whispered in her ear, "we could stay here a little while longer."

The feel of his breath against her flesh made her shiver with desire. But his words sent up a red flag. "*A little while longer?* Were you planning to go somewhere afterwards?"

His arms loosened. She could feel his reluctance, but he pulled away. When she turned to face him, he ducked his head.

"I remembered something," he said. "Or at least, I think I did. Maybe it was just a dream. But I think there's another way out."

All languor, all longing to spend her last moments in forgetful lovemaking disappeared. "Where?"

"Farther down the hallway. There should be another corridor branching off from the main one. It leads to the surface. It's"—he paused, looking abashed, even guilty—"I'm pretty sure it's how we got away the first time. When the bombs fell, most of the doors malfunctioned. Or maybe the scientists opened them so they could escape. But if the door I'm thinking of is open and the passage hasn't been blocked by the explosion, we might be able to get out."

She should have felt hope rekindle in her breast, but a splinter of skepticism worked its way beneath her skin. "There's something you're not telling me."

He lowered his eyes, shielding them beneath his long lashes. It was a gesture she'd learned too well not to notice. She took his face in both hands, tilted it upward, and planted a kiss on his lips.

"Kareem," she said, "you can tell me anything. I trust you."

"Okay." He drew a deep breath before continuing. "If we both leave, the Skaldi will sense a difference between the two of us. The same way they did in the desert. I don't understand it completely, but I think it's because I've been exposed to them so many times. They'll be drawn to someone whose energy hasn't been tapped yet. Someone who's ... "

"Fresh meat."

He cringed at the expression, but went on. "They're always hungry, Michelle. They're in agony when they're deprived of another life source. It was actually painful to watch them straining to reach their prey while the scientists drove them off."

She tried to picture it, then tried just as quickly to drive the image from her mind.

"But once they've fed on someone a few times," Kareem continued, "they start to lose interest. It happened quickest with the littlest children, probably because their bodies contained less of the energy the Skaldi wanted. After a while, the creatures would ignore the victim that was offered to them and start looking around for someone else to fulfill their need."

"I get it," she said. "So if I leave the room first, they'll forget about you and follow me."

His expression transformed instantly to horror. "That's not what I meant. I—"

"But it's true, isn't it? If they're chasing me, you'll have a chance to escape. I'm faster than you, Kareem. And you're the one who knows the way out."

"*I'm* going to go first," he said defiantly. "They'll be interested in me the way they would be with anyone, but they won't be as quick to attack. And then, when I draw them away from the door—"

"But they won't follow you if they sense me inside," she said. "This is a siege, not an assault. They've obviously figured out that they can't get in, which means they're going to sit by the door and wait either until we leave or until we're dead and they don't feel our life force anymore."

"They won't last long," he argued. "Like the ones in the

desert—look what happened to them. We could wait them out … "

"And die of dehydration while we're waiting?" she asked. "*You* might be able to outlast them. Whatever the scientists did to you in this place, I've seen how quickly you heal. But I'm not like you. I'll be dead in less than a week, unless you open a vein and let me drink your blood. Is that what you want?"

His face fell. "I would let you … "

"I know you would," she said. "But I wouldn't."

She hurried away from him for a second, kneeling to retrieve one of the vials that had scattered across the floor. When she returned, she enfolded him in a hug, her cheek against his bare chest. His steady heartbeat belied the turmoil she knew was in his mind.

"I want to do this," she murmured. "If I can outrun them, we'll both be safe. If I can't, at least I'll know that you got away."

"But I promised. I said I wouldn't let them … "

"I know. And I love that you promised me. But that was when we thought there was no way out. Now that we know there is, you have to make me another promise."

He gazed at her, his Adam's apple moving, unable to speak.

"You have to promise me that you'll live," she said. "That if they catch me, you won't try to save me. That you'll go far away from here, somewhere the Skaldi haven't reached yet. Out west, maybe. And when you get there, you'll bury this." She pressed the vial into his hand, and he clutched it without looking. "And then, after you've put what's left of me in the ground, you'll say my name out loud—the name you gave me—and release my spirit to the sky."

Kareem opened his hand and stared at the vial. She'd plucked a couple of strands of her hair and placed them inside, and—though he couldn't know this—she'd touched her finger to her lips, her lashes, and let the salt of a tear slide into the vial before sealing it. Now she gave him a final kiss on the cheek and folded his hands over the offering before letting him go.

"I need to get ready," she said. "There's no way I'm going out there like this."

She dressed hurriedly in her bra and underpants, then threw on one of the sweat suits. With each item of clothing she placed on her body, she felt as if she were closing a door to her past, her life, her heart. When she'd garbed herself fully and tightened the laces on the fresh pair of boots from the footlocker, she moved to the door like an automaton, precise and unemotional. Kareem reached out for her one more time, but she'd already said her goodbyes.

"How far is it to the other exit?" she asked.

His face was pure misery. "About two hundred meters. The branch is to the right from where we are."

She pulled open the slot and looked over the bowed heads of the Skaldi. The exit was too far away to see in the dim light of the corridor, but she trained her eyes on the distance, silently counting off steps.

"Give me sixty seconds to be safe," she said. "I'll double back and meet you if I can."

He tried to say something, but failed and hung his head. She would have been tempted to stay and comfort him if she hadn't closed that door last of all. Her eyes were dry and her gaze focused on the path ahead as she pulled the bolt and slipped outside.

The Skaldi surged upward as one, but before they'd gained their feet, she vaulted over the first row of them and ran.

They clutched at her, but she was moving so fast that by the time they turned, she'd leaped over the succeeding rows and was fleeing down the open corridor. She heard them following, claws scraping the floor, moans echoing. Their smell enveloped her, but they seemed sluggish, lacking the inhuman swiftness she'd witnessed on the video and in the desert. Maybe the adults died as quickly as Kareem said, and these ones had little energy left. The half-open door to the exit tunnel flashed by her in a beam of weak blue light, and the Skaldi streamed past it in her wake. In another few seconds, she'd have lured them far enough away for Kareem to reach the escape passage across the open space she'd created.

She heard the bedroom door scrape open behind her, and Kareem's voice echoed down the corridor.

"Hey! Back here! I'm right behind you!"

The pursuit fell off at the sound of his voice, the Skaldi's rancid smell and odious presence vanishing like a flame extinguished by a gust of wind. She threw a look over her shoulder to discover that the creatures had reversed course and were flooding toward the lone figure in black sweatpants and shirt who stood waving his arms in the dimly lit hallway. He made no move for the exit, and that delay allowed the monsters to swarm back between him and safety. She realized what Kareem was doing: she was well past the exit doorway now, and with the Skaldi converging on him, she'd succeeded in opening an escape route not for her lover but for herself.

He had lied to her about the Skaldi's choice of prey, gambling that if she left first, he could save her life at the cost of his own.

"Run!" he shouted, his voice echoing down the corridor before she lost sight of him over the heads of the maddened creatures.

"Kareem!" she cried out, but there was no answer.

Without hesitation, she sprinted toward the milling mass that choked the passageway, then flung herself at the nearest pale forms. Contact with their skin froze her blood, but she struggled through the squirming bodies, feeling lightheaded and disconnected, her thoughts a blur. There was no pain; none of the scars opened to draw her in. But the mere touch of their flesh peeled slices of her memory away, until she felt exposed and numb, unsure of who or where she was. Only a single word was left to her, and she clutched it as tightly as she could, raising it before her as a shield against the void.

Chelle.

A hand gripped hers, and she squeezed reflexively. When she pulled, a human figure came free of the pile, a boy with black hair and thick, curling lashes. He was shouting at her, his mouth stretched wide, but she could hear nothing over the moans of the things that surrounded them. She stared at him dazedly, her mind trying to decipher his words, her tongue to shape his name. Then he was pulling her along behind him, out of the pile of monsters, along the hallway. Light and life bloomed in her chest as memories returned to her: his body, his voice, his vow. The tips of claws raked her heels, but she ignored the freezing pain as she and her partner flung themselves through the exit door, then slammed it in the creatures' blank faces.

She raced up a new blue-lit tunnel, holding his hand, putting as much distance as she could between the two of them and the nightmare behind. Her heartbeat throbbed in her head, her vision clouded with lack of breath, but her arms and legs continued to churn mechanically. She heard a sound close to her ear, a soothing sound that was nothing like the moans of the creatures, but she was focused only on escape. After an impossibly long time, the sound resolved into a voice, speaking words in a soft yet urgent tone.

"Michelle. It's okay. You can slow down."

She shook her head, trying to clear the fog that remained. His face appeared before her, dark eyes soft and pleading.

"Really," he said. "They can't reach us here. The door must have locked when we closed it. We're safe."

She sank to the ground in exhaustion, and he held her while her lungs fought for air. Slowly, painfully, she came back to herself, felt the ache in her stomach where she'd been wounded, the deeper ache in her chest where pieces of her past had been stripped away. She remembered her name, the place she'd lived for seventeen years and the life she'd lived there, the people she'd loved and lost. She recalled what the world had become, the monsters she now shared it with. Their touch had diminished her as it had in the desert. If not for the one who held her in his arms, she wasn't sure there would be anything left of her.

Weakly, she pressed her fists against his chest. "Don't ever do that again."

"I couldn't let them take you."

"Not that." She gazed at him long and hard, until his face swam into focus. "Don't ever lie to me. *Ever.* You can tell me the worst thing in the world, but don't lie to me. Do you understand?"

He said nothing, but his eyes dodged hers. Her hands clumsy with fatigue, she forced his chin up.

"And don't do *that*," she said. "I know when you're not telling me something. It's the same as lying."

"There are some things that are too bad to tell."

"*No*," she said. "There's nothing you can't tell me. Nothing I can't take. Don't you understand what last night meant?"

"I—"

"It meant no lies," she said. "It meant you can tell me anything. It meant you *have* to tell me everything. My God, Kareem"—his name had just come back to her, along with the soulful image of his child-self in the photograph—"you could have died back there. And you didn't even think what that would have done to me."

"You were willing to die for me," he mumbled.

"But I *told* you!" she said shrilly. "You *knew*. I told you the truth, and you—you repaid me with lies."

His hands jumped away from her as if she'd administered an electric shock. She wondered if she'd gone too far, or not far enough—if instead of reproving him, she should have fallen into his arms and kissed him, then told him the thing she hadn't had the guts to say. Maybe she'd learned it only this moment, when she thought she was going to lose him. And when she realized she hadn't been entirely truthful with him either, she softened, reaching out to touch his face.

"I love you, Kareem," she said. "And I need you to tell me the truth. Even if you think it'll hurt me or scare me

239

away."

She expected him to return to her arms, but he shook free of her caress and stood. He walked a short distance down the hallway, his face turned from her. Her legs felt too weak to stand, so she remained on the cold cement floor while he paced the narrow corridor, looking like a caged creature that had learned long ago that no escape was to be found.

At last he stopped. He turned back to her and lowered himself to the ground at her side. He didn't touch her, and his face was surprisingly harsh in the tunnel's blue light.

"I don't know the truth," he said, his voice as unforgiving as his expression. "That's my problem, remember?"

"I'm not asking you to tell me anything you don't know."

"But you keep hoping, right? That I'll remember?"

"Of course." The accusation in his voice shocked her, especially after what she'd just confessed to him. "I want you to remember for *you*. Not for me."

"But it would make things a lot easier for you, wouldn't it?"

"Kareem," she said, and now that her body had stopped quivering from exertion, she felt her veins throb with the first stirrings of anger. "Nothing about this has been *easy* for me. Not from the moment I lost my way in the woods. Not from the moment I found you." Trying to keep things from getting worse, she added in a softer tone, "But I am glad I found you. And now that we've gotten away from them, I do want to stay with you."

He let out a short laugh, ugly in its finality. "You'll change your tune when you hear what I have to say."

She recoiled from the callousness in his voice. "What is it?"

"It's what I figured out when the Skaldi attacked me back there," he said. "Maybe that's why I didn't try to get away. Maybe I was hoping I'd die, and then at least I'd know who I was. *What* I was."

She reached for his face, but he flinched away.

"The Skaldi only attack the living," he said. "They're empty vessels, and they don't waste time on things that can't fill them up. The scientists tested them to see if they'd feed off each other, but they couldn't get Skaldi to attack other Skaldi."

His face was half-turned from her, but it was the face of the boy she knew, the face she'd come to love. She'd dreamed of it before she knew it well, and since then she'd memorized every line, every look. It couldn't be the face of the other, the blank emptiness staring out from behind his dark eyes.

Could it?

"Oh, God," she said, but he didn't seem to hear.

"They couldn't kill me," he said, "because there was nothing left to kill. Which must mean I'm already one of them."

Chapter 16

She crept to him on hands and knees, trying to convince him this terrible thing couldn't be true.

"I've been with you all along," she said. "They never had time to ... to take over."

He refused to look at her. "It could have happened before you got to the city. Or when I left to take a shower. They've had plenty of time."

"But if you were one of them," she said, her mind racing, "you would know."

"Would I?" he asked. "Maybe Skaldi don't know what they are, and they think they're still human when they take over."

"But you remember ... you remember my name?"

"Of course I do. But I told you before, that doesn't prove anything. If I'm not me, I might still have my memories." He laughed bitterly. "This is crazy. I couldn't remember who I was before. Now I don't even know if I'm *me*."

"But," she tried again, "if you were Skaldi, you would have attacked me. You wouldn't have ... " She wished she could finish, but the place where that thought led was too awful for her to say the words out loud.

"That's no proof either," he said with a combination of pity and cruelty. "Maybe I wasn't fully Skaldi before just now. Maybe what the scientists did to me gave me the power to resist them, and I didn't transition completely until they laid hands on me back there."

She tried to think of something more to say, anything to get him to stop talking like this. He still looked like himself, sounded like himself, *thought* like himself. The touch of his hands had been warm and gentle, nothing like the searing, mind-numbing chill of the Skaldi's claws. But she knew so little about their power of mimicry. Could that power be so perfect it deceived not only its victims but the Skaldi themselves?

And if so, what unholy thing had she given herself to last night?

"Whatever I am," he went on when she didn't contradict him, "it's dangerous for you to stay with me. Possibly there are enough traces of me left that you're safe for the moment. That could change."

She reached up to touch his hand, but he yanked it away. "You would never hurt me," she said.

"I don't want to," he responded. "But I don't know what I might do down the road. Do Skaldi start out wanting to kill, or do they start out just wanting to survive? Even when they're dying, when the only way they can stay alive is to take another's life, they might hate themselves for doing it. But they do it anyway, don't they?"

His face was hidden in the shadows. Now he turned and fixed her with a look that was half despairing, half pleading. His outstretched hand gripped the vial she'd given him—but the glass was broken, the shattered end sharp as a knife.

"You have to do what we talked about," he said. "What we promised. You can't take a chance with your life. And you can't let me go on like this."

The realization of what he was asking her to do struck her like a physical blow. "I can't do that! What if you're wrong?"

"Then it won't be your fault. And at least you'll be safe."

Tears flowed down her face, and she reached out with both hands to touch him, but again, he rebuffed her. "I can't do it, Kareem. I can't! Please, I'll do anything, but not that."

He considered her, his expression hard and cold. "If you truly loved me, you'd do it."

"Don't say that," she begged. "If I kill you now, Kareem, I die with you. The dagger I use to slit your throat is the same I use to cut my own."

"Then I'll do it myself," he said, and held the shard against his wrist.

"Don't!" She scrabbled for his hand, trying to tear the vial from his grasp. He pulled back wildly, and the glass slashed across the backs of her fingers. Through the pain, she stared at the cut on her knuckles, the bright red spots welling like a string of scarlet pearls.

"They don't bleed," she said softly, then spoke it again. "They don't bleed! Kareem, Jason did a blood test on everyone who joined his camp, because he must have known that the Skaldi don't bleed. And the one I shot in the desert—I put an arrow straight through its heart, but there was nothing, only dust."

He stared at her as if he couldn't make sense of her words.

"You were bleeding last night," she said. "Your face,

your hands. You were … "

The words failed in her throat. She reached out for the shard of glass.

"Let me do it," she said. "If there's no blood, I promise you"—she swallowed, and had to struggle to go on—"I promise you that when I can make fire again, I'll do what you ask. That's fair, isn't it? Please, Kareem. I promise, as I love you, that I'll do as I say."

Shakily, he handed the broken vial to her. His eyes were wary, as if he suspected this was some kind of trick. With all the tenderness she could summon, she held his hand palm up and slowly drew the sharpened tip of the vial across the pad of his index finger. Then she pinched his fingertip and watched the cut for signs of his salvation, and her own.

The next thing she knew, she was sobbing uncontrollably, flinging herself into his arms as he knelt there in a daze, his eyes fixed on the evidence of his own finger.

"I would have done it," she said through her tears. "You have to believe me. But I knew you weren't one of them. I knew you were *you*."

His arms rose to grasp her shoulders and pull her to him. Where his hand touched her cheek, she felt the smear of blood from his fingertip.

"I'm sorry," he whispered into her hair. "It wasn't fair to ask. They've been playing with my head so long, I didn't know what to believe. I couldn't stand the thought of hurting you."

They held each other until she stopped shaking and he ran out of ways to apologize, though she let him repeat the same apologies at least twice more. She listened to him babble, thrilled by the sound of his voice, the warmth of his breath against her hair. She didn't mind his kisses either, one for each tear, which added up to a lot. When he was done, he spoke the words that canceled all of his past debts and forestalled future ones he hadn't yet accumulated.

"I love you," he whispered, following the incantation with the sound of her newly given name.

She wrapped his cut in a strip of tape from her own wound, binding the broken vial in another strip that she tucked into the pocket of her sweatpants. The corridor stretched ahead of them, lit sporadically by the blue track lights, receding into darkness.

"How far is it to the exit?" she asked Kareem.

"You're going to hate me for saying this," he remarked with a bashful grin, "but I don't remember. I have a vague memory of walking it with the others and exiting into the forest, so it must go on for a pretty long distance."

"That's at least a day to pass under the desert," she said. "Are you sure you're all right?"

"I will be," he said, taking her hand. "Now that I'm with you."

She kissed him for that, and they started down the tunnel.

They walked at an untaxing pace, one Michelle felt confident they could keep up for as long as necessary. Her own strength had come flowing back in the last few minutes, as if Kareem's miraculous rebirth had been hers as well. Without a supply of water, she knew that they'd have to get out of here in a day or two to avoid dehydration. But like the tunnel through which they'd entered the SKLDI facility yesterday, the exit tunnel was cooler than the surface, so they wouldn't lose fluid as quickly. She couldn't detect any warning signs in her throat or in the condition of her body and mind, so she felt content to spend the journey, however long it took, in a companionable quiet she hadn't known for days.

They passed through stretches of tunnel where the blue lights were all intact, other areas of checkered glow and shadow. Occasionally, they encountered a section that was nearly pitch-black, with only a single light to mark the way. Michelle wondered whether the tunnel had been damaged in places like this by Jason's pulse device, or by the earlier bombs that had obliterated the city above their heads. The thought that they were walking underneath such devastation would have rattled her if not for the feel of Kareem's hand in hers.

Once, after they'd been walking for several hours, they came across a sector that had lapsed into utter darkness. Kareem gripped her hand more tightly, and the two of them felt their way forward with fingertips outstretched, discovering that debris from the ceiling had blocked the tunnel. For a moment, she felt despair descending. But working silently and by touch alone, the two of them managed to clear enough rubble that a dim blue beam showed through. That gave them the visibility and the motivation to attack the pile even more aggressively, and within another hour, they'd opened a space they could slip through by turning sideways and sucking in their stomachs. Michelle was thankful for the drastically reduced-calorie diet she and Kareem had been on for the past several weeks, especially when, just as he wiggled through the gap behind her, the precarious pile shifted and filled the opening they'd made. Standing in the blue light and staring at the blockage, she doubted they'd be able to clear the passageway again—or that they'd have had the heart to try the first time if they'd been able to see how bad it was.

Kareem, covered in dust, wiped his hands together. "Let's hope there's no more of that."

She brushed a chalky cloud from his hair, kissed him, and took his hand once more.

They'd been walking for a long, peaceful time without further obstruction when Michelle felt the first hints of headache and weakness that signaled her body's demand for water. Earlier, they'd come across an exposed pipe in the tunnel wall that leaked a foul-smelling dribble, but she'd warned Kareem away when he made a move toward it. Now, she wondered if they should have taken their chances with that almost certainly polluted seep. If, as she hoped, they'd left the area under the city and were making their way beneath the desert toward the forest, there'd be no water magically raining from the ceiling. In the past several hours, they'd seen periodic doors on either side of the tunnel, one every mile or so—but they were all closed and inoperable, except for the half-open one that led, maddeningly, into a shallow nook that might once have served as a utility closet. But even if they found a door to the outside, there was no guarantee it wouldn't deposit them into the middle of a sand dune. She told herself that if they ever got out of here, she'd have to be much more careful about water. They couldn't count on finding it in the hostile environment they were headed for.

They stopped to rest after they'd been walking for what seemed like most of the daylight hours. Reluctant as she was to lose any time now that dehydration had reminded her of its

248

looming threat, her feet and legs were absolutely killing her. Kareem, she noticed with concern, was in even worse shape than she was. He'd seemed strong when they started out, but no sooner had they sat down than he closed his eyes and rested his head against the wall, giving her a chance to study him in the dim blue light. His face looked worn and gray, the way it had looked days ago—ages ago—in the Argo's infirmary. When she wrapped her hands around his, they felt not cold but overly warm, as if a fever were dawning. She wondered if he'd hurt himself breaking through the jam in the tunnel. More likely, he was simply starved and exhausted. She watched him anxiously as she smoothed thick black hair over his forehead.

"How are you feeling?" she whispered.

He opened his eyes and smiled. "Tired."

"Do you want to sleep?"

"We should probably get going soon. I don't want to spend any more time in this place than we have to."

"Okay." But she let him decide when "soon" was, and more than an hour passed before he pushed himself from the wall and announced, "Let's go."

She stood first. He needed her help to climb to his feet.

They set off down the tunnel again, but they'd gone only a few more miles before Michelle was forced to admit that his condition was getting progressively worse. Hours ago, they'd been walking leisurely, holding hands like the young lovers they were; now, it seemed as if they'd turned into an old married couple, with his hand looped through her arm the only thing that enabled him to continue. His gait had slowed, while his movements were gingerly, his breathing labored. At the same time, his fever had metamorphosed from dim shadow to glaring certainty: she could feel it not only in the heat of his skin but in the quiver of his hand. From what he'd told her about his time in the lab, it seemed the SKLDI scientists had built up his strength to help him resist their creations—or, she thought now, to give the monsters extra energy to feed on. That additional vigor probably explained both his quick healing power and his ability to fight the infection that had threatened his life when she first met him. At the same time, it was obvious that repeated exposure to the creatures had worn him down, and she wondered if his exertion over the past days had finally been too much for him. Maybe, like his memory, his body had been permanently weakened. Either way, she doubted he had the strength to reach the exit, wherever that might be.

And if—when—they did reach it, what then? What would happen when they finally emerged from the tunnels into the desert or what remained of the woodlands? It wasn't as if they could settle down in a rustic cabin and live out the rest of their days happily ever after. Jason and his camp were still there, and his scouts might discover them at any time. The leader of the Argo wouldn't hesitate to take her life, and Kareem's, if he learned that they'd survived the assault on the city. Though the Skaldi appeared to be contained, she couldn't convince herself they'd stay that way forever. Sooner or later, she and Kareem would have to move on, and she wasn't sure her companion would regain the strength to do so.

She glanced at him out of the corner of her eye. He stared doggedly ahead, as if he required every ounce of concentration to set each foot in front of the other. At this rate, they'd have to rest again soon, and they'd almost certainly need to repeat the process with increasing frequency as the journey wore on. A new urgency overtook her, as the enclosure that had started out seeming like a welcome respite from danger now felt like another trap they needed to free themselves from as soon as possible. She picked up her pace incrementally, willing Kareem to follow suit. If they could only get out of this place, she told herself, she'd work on securing their future then.

But it was no use. Kareem tried to match her quicker strides, but she could feel his body dragging against hers, an anchor pulling both of them backward. Finally, in his effort to speed up, he got tangled in his own feet, and she had to catch him before he fell. Keeping her arms around him, she lowered the two of them to the floor.

"Maybe we should take another break," she said.

"Yeah." He tried to smile at her, but the smile looked more like a grimace of pain. "I'm really beat."

His head fell so heavily against the wall she winced in sympathy. In the unusually strong light that prevailed in this section of the tunnel, she saw what she should have seen hours ago, maybe *had* seen but refused to accept: his face wasn't just pale but waxy and emaciated, his eyes sunken and the curve of his aquiline nose so prominent it appeared hawkish. *A death mask*, she thought, and shuddered. She'd convinced herself he was strong: in his fight against the immature Skaldi he'd appeared nearly invincible, and though the memory made her cheeks grow warm, she could never forget his seemingly inexhaustible lovemaking. Now, he looked as beaten and broken as the children he'd described succumbing to the Skaldi.

That thought made her shake him gently, searching for a

response. Thankfully, his eyes opened, but his gaze wavered, fever bright.

"Time to go?" he asked weakly.

"Not yet." She leaned down to kiss his forehead, and was shocked by how hot and dry he'd become, his flesh burning like desert sand. "We can rest here as long as you want."

"Okay." He settled back against the wall, but his eyes remained open. "What's in the west?" he asked out of nowhere.

"I'm sorry?"

"You said before that I should go west." His voice had that dreamy quality to it, and his eyes were having trouble focusing on her face. "So what's out west?"

It took her a long time to remember saying that. When she did, she wasn't sure how to answer.

"There are mountains," she said at last. "My parents took me there before my little sister was born."

"You have a sister?"

"I had a sister. She's gone now."

He laid a hand over hers. "Tell me about the mountains."

She closed her eyes and tried to remember. At first, all she could see was Rosie's face. She spoke, haltingly, and as she did, the veil lifted and the memory returned.

"I was about five years old," she said. "My mom was pregnant with Rosie, although I didn't know it at the time. I think taking me there was meant to be a treat—you know, a way to soften the blow of inflicting a sibling on me. So they took me camping. It's the first vacation I can remember. One of the first things I remember distinctly about my life,

252

period."

He was silent, stroking her hand, gazing unsteadily into her eyes.

"I don't remember all of it," she confessed. "The things we did, the places we went. But I remember the mountains. They were beautiful. The peaks went up into the clouds, and the streams were so clear you could see the backs of fish shining in them like nickels and pennies. The grass was long and covered in wildflowers, and when the wind blew, it would ripple in a way that reminded me of satin. I remember the feel of it, sinking into that soft grass and lying there staring up at the sky. Maybe I did know that something was coming, something that was going to change my life forever, because I remember I'd lie in the grass to hide. As if my parents couldn't find me if I kept perfectly still, and then I could stay there forever and become part of the trees and rocks and streams. They knew where I was, of course, but my dad would play along, calling out to my mom, *Do you know where Michelle's gone?* while I lay there and smiled to myself to think how clever I was. It's what I used to visualize to calm my mind before a race: lying there in the grass, invisible to everyone, except maybe to the mountains themselves."

"Could we go there?" he asked, so earnestly it was as if he were a child asking.

"We could try," she said. "It's a long way from here, but there's no reason we couldn't go together. I know how to survive in the woods now. And we're not in a rush anymore, are we?"

"I guess not." He laid the tips of his fingers on her cheek. His hand shook. "Now that the Skaldi are gone."

She closed her eyes so he couldn't see the tears form.

When she opened them to smile at him, his had already closed.

"Get some rest," she said. "I'll keep watch."

He smiled wanly, and she kissed his hot forehead and saw his face relax.

For as long as he slept, she did keep watch, but only of him. She wished they hadn't ended up in this spot, where the light proved so merciless in feeding her anxiety: it showed her every vein beneath his pellucid skin, every hitch in his ragged breath. During the hours of her vigil, she charted the rise of his fever, felt his forehead grow unbearably hot and tight, the roots of his hair turning damp with droplets of sweat. He shivered in her arms, and his teeth chattered. The sickness came on as swiftly as his cuts and bruises had departed, and through her dread, she wondered if the experiments that had been performed on him had made him both inhumanly quick to heal and uncommonly susceptible to relapse. If it was true that the Skaldi consumed people's energy, their life force, could it be that after such prolonged exposure to them, his own life force had become unstable, rapidly consuming itself after abnormal bursts of power? Could it have worsened to the point where, as with the creatures that had preyed on him, the process of decay had become irreversible and final?

Speculation was useless, she told herself. She couldn't remain here and hope he'd recover. But she couldn't carry him the rest of the way out of the tunnels, and even if she could, what awaited him there was no better than what was happening here. He needed help, medicine, a doctor. And there was only one place she could go to find those things.

Should she wake him, tell him what she planned to do? Or would that only frighten him? Surely he'd be even more frightened if he woke and found her gone. She wrestled with herself, every precious second that slipped through her hands feeling as if it were the countdown to a death sentence. She stared down the tunnel, but no doors were in sight, and she wondered if Kareem had been mistaken, if this tunnel led to nowhere. If she found a door, would it open? If she exited into the forest, how much farther was it to Jason's camp? She'd determined that she couldn't leave without rousing him when her eyes fell on his face and she saw that he was awake.

She leaned over to brush her lips against his. They blazed back like hot coals. "Feeling better?"

"A little," he said, though his voice told her differently. "Is it time to go now?"

"Not quite," she said. "I was thinking I might … explore up ahead for a little bit. See if we're close to an exit."

He didn't respond, other than to flick his eyes across her face.

"Will you be okay by yourself for a minute?" she asked. "I promise I'll be right back."

He gazed at her with bright eyes. "I'll be fine."

She leaned down to kiss him once more. Though she knew he could taste her tears, she kept her lips pressed against his for as long as she could bear. "I'll be right back. I promise you, Kareem. Nothing will touch you until I come back."

He sank against the wall, eyes closed. If he heard the lie in her voice, he didn't say anything.

Michelle stood and took a long look down the tunnel. *There's no time*, she thought, but she couldn't have explained to herself what she meant. No time to waste, no time to save the one she loved. No time to give in to doubt or fear or despair.

She hesitated the merest second to make sure he was asleep, and then she was off.

Chapter 17

She ran faster than she'd ever run before.

Her flight from Caeneus, her nighttime pursuit of Kareem, her attempted escape from the Skaldi in the desert—all were nothing compared to this. The tunnel lights blurred as she streaked past, the wound in her side leaking a steady stream into the padding Kareem had taped there, but time and space and pain were nothing compared to the strong, steady pull of her resolve. Her weary body whispered that she couldn't maintain this speed for the distance she'd have to run to reach the exit, much less to arrive at Jason's camp. But her heart wouldn't listen, telling her that there was no limit to how fast and far she could run. As the miles fell behind her, the dream that gave her feet wings was of green fields, crystal clear streams, and soaring, cloud-capped peaks, all of them awaiting her and the boy who rested against the tunnel wall, the boy she had no doubt she would save. It was impossible to believe otherwise. His life and hers were a single force, and his could never be extinguished while hers burned so bright.

She couldn't guess how far she'd run when she came upon a solitary door in the tunnel, partway open like the ones in the SKLDI facility. She was moving so fast she nearly flashed by it, but she braked hard and barreled into the door,

JOSHUA DAVID BELLIN

which offered no more resistance than air. A ladder of iron
rungs climbed the cement wall on the other side. Sunlight,
unmistakable after all the hours in darkness and artificial
illumination, streamed down from above. She scaled the
ladder in seconds, never slowing, the torment in her arms and
legs and chest just another physical impediment she shook
off like a forgotten insult. Shouldering aside a door that had
come partly off its hinges and lay askew on the ground level
exit, she emerged into the afternoon brightness of a forest
clearing. Without a moment's hesitation, judging her position
less by sun and surroundings than by instinct, she resumed
her dash through the forest, heading for Jason's camp. She
couldn't see the Lethe or sense any sign of human presence,
but she knew that the Argo and its life-saving medicine lay
only a few more miles, a few more minutes away.

She also knew that, once she got there, the dreamlike
freedom of this run would come to an end. She'd have to
slow down to evade the sentries, or to talk her way past them.
Failing that—and she surely would fail that, especially if
Arachne was back on patrol—she'd have to overpower any
resistance she met and take her chances with what followed.
At the camp itself, she'd have to find Circe, pray that Jason
hadn't taken the opportunity while she was gone to imprison
the doctor or worse, and hope that the woman would show
sympathy toward her as she had the morning of Michelle's
departure. Assuming she could pull all that off and get Circe
to come with her, she'd probably have to carry the older
woman on the return trip, which, no matter how strong her
legs felt at the moment, would unquestionably slow her
down. Maybe she was fooling herself. Could she really run
through the woods with a full-grown woman, even a woman

258

as small as Circe, on her back? She hadn't marked the tunnel exit; could she find it when they returned? If she found it, could they reach Kareem in time?

Yes, she told herself. *Yes*. Failure—or even doubt—were not options.

The first sentry rose in front of her as she exited the woods. She raced past, ignoring the man's shout, barely registering his order for her to stop. The command wasn't repeated before she heard the crack of a rifle. She kept low, zigzagging across the open space as bullets tore the turf around her. She spared a moment's reflection to wonder which member of camp it was who'd been willing to kill her, but she decided it didn't matter. Jason would have given the same orders to all of his followers, and she wouldn't know until she reached the Argo if anyone—including Circe—would defy those orders. The only thing that mattered now was that the next sentry would be ready for her.

As it turned out, the next sentry was Arachne, who lay in wait behind a boulder on the headlands overlooking camp. She'd strung a tripwire across the pass to slow intruders down. When Michelle neared, the sentry stepped out from behind her redoubt with rifle already raised, but before she could fire, Michelle was hurdling into the air, using the tripwire's tension to vault for the outcropping where Arachne had hidden herself. As she left the ground, she had the sensation of soaring free of earth's gravity, her foot touching the rock briefly before propelling her past the startled sentry. Then she was plunging down the hillside that shadowed the River Lethe, the rocky path providing cover as Arachne rained fire mingled with obscenities after her. Several bullets chipped fragments from the boulders near Michelle's head, but none struck home. There was a hiatus filled only with Arachne's curses as the woman paused to adjust her aim, but by the time the hunter had her weapon trained again on the path, Michelle had left it and was sprinting through the trees that led to the women's quarters.

Please, she said silently, *let Circe be there.* She knew that Arachne would radio ahead to Jason, who'd rouse his soldiers to hunt for the outlaw. She'd have only minutes, maybe less, to plead for Circe's help. And even if the doctor agreed, the two of them would have to elude everyone else in camp long enough to lose themselves in the forest once more.

Her mind told her it was impossible, but her heart refused to believe.

She paused at the edge of camp, peering out at the alternating bands of sunlight and shadow that striped the grounds. She was surprised to find the settlement quiet and seemingly empty: no figures patrolled the compound, no voices rose from the cabins. She'd kept to the trees for as long as she could, but now she'd have to cross the open space in front of headquarters to reach the women's lodging. Would Jason be watching? He wouldn't even need to step onto the porch to spring his trap: he could have repositioned his tripwires, dug new pits since she'd been gone. After all the miles she'd put behind her, the hundred-meter dash across the compound's central area could be the end of her run.

There was nothing to do but risk it. Every second she hesitated was a second Kareem didn't have to spare.

The decision made, she shot from cover and aimed straight for the women's quarters, moving at a dead sprint. Out of the corner of her eye, she thought she saw a shadow passing in front of the infirmary window, but she didn't slow to study it. She expected shouts, the crack of rifles, the ground giving way beneath her feet or a hidden garrote strangling her throat—but there was nothing. Within seconds, she'd reached the front steps of the women's barracks and burst through the door.

There was no one there.

Her eyes told her that instantly, but disbelief held her for long minutes while she tore through the building, looking for someone who couldn't possibly have hidden from her in the small, boxy room. She knew it was useless, that Circe and the others were gone—where, she couldn't imagine—but she searched anyway, checking corners and dropping to the floor to peek beneath beds. Empty as the barracks appeared, there was something she couldn't identify—a silence like a held breath—that kept her from giving up. Did she hear a noise? Catch sight of a small shadow? Too small to be one of the women or the twins, but small enough to be—

"Tyris!"

She lunged for Circe's daughter just as the little girl rolled from beneath the bed closest to the room's solitary window and tried to exit that way. Tyris was struggling to climb, kicking her legs helplessly against the wall, when Michelle caught her arm. Without a second's pause, the five-year-old redirected her kicks at Michelle's shins.

"Tyris, stop!" She grabbed the girl's hands, tried to fend off her feet, but Tyris was as fierce as a feral kitten. Michelle found it necessary to wrap her arms around the little girl's body and lift her from the ground, where she continued to kick futilely at the air.

And scream. "Mommy! Help! Mommy!"

Michelle had never heard the girl raise her voice, but

now her piercing cry seemed as loud as the warning siren on the night Michelle and Kareem escaped the Argo. As the child's voice escalated in volume and pitch, she stopped invoking her mother's name and gave vent to mere inarticulate sounds, shrieks of terror without sense. Michelle tried to stifle the noise, but Tyris bit at her fingers when they neared her mouth. Fear of staying too long, of Jason finding her, of Kareem dying in the tunnel while she delayed, made Michelle much rougher than she intended, and that didn't help the girl's panic. All Michelle could think to do was squeeze Tyris against her and pray she'd grow still.

"Tyris," she spoke as calmly as she could over the girl's racket, "I'm not going to hurt you. I just came to see your mom. Do you know where she is?"

It was no use. Tyris flailed against her with renewed energy, her screams rising even higher. Michelle knew that if she held the girl any more forcefully, she'd hurt her.

What kind of monster must she think I am? Michelle thought as she let go.

At once, Tyris sprang for the window. She'd managed to brace a foot on the sill when the door slammed open behind them and a commanding voice filled the room.

"Tyris! Get down from there!"

Michelle turned to see Circe storming into the room, a clanking sound as of heavy keys accompanying her steps. When Michelle's gaze dropped to the doctor's ankles, she found them encased in twin manacles, a short length of chain between them preventing her from taking full strides. Without a glance at Michelle, the older woman approached her daughter, who dropped obediently from the window and threw herself at her savior.

"Mommy!"

The girl collided with Circe, wrapping her arms around her mother's waist as if she alone could fend off the intruder. Circe hoisted her into her arms and turned to face Michelle, Tyris clinging to her neck and resting on a hip.

That was when Michelle saw that the right side of Circe's face was badly bruised, her eye swollen nearly shut. She tried not to stare, but Circe smiled grimly.

"Jason needs me too much around here to put me in the box," she said. "But he wasn't above a little creative redecorating."

"He did this to you? Because you talked to me?"

"Because I challenged his authority. Arachne's the leader of the women's camp now, and I'm just another one of his tools, useful so long as I keep my mouth shut and stay in line."

She shook her head, while Tyris laid her curls on her mother's shoulder and softly, in imitation of Circe's comforting gesture, stroked the woman's hair.

"But what are you doing here?" Circe asked in a sharp whisper, pointless though caution was after Tyris's squall. "Jason said he left you in the city."

"I came back for"—Michelle paused, feeling faint and out of breath—"for you. And for medicine."

Circe's expert eye took in the wet stains on Michelle's sweatshirt where the bandage had loosened and her wound had wept tears of blood. "What happened to you?"

"There's no time," Michelle answered. Now that her legs had been motionless for minutes, they trembled beneath her, feeling hardly strong enough to bear her weight. "We have to get back to the forest."

Circe let her daughter slide down her hip and approached Michelle while the little girl clung to her mother's leg. The doctor's fingers carefully lifted the sweatshirt and probed the area around Michelle's wound.

"You're not going anywhere," Circe said. "Who patched you up like this? You need stitches."

"I can't," Michelle said, and this time her legs did give out, folding beneath her so that she landed awkwardly on the floor. "Please, Circe. I need your help."

Circe pursed her lips and studied Michelle. Tyris, calm in her mother's presence, was humming the notes of a nursery rhyme beneath her breath.

"If Jason finds you here, you're finished," the older woman announced. "We're both finished. But you can't leave, Diana. You're bleeding badly. Just look."

Michelle followed Circe's finger. The floor beneath her was a puddle of blood.

"I'll have to take you to one of the outbuildings," Circe said. "With luck, Jason won't think to look for you there." She shook her head, glowering at Michelle. "You had a chance to get away from him. And you didn't have the sense to *stay* away."

She reached beneath Michelle's arms to lift her from the floor, but Michelle threw herself at the older woman and clutched her waist as Tyris had done. The little girl's lullaby stopped abruptly, her face tightening and a whimper escaping her.

"I had to come back," Michelle said. "It's ... it's Kareem. He's sick. Maybe dying. Please, Circe. I wouldn't ask if I had anywhere else to go."

She pawed at the doctor's arm, beseeching her with her

eyes. Tyris, aware that she'd been displaced in her mother's attention, progressed from whimpers to wails.

"Tyris, be still!" Circe ordered. The girl sniffled, but obeyed. Circe squatted painfully beside Michelle, the ugly chain restricting her movement. "Where is he?"

"In the tunnels. Beneath the desert. I ran all the way here."

"You ran—?" Circe stared at her in disbelief. "And you expect me to head back there with you, loaded down with medical supplies? Look at me, Diana," she said, clutching the chain in a deeply veined hand. "I can't run after my own daughter, much less chase someone else's foolish dreams."

Michelle had no more strength for protest. The words *I'll carry you* died on her tongue as she realized she could never fulfill that promise; she didn't think she could carry Tyris, let alone an adult burdened by chains. She stroked Circe's arm, stared into her eyes. Consciousness drifted like a leaf, bobbing and twisting in the air above her. The effort to hold her head up finally became too hard, and she slipped to the floor and lay in the stickiness of her own blood. A pounding in her skull overwhelmed all other sounds in the room, so she wasn't sure she'd heard correctly when Circe next spoke.

"I'll send the twins with you," she said. "They can find their way through the woods. And they've watched me enough times to know what to do."

Tyris, possibly realizing this meant her mother wouldn't leave her, looked up at Circe and smiled.

"But I have to stitch you first," the woman said. "And we'll need to get some blood into you if you're going to go anywhere."

"There's no time," Michelle said. "Please, Circe. Just the

stitches and some water. I'll be fine."

Circe looked at her with doubt carved in every feature. Then she shook her head and laughed.

"I shouldn't be letting you go at all," she said. "And if anything happens to the girls, you'll hear from me, do you understand?"

Michelle nodded, wishing she had enough strength to summon the right words of thanks.

Circe led her across the silent campground to the infirmary, the older woman limping badly and Tyris prancing along at her mother's side. While she gathered her instruments and Michelle changed into a fresh uniform top, Circe gave her patient a status report on Jason's activities since his return the morning after he and Michelle left camp. His first order of business had been the public punishment and humiliation of his camp doctor, which he'd justified by seeding rumors of an immediate threat from the outside. Everyone in camp was on high alert and hair-trigger nerves. Then he'd disappeared into the bunker with Argus and Arachne, emerging hours later. He'd rounded up the majority of the camp's members, armed them with rifles and flamethrowers, and set off into the woods, leaving Circe behind with her daughter. The twins had remained as well, along with Arachne and a handful of other sentries. The entire remaining population of the Argo had marched off to join him on his mysterious expedition, and those who'd stayed at camp hadn't heard from him since.

"That was yesterday afternoon," Circe said as she prepared the sutures. "Jason wouldn't utter a word about where he was going, though I overheard him saying something about how he needed to make sure 'they' didn't get loose. When I tried to pry the answers from Argus, he wouldn't talk, either. This will pinch."

Michelle gritted her teeth as the needle penetrated her skin. She'd refused numbing medication on the grounds that she needed her body to be fully under her control. "Jason had me carry a bomb into the city," she said. "And the part about *them* getting loose—well, I can tell you about that."

Briefly, while the needle poked and pulled, she told Circe what she'd learned about Jason, the SKLDI facility, and the creatures that were spawned there. Though Circe showed no surprise when Michelle described Jason's secret history, she frowned at the teen's tale of monsters.

"You've been through a lot," she said. "And sometimes, when our bodies are under that much stress, our minds play tricks on us."

Michelle tried to remonstrate, but Circe waved her off, her concentration focused on her task. Michelle decided there was no point in wasting time or breath on a story she wouldn't have believed if she hadn't seen the truth for herself.

When the operation was done, Michelle rose and stretched, feeling the hot tightness where the stitches had gone in. She sipped carefully from a bottle of water until her vertigo passed and her legs felt strong enough to walk on her own. She'd described Kareem's symptoms while Circe worked, and now Tyris presented her with a satchel full of supplies. Michelle slipped it onto her back and tightened the straps.

"He might not make it, you understand," Circe warned her. "I've taken my best guess based on what you told me and what I observed when he was here before, but emergency medicine isn't the place for guesses. Even if I had him in camp and could treat him myself, there's no guarantee he'd survive."

Michelle's throat clenched. "I know."

"But I think you made the right decision," Circe said more gently. "Coming here for help gave him the best chance he was going to get."

Tyris scampered off to find Nausikaa and Aristodeme, who met them at the door a few minutes later, their drifting movements reminding Michelle of ghosts. She'd taken her first step down the front stairs to join them when Circe touched her arm.

"You asked me once about my past," she said. "I never told you about Argus."

Michelle looked at her blankly. "Argus?"

"My husband." Circe smiled, the lines around her eyes deepening. "We lost our first child to cancer, which is why Tyris came so late. Her big sister would have been about your age by now."

"I'm so sorry," Michelle said.

"That's all right," Circe said, though her chin quivered. "Argus blamed me, the doctor. Said I should have been able to save her. He left home to take a spiritual journey—his words—and met Jason. When he urged me to join the Argo, I said yes. I was grieving, too. But after Tyris was born, I knew I could never leave."

Michelle reached out for Circe's hand, and the two women's fingers clasped. "You could come with us. Both of you."

"They'd hunt us down," Circe said. "You, Jason might let go. Tyris and me, never. Even if I was a younger woman, I couldn't risk it." She smiled sadly. "We give up much for love, Diana. Maybe too much."

"It's Michelle."

"Helene," the doctor said. "Keep the girls safe, Michelle."

She hefted Tyris in her arms and hobbled into the infirmary, the child waving goodbye over her mother's shoulder.

The journey back passed in a timeless haze. The three travelers climbed the cliff warily, the twins proving as silent of foot as they were of voice. When they found Arachne's station deserted, Michelle sensed a trap, but they made it safely to the woods and slipped past the outlying sentry. Despite her urgency, Michelle found that she couldn't match the pace she'd set before. Fear of Jason's forces slowed their steps, and now that she'd come back to earth, she had to admit that her body simply wasn't equal to the task. The newly sewn stitches yanked at her, while the fatigue of her earlier run settled in her quads like lead. Her thoughts blurred as they advanced deeper into the forest, and the image she'd tried to hold of Kareem's face—his smile, his dark eyes, his thick lashes—gave way to a pale emptiness without solid form. She struggled to convince herself she was merely suffering from exhaustion, but a voice at the back of her mind whispered that she'd seen that emptiness before and was rushing to meet it once again.

The sun dipped below the treetops while they made their way through the forest. From that point on they moved in darkness, their only light the dancing beam of the flashlight Nausikaa shined against the boles of trees. After hours of dodging shadows that seemed to leap at her out of nowhere,

Michelle realized that she'd long since stopped leading the pack. Nausikaa and Aristodeme had taken over, and were making their way toward the exit Michelle had described. Her foggy mind had a moment to ask how they knew the direction, whether this was the way they'd fled from their former enslavers to the new slavery of the Argo, when Nausikaa held out a cautioning hand and spoke.

"*K'chortu.*" Michelle didn't know the language, but it sounded like a curse.

Nausikaa doused the beam, and the three of them shrouded themselves in the total blackness behind a tree. Up ahead, a collection of shimmering lights hovered in the darkness, reminding Michelle of fireflies. Except it was too early in the year for fireflies, and the lights didn't flash on and off but held steady at waist height. Reluctantly, she admitted to herself that what she was seeing was a collection of flashlights, all of them clustered together as if the people holding them had circled for a conference. She could think of only one reason they'd do that out here in the woods, and her heart pounded as she signaled the twins to stay back while she crept closer to the source of the light.

The first thing she realized was that they weren't in the clearing where she'd exited the tunnel; the trees were as thick here as she'd ever seen. Beneath the giant trunks, she was able to discern the shadowy bodies of the people holding the flashlights. She couldn't pick Jason out of the crowd, but she heard his voice.

"Did you find anything?" he asked.

"Not yet," a single member of the Argo answered. To her surprise, Michelle recognized the raspy voice of Caeneus. "You sure about this, boss?"

"I saw the two of them in the city," Jason said. "Before they went to ground. Keep looking. There are plenty of ways in and out."

"Will do," Caeneus said. "Let me check with ... wait." His voice fell silent, then resumed a minute later. "He's bringing one up now."

"Stay back," Jason said. "And keep your weapons ready."

There was movement among the lights and shadows. Caeneus's limping form emerged from underground, followed by Argus, his bald head and bushy beard rimmed by the flashlights. The big man was carrying someone over a broad shoulder. To either side, members of camp aimed rifles and flamethrowers, ready to shoot if the captive tried to escape. It was obvious to Michelle, though, that Argus's prisoner was in no condition to resist. He hung limp and unmoving across the lieutenant's chest, and when Argus laid him on the ground, the most he could manage was to moan weakly and roll onto his back. Michelle's heart fell as the flashlights revealed his thick hair and pale face, the bright red letters stitched across his chest.

It was Kareem. Jason had found him first. If she'd waited any longer by her lover's side, if the captain of the Argo hadn't taken this alternate route into the city, he would have captured them both.

She was trying to decide what to do when the cold barrel of a gun pressed against her temple.

"Nabbed you at last, little bug," the voice of Arachne spoke in her ear. "One move and I'll bleed you dry."

Chapter 18

They returned to camp while night paled to dawn.

As Circe—Helene—had said, the majority of the Argo had accompanied Jason, almost thirty men and women in combat fatigues. Michelle wondered how the injured Arachne had joined the party, but her question was soon answered: the sentry had driven Jason's moon buggy, which explained as well why she hadn't pursued Michelle into camp. She sat behind the wheel and slowly steered the ATV through the woods in front of the others, beaming her headlights to show the way. A single passenger occupied the seat beside her: Kareem, his hands bound with rope and his head lolling to the side as if he'd never awakened since Michelle left him. She and the twins walked behind the vehicle, their hands bound as well, Jason's hunting knife held in warning against Michelle's back. Arachne had confiscated the satchel full of medical supplies, but in her haste and excitement, she'd neglected to check the pocket where Michelle had secreted the broken vial from the barracks. With her hands tied, though, she couldn't reach it. And even if she'd had any thoughts of escape, the soldiers who marched on either side of Kareem as Arachne crept through the forest would have made it impossible for her to act.

She asked herself, briefly, why Jason was going through the bother of bringing them back to camp when he could have slain them out here and left their bodies to rot in the woods. But no sooner did she ask the question than she arrived at the answer. He was planning to mount a show trial in the presence of the camp he'd founded after he'd left the SKLDI facility. A trial where he was the sole judge and jury, and where the only possible outcome was an execution.

The sun peeked above the treetops by the time they stood on the cliff overlooking the River Lethe. Arachne jumped with surprising nimbleness from the vehicle, circling to the passenger side to shake Kareem until his head snapped up and his eyes flickered open. The sentry dragged him from his seat before he seemed fully aware of what was going on, with the predictable result that he tripped and sprawled on the ground. She drew back her foot—the one with the heavy plastic boot—to kick him, and Michelle was about to risk Jason's blade when he intervened.

"That's enough for now," he said. "Argus, take him below. The rest of you, keep the flamethrowers ready."

Argus hooked a hand in the rope that bound Kareem's wrists and hauled him to his feet. Michelle saw how gaunt he had become, a walking skeleton who looked nothing like the boy who'd held her in his arms just days before. What had seemed a trick of the darkness and wavering flashlight beams became cruelly visible in the morning light: his black hair had actually grayed, as if he'd aged thirty years since she last saw him. When his bloodshot eyes turned in her direction, he looked right through her. It was as if, accompanying this final, terrible decay of his body, his memory of the past few days had turned to dust as well.

She would have said something to him, spoken his name, but the knife in her back kept her lips sealed.

The roar of the falls filled Michelle's ears as they threaded their way to the campground. Kareem stumbled blindly forward at the head of the pack, with Argus shoving him and the guards standing just behind. How he kept his feet at all on the steep, rocky trail, she couldn't imagine. When they reached level ground, Jason sheathed his knife and handed Michelle over to his huge lieutenant, the men with the flamethrowers keeping them trained on Kareem. She wasn't sure what expression she expected the leader of the Argo to wear as he stood before his followers: triumph, malice, bloodlust. She was surprised when she saw what she could only describe as mingled eagerness and relief. He looked like someone who'd been carrying an impossibly heavy burden for years, and who'd finally been given a chance to lay it down.

"Should I take these three to the box?" Argus asked, indicating Michelle and the twins.

"No," Jason said. "I want everyone to see this." He gestured to Arachne. "Fetch Circe and her daughter. Meet us at headquarters."

The sentry nodded and marched off, her strides military-crisp despite the cast. Michelle felt a jerk on her bonds and moved forward mechanically, keeping an eye on Kareem's wavering steps and the menace of the flamethrowers on either side of him.

That's when it clicked.

The flamethrowers.

For any other prisoner, Jason would have armed his guards with rifles such as those the majority of his soldiers carried. The fact that he'd reserved the flamethrowers for Kareem could mean only one thing.

He was treating Kareem as if he were Skaldi.

Michelle's own steps faltered as she remembered the awful scene in the tunnel after she and Kareem escaped from the barracks. His blood had saved him then. But in all the hours he'd been alone, was it possible the Skaldi had broken through, found him, overpowered him? Or was it as he'd suggested, that a person exposed to their assaults time and again might need only the slightest push—a single touch from one of the creatures' hands—to succumb completely? The thought that she'd abandoned him when he needed her the most opened a fresh wound of guilt in her chest. She should have kept her promise and stayed beside him, watching until she was sure he was no longer himself, and then somehow—she had no idea how—she should have ended his life, or died trying.

But, she pleaded silently, *I didn't know*. Even now, she wasn't sure Jason *knew* that Kareem was infected with the Skaldi plague. All she knew was that, whether Kareem was still himself or not, his former jailer wouldn't let someone he considered a threat to the Argo survive.

The woman Jason had renamed Circe was hobbling toward them, Tyris in her arms and Arachne stalking in their rear. Though Michelle was sure the doctor had treated every member of camp at one point or another, many of the soldiers smiled viciously as they watched her struggle forward with the twin burdens of her shackles and her child. As she came abreast the camp's leader, Helene offered Michelle a look filled with pity and understanding.

"Jason," the doctor said. "I see you've brought back my

patient."

"You can't cure what he's got," Jason said. "Only one thing can."

"Let me be the judge of that," Helene said, taking a step closer.

Jason pulled out his knife and pointed it at the doctor. "You chose your fate, Circe. Now back off, or there'll be more than one dead body for you to deal with."

Helene didn't answer, but she gripped Tyris fiercely and edged away. The little girl buried her head in her mother's shoulder as if she knew what was about to happen. Seemingly satisfied with the doctor's submission, Jason raised his arms to address his followers.

"This is an important day," he said in a quiet voice that nonetheless carried over the crowd. "A day that's been in preparation for years, even if none of you saw it coming. It's what we've been living for all this time, waiting for, working for. Now that it's come, it's fitting we should share the responsibility for seeing it through."

He paused and took a look around the circle of his followers. Kareem showed no sign that he was listening; he stood between the armed guards with his head bowed, his eyes closed. Maybe he was too exhausted to care what happened to him anymore. Licking his lips in anticipation, Jason continued.

"You've all followed me for years, knowing the challenges that come with our unique charge. You never doubted me"—his eyes shot to the camp doctor—"but I wouldn't blame you if you wondered. I wish I could have told you the whole truth, I honestly do. But there were too many threats to my wellbeing, too many risks to exposing myself.

The Argo stands or falls with me, and I knew that if it fell, the dangers it was designed to contain would be unleashed on the world."

The faces of the men and women in the circle showed neither surprise nor bewilderment at Jason's announcement. They seemed willing to wait for him to finish, just as they'd waited for as long as they'd been bound to his camp for some revelation to show itself. The coming of the yellow fire hadn't been enough for them. Whatever it was that these people wanted, Michelle doubted their restless longing could ever be satisfied, whether through blood or fire.

"Enemies surround us," Jason went on. "You've always known that. Weeks ago, some of them struck, to devastating effect. It wasn't due to any failure on my part, or yours, that we were unable to prevent their attacks. The Argo was placed on this earth to fight a specific enemy, one that's lain hidden for years in the city that sits just beyond our sanctuary. Until that threat was dealt with, I couldn't risk letting anyone, not even my closest advisors, know the fullness of the truth, in case it might be used against me."

Michelle couldn't be sure, but she thought that Arachne, who stood across the circle with Helene and Tyris under her watchful eye, frowned at these words.

"But the time for secrets is past," Jason concluded. "Today, I can tell you what I couldn't make public before. Today, you'll see what we've been preparing for through the long years of our vigil. Argus, if you would bring the prisoner forward."

The lieutenant stepped away from Michelle's side and grabbed Kareem roughly by his arm, throwing him to the ground. Kareem landed on his knees, his head lowered as the flamethrowers loomed above him. Michelle would have run to him if Caeneus, sidling up to her with an ugly, gap-toothed grin, hadn't placed the hunting knife he must have earned for good behavior against the base of her spine.

"You and me, sweetie," he hissed in her ear, "we never did get a chance to settle up."

Jason stepped forward to stand over Kareem. The crowd fidgeted, murmuring, as their leader flourished his knife above the drooping, gray-haired head.

"Ten years ago," Jason said, "I knew this boy. Too much time had passed for me to recognize him when he came to our camp. He's changed so much—his body, his face, even his name. When I knew him, he had no name. He was simply Kenos Subject One, or K-1 for short. The new name he took—or was given—came to him after he'd left the site where he and I first met, the site that lies beneath where we're standing right now."

Michelle stared at Jason and his prisoner as the photograph she'd found in the SKLDI facility flashed through her mind. A wooded area, where the scientists under the command of the Tall Man had begun what they called the "pre-trial" phase of the Skaldi experiments—that photo must have been taken *here*, in the forest above the Argo's tunnels. Kareem's memory had failed him when he'd described Jason's role in those experiments. It wasn't that Jason had vanished. It was that Kareem and his brothers had been moved to a new site in the city while Jason remained behind.

"That's right," Jason said, and Michelle had to shake her head to overcome the creepy feeling that he'd read her thoughts. "The Argo wasn't always the Argo, and I wasn't always the man I am now. Back when I was a boy, this place

Daughter of Dust

was a secret military installation, similar to but much smaller than the one in the city, whose tunnels extend for miles in every direction. I lived here, and worked here. My job was to take care of subjects like K-1. The man I worked for, the man who ran this place, was my father."

Michelle's gasp was swallowed by the crowd's. The only person who kept silent—other than the twins and the cowering Tyris, whose head remained buried in her mother's shoulder—was Arachne, and this time, there was no doubt that her eyes narrowed suspiciously.

"I didn't witness the completion of the work my father started," Jason said. "A day came when he decided it was too dangerous for me, and so he left me here and moved to a more secure site in the city, where the project took a direction whose implications I couldn't have foreseen at the time. All I knew was that, when he left, he promised me he'd halt the work if it threatened his safety or the safety of others. I believed him. He left behind one of the prototype weapons he was developing, and he provided me with the resources I needed to build an outpost at the site of the old installation. He told me to be watchful, and to stay prepared. I gathered my forces and waited for him to return, or to call me when he needed me."

"So the Argo"—it was Arachne speaking, or more like spitting, the question—"the Argo was nothing but a little family project? A science experiment between you and your daddy?"

Everyone's eyes turned toward the sentry, then back to Jason. He glared, and when he spoke again, his voice carried the dangerous edge Michelle had first heard on the day of her rescue—her capture—in the woods.

"It was much more than that, Arachne," he said. "It was a massive bioweapons experiment with the potential to wipe out all life on earth. Like I said, I didn't recognize it for what it was at the time. I understood that the work was risky, but I let myself be convinced that it was *necessary*"—his voice curled sarcastically around the word—"for our national security. When my father went away, I let myself believe he'd keep his promise. It wasn't until the twins showed up that I knew he'd lied."

Michelle focused her attention on Nausikaa and Aristodeme, but their faces revealed nothing. It was only then that she realized the significance of that fact.

Their faces revealed nothing.

"My God," she breathed, and Jason heard.

"Yes," he said. "These girls were two of the experimental subjects my father was working on in the city. I don't know whether they escaped or were released, but they must have made their way to the Argo via the tunnel where we found K-1. The day they came to us, I realized that, far from halting his project, my father had accelerated it. I tried to contact him, but he'd closed off all communication between us. It was from that day that I started keeping my eyes open for people with gaps in their memory and deficiencies in their blood roaming my woods."

"What are you talking about, Jason?" Helene challenged him from across the circle. "The girls were suffering from severe anemia and traumatic memory loss when we took them in. But we all know why. You *told* us why."

"I told you what you wanted to hear," Jason said. "What you were able to accept. But I knew what my father was working on, and though he left me behind before he completed it, I know when I see the finished product. I know it—because I see it before me now."

His knife pointed like an accusing finger at the bent shape of Kareem. Helene shook her head, glaring darkly at the Argo's leader.

"You've planted this crazy idea in the head of Mi … of Diana," she said. "And I'm sure it suits your purposes to scare us all with ghost stories. But this poor boy is sick, just like the twins were sick. Just like *you're* sick, with grief and anger of your own."

"You think so?" Jason asked. "Argus, get the girl."

The big man responded instantly to his leader's command, stepping across the circle and tearing his child from his wife's arms. The five-year-old screamed, but when Helene grabbed for her husband, he backhanded her with all his strength, and she spun to the ground. She lay there for a moment, dazed, before rolling to her stomach and struggling to her feet, the chain hampering her movements. Tyris continued to flail in Argus's rough grip, her screams pitching higher and higher as her panic mounted.

"Tyris, honey, it's okay," Helene crooned to the struggling child. "Stay with Daddy."

For once, Tyris failed to calm at her mother's voice. Jason looked on in satisfaction as Argus wrapped his daughter in his arms, clamping a beefy hand over her mouth to stifle her screams. Helene's face crumpled at the sight of Tyris's distress, but she drew herself up and faced Jason.

"You'll answer for this," she warned in a voice that shook with anger. "You will as well, Arthur," she said to her husband. "Now both of you, step aside and let me tend to this boy."

Jason's lips twisted into a smile. "Tend to this, old woman."

Moving so swiftly Michelle couldn't have stopped him if she'd been standing right next to him, he plunged his knife into the kneeling figure at his feet.

"No!" she screamed, but it was too late. The knife struck Kareem in the chest, his body going rigid at the impact. Michelle tore at her bonds, but Caeneus held her tight. She could do nothing but stare at the knife protruding from Kareem's chest above the red letters, and wait for him to fall.

But he didn't fall.

The crowd took an involuntary step backward. Only Helene moved toward the prisoner, catching Kareem as he swayed. The doctor held him upright, her normally sure hands fluttering around the knife. Across the distance, Kareem's eyes sought Michelle's, sending her a look of such sorrow she felt as if she would swoon.

Helene backed away from him slowly. She stared at her hands as if she couldn't believe what she was seeing.

Where the knife jutted from his chest, no blood flowed.

"You see?" Jason's voice rose hysterically. "This is one of *them*. And now he's ours."

Michelle's legs gave out, and Caeneus seemed too shaken to catch her when she fell. Through tears, she looked across the circle at the boy she'd known and loved, the boy she no longer knew and could never love again. He met her eyes with the same sorrowing look as before, as if he were begging for forgiveness, knowing it was no longer hers to give.

"I'm sorry, Diana," he said. "I tried to fight it, to be what you saw in me. I didn't want to live this way ... to die this way ... "

His voice failed, but his eyes continued to plead with her. She couldn't stand that look any longer, and so she hung her head and wept. Over the sound of her grief, she heard Jason's voice.

"*This* is the result of my father's experiments," he said. "A creature with the power to drain life energy from human beings, appearing in their guise to infiltrate the ranks of enemy combatants. I don't know how many of these monsters in the shape of men he bred, what part they played in last month's attacks. It's my belief that most of them have fallen prey to the weapon I delivered to the city, and in the days and weeks to come, we'll return to hunt down any that remain. But today—*now*—we're going to put an end to this soulless abomination, the proof of my father's deadly work."

"How are we supposed to do that?" Arachne's voice fell on Michelle's ears.

"There's only one way to kill these creatures," Jason said. "Their bodies can take any amount of damage from bullets or blades, but they can't survive burning." He paused, and in the silence while his followers waited for his command, Michelle heard the sound of him sheathing his knife. "So we're going to have ourselves a little bonfire."

Her head jerked up. Jason was smiling, his eyes alight. He raised his hand to give the signal to his guards.

At that moment, Michelle struggled to her feet and flung herself in front of Kareem. Before the men with the flamethrowers could pull the triggers, she bent over him, shielding his body with hers.

"No," she said, addressing Jason alone. "Let me take him. I promise, you'll never hear from either of us again."

Jason sneered. "I won't have any more blood shed on

this monster's account."

"But he's innocent," she said. "He didn't choose to be what he is. Please, Jason. We won't trouble you. We'll go somewhere far away from this place, and then he can … "

Die in peace.

"You think that's merciful," Jason said. "It could be days before this one dies. You saw what happens to them. Is *that* what you want?"

She remembered the creatures from the desert, their bodies crumbling to dust as they pursued her. Kareem's face and hair had already turned the color of ash. Could she bear to watch the rest of his body dwindle to nothing?

"But that's not what'll happen," Jason went on. "The beast won't let itself die if there's a way to save itself. The minute you're out of our sight, it'll take *your* body, and then it'll move on. It'll be too smart to return to the Argo. It'll seek other survivors, and my father's curse will spread across the land."

Michelle tried to meet Kareem's eye, but he wouldn't look at her. Was it grief that made him hide his face, or shame—shame at what he was, at what he couldn't deny he might do to her if that was his only way of staying alive?

"I can see this one's gone to work on you," Jason said. "They're insidious, Diana. It's how they operate. What, did you think it was your friend? Or"—his tone darkened as he seemed to glimpse the truth—"*more* than a friend? That's it, isn't it?" He laughed maliciously. "I guess they can mimic everything else. Why shouldn't they be able to mimic that as well?"

His laughter cut her to the core, and she wished she could tell him *her* truth. How Kareem had rescued her, fought for her, loved her. How he'd been willing to die for her. If all he'd wanted was another body to steal, there'd been no shortage of opportunities for him to take hers. But he hadn't. He'd even begged her to kill him when he thought he'd become one of them. *I tried to fight it, to be what you saw in me,* were the words he'd said just now. Would it be different with his unnatural life coming to an end? The moment he got her alone, would he strike without remorse, without a memory of what they'd meant to each other?

She didn't know. Jason might be right. Maybe it was better to end it now, before she learned something that would shatter her soul forever.

"It's over, Diana," Jason spoke from the emptiness that had descended on the world. "Now step away and let us finish it."

She struggled to obey, but found herself frozen, unable to command her legs to propel her away from Kareem. She couldn't bring herself to touch him, but she couldn't bear to let him go. She wished that Jason would give his executioners the order to shoot, so that her grief and uncertainty could be washed away in a cleansing wave of fire.

"Last chance, Diana," his voice came as if in answer.

My name is Michelle, she thought, but even that something she could no longer be sure of.

"Have it your way," Jason muttered, and she braced her body for the fire.

The flamethrowers coughed and roared. Searing heat blossomed against her face, wrapping her in its hands. She smelled gasoline, detected the scent of singed clothing and hair. Whether it was hers or Kareem's she couldn't tell. She knew that she was dying, that the night of yellow fire had only been delayed. She closed her eyes and waited for the bright light beyond her eyelids to fade utterly to black.

Then she was flung free of the heat and lay choking on the ground, struggling for breath. Another body landed on hers; hands beat at the flames that licked her cheeks, her hair. The inferno should have consumed her, but it hadn't—every nerve in her body was engulfed in pain, but she was alive. She heard screams, multiple rounds of gunfire, running feet, all of the sounds combining into a single chaotic roar. She opened her eyes to see what had saved her, and her mind reeled as she took in the hellish sight.

Kareem was on his feet, his hands freed of their bonds, but his body was no longer his own. It had split in a ragged line from his forehead to his stomach, leaving nothing from the waist up but a gaping scar like a huge, vertical mouth without teeth or tongue. Inside that awful maw, there was nothing—no heart, no bones, no blood, only a wet gray emptiness that reeked of rotting flesh. The snapping jaws had left one of the men with the flamethrowers torn and bloody on the ground; the other guard had dropped his weapon and run. The remainder of the camp had fled as well after emptying their rifles into the unstoppable creature, leaving only Arachne, the twins, Jason, and Argus to face their foe. The camp's leader and lieutenant, along with their chief sentry, had drawn together to defend themselves against the Skaldi, but the only weapons that might have saved them lay at the creature's feet, its deadly mouth putting those weapons beyond reach.

Michelle heard a thin wail, a child's cry. Gasping against the pain that gripped her with every movement, she turned her head to see Tyris on the ground, the girl tugging at her mother's inert body. Michelle realized that it wasn't Kareem who had saved her from the flames; it was Helene, whose own face and hands were badly burned by the effort. No matter how loudly Tyris screamed her mother's name, no matter how urgently she pushed and prodded, the woman didn't respond. It wasn't long before Michelle saw why: the doctor's chest was bloody and motionless, the bullet that someone had fired in panic having hit her.

Michelle struggled with her bonds and felt them give, possibly charred by the fire. With a violent sideways motion, she raked the last threads against the broken vial in her pocket. Pain lanced her wrists and blood flowed, but her hands came free. She began the agonizing crawl toward Tyris, wishing it didn't have to be her who explained what had happened to her mother, seeing in the child's stricken face that she might never recover from the horror of this day.

Michelle was reaching for Tyris's hand when the Skaldi struck.

It clutched her in its jaws and flung her to the ground. She landed with excruciating impact, then dazedly raised her head to see the creature's mouth descending on Tyris. With a shout, Argus barreled toward the monster, taking advantage of its focus on his daughter to throw himself at it from behind. But no matter how fast the big man moved, the Skaldi moved faster. It lashed out like a snake, the hideous mouth snapping closed on Argus's broad chest. Blood sprayed, and Argus fell without a sound, his beard so matted with gore Michelle could no longer find his face. In the moment's pause while the creature was spitting Jason's dead lieutenant from its maw, the leader of the Argo ducked beneath its reach and put a hand on the nearest flamethrower, raising the nozzle to fire.

"This is *my* camp!" he shouted. "*I'm* the hunter here, not—"

His voice ended in a strangled scream as the mouth clamped down on his throat. Jason struggled to free himself from the monster's grasp, but his strength was ebbing as blood poured from his neck to soak the charred ground. His head turned to the side, his unnaturally blue eyes directed at Michelle, but they were glassy and sightless. When the creature released him, the head fell from the man's body and rolled to a stop facing away from her and the Skaldi's other victims.

The creature turned to those who were still alive. Tyris continued to keen and roughly pull her mother's arm, desperation making her wild. The twins had backed away from the Skaldi, while Arachne had positioned herself in front of them. The sentry had no weapon but her rifle, but she faced the ravenous mouth nonetheless.

Michelle rose. She tottered on legs that were bruised, burned, and weak with anguish. Her hands, reddened by fire and dripping blood, curled like claws at her sides. The Skaldi swiveled to face her, its mouth wide, its corpse-stink bathing her. Every trace of the boy she'd loved had been swept away by that pitiless maw.

But she spoke to it, using his name.

"Kareem. Hear me. As you loved me, listen to me. Let them go."

It stood motionless, as if there were something inside its empty shell that could still respond to her voice.

"Jason is gone," she said. "His camp dies with him. Let it end now, not with more suffering and death."

A hissing noise emerged from its inhuman body, and Michelle covered her ears, all willpower draining from her as she confronted the thing he had become. Then she realized the creature was forming words—thin, faint words she heard in her head as if from a long forgotten dream.

All things suffer, the voice said. *All things die. Why should you resist? It's better to let go, better to forget than to bear the burden of memory. I was once Kareem, but now I've cast that aside. Join me, and you can be truly free.*

The creature took a step closer. The smell of the grave enveloped her as the soft voice caressed her inner ear.

Let me carry you away, it said. *Let me consume you, and your own legs can run from this field of death. We'll find the place you spoke of. A place where no one will trouble us, where all sorrow vanishes into thin air. Isn't that what you want? To be done with this place, this time? To forget that you ever loved, that you ever lost?*

Yes, she answered it silently. *I'm so tired, Kareem. Tired of running, tired of fighting. Tired of mourning people I'll never see again. Can you make it all go away? Do you promise?*

I promise, the voice said. *Come with me now, and I'll show you.*

She raised her head to face it. The scar had split even wider than before, looking less like a mouth than like arms held out for an embrace. A single step, and those arms would enfold her, wrapping her in the eternal amnesia of death.

If the world is to be erased, she said to herself, *let me be erased with it. Let my name vanish with the songs of the birds and the cry of the wind. Names are for things that last. Let there be silence forevermore.*

She took the final step. Darkness blotted her vision. She shivered in the cold, and she knew that no human touch would ever warm her again. The Skaldi's scar opened wider still, and to Michelle, it looked like a welcoming smile.

"I'm sorry, my love," she spoke out loud. "But I made a promise, too."

The mind of the Skaldi flickered with doubt as she grasped the flamethrower that lay discarded at its feet and pulled the trigger.

The stream of fire struck the creature in the depths of its body, in the heart of the hollowness she'd permitted to encircle her. Instantly, the Skaldi cringed away, releasing its hold on her as it sought to evade the flame. But it had allowed her to come too close, had let its mind stray from the only weapon that could destroy it. Michelle advanced on it as it caught fire from within, its corpse-gray flesh blackening and shriveling like paper. It fell to its knees, and what was left of its body seemed to spread wide like arms beseeching her to stop. But she didn't stop. Tears blurred her vision and the heat of the fire seared her own flesh, but she continued to burn the evil thing before her, fulfilling her promise to the one it had replaced.

At the last moment, when it was nothing but an empty, smoking husk, so fragile she knew that the next gust of the flamethrower would blow it to ash, she released her finger from the trigger and stared at the shapeless mass at her feet.

Memories assailed her. Memories of him, of their flight through the woods, their battle against the Skaldi, their night in each other's arms. Memories of Rosie, and her family, and her hometown, and the friends who'd vanished from her life in a burst of yellow fire as this creature would soon do. Memories she swore to herself she would never lose, even if they tormented her to the end of her days. She raised the flamethrower once more and aimed it at what remained of the Skaldi.

It spoke a final time. It spoke with Kareem's voice, and she heard the word aloud, a grateful sigh like a child settling to sleep.

"Chelle," he said.

Then she pulled the trigger, and the last traces of him exploded in a spray of flame and dust.

Epilogue

They made ready to set out for the west.

It was a week since the Argo's final battle. The survivors had removed the shackles from Helene's legs and buried her body, then incinerated the remains of the others who'd fallen victim to the Skaldi. Fortunately for Michelle, the twins were as adept pupils as their predecessor had promised, and though they remained stony-faced and silent while they worked, the lacerations and burns she'd suffered in the Skaldi's final moments had been treated so carefully she could walk with only a modest degree of stiffness and pain. Whether she'd be able to run again was an open question. When she gazed at herself in the bedroom mirror, she thought the scars that crisscrossed her face and hands made her look like an old woman. She wondered if they'd ever soften, or if she'd bear them for the rest of her life.

To her great surprise, several of the remaining members of Jason's camp pitched in to help while she was on the mend—including Arachne, who never once mentioned the attempt she'd made on Michelle's life just days before. Most of the adults, however, followed the example of Caeneus and his two companions, who vanished without telling anyone where they were going. Over the course of the week, the camp emptied, leaving only Michelle, Arachne, Tyris, Calypso, the twins, and three men whose names she didn't know. Possibly the rest had headed for the city, but Michelle suspected that they had merely wandered off into the woods. Whether they would find a means or a reason to survive now that Jason was gone was beyond her capacity to guess.

Her hands were too full with Tyris to give them much thought. The little girl spent the first three days after the death of her parents in obvious shock—eating no food, talking to no one, perched with her hands folded in her lap and her legs dangling from the side of the cot she'd shared with her mother. Once Michelle was cleared by Nausikaa and Aristodeme, she spent every moment she could with the girl, sitting beside her to hold her hand, stroke her hair, whisper words of comfort to her apparently deaf ears. It took another two days of this routine, but finally Tyris came back to life, the first sign of her resurrection being the torrent of tears she shed on Michelle's shoulder. Next, she allowed Michelle to spoon-feed her, then to bathe her, and finally to hold her in her lap and read from the child's favorite and only bedtime book, *The Runaway Bunny*. By the end of the week, she was tagging along behind Michelle everywhere the latter went, as if she were fearful that her new caretaker might disappear if she didn't dog her steps as closely as she had her mother's. When Michelle gazed into her little shadow's eyes, she perceived a depth of sorrow and understanding that she doubted would ever disappear. Tyris was only five, but she'd become like the rest of the grownups, like Michelle herself. She was at once Rosie's replacement and her revenant. The girl had ghosts.

When Michelle told her one night while they were

preparing for bed that she wanted to leave camp and travel west, Tyris didn't question. She looked at the teen sitting beside her and tilted her head, smiling an oracular smile.

"It's pretty there," the little girl said. "Can I come, too?"

Michelle hugged her in answer. Tyris was already so much like her mother. She'd inherited the healer's gift.

The few members of Jason's camp who remained were quick to approve the exodus as well. Even Arachne offered no resistance. The woman had trimmed Michelle's fire-singed hair—gently this time—and had taken to wearing Jason's too-big jacket over her black top, an obvious sign that she considered herself in command.

"There's only one thing," she said after she okayed the plan.

Michelle cringed. She hadn't mentioned the mountains to anyone, and the formidable sentry was the last person she wanted to broach the subject with. "What's that?"

"Our name," Arachne said. "We're not the Argo anymore, so who are we?"

Michelle thought about it. "The Argo Nots?"

Arachne looked blank for a moment. "Oh. I get it."

"How about … " Michelle counted the camp's remaining members. "Well, there are nine of us, so how about … the Nine Survivors?"

Now it was Arachne's turn to cringe.

"The Survival Colony Nine?" Michelle tried.

Watching the woman's dour visage break into a smile was as much of a surprise as anything Michelle had seen in this new world. "I'll tell the others," Arachne said.

The others liked it, too. All except Tyris, who didn't know what a colony was. But she trusted Michelle's awesome powers enough to give the name her guarded approval.

The morning they were to set out, Michelle rose before anyone else, slipping silently out of the bed she shared with Tyris and padding barefoot to the door to avoid waking her bunkmate. She shouldered her backpack, laced her boots on the porch, then walked as quickly and quietly as Jason had taught her to his erstwhile headquarters. The camp was silent except for the songs of forest birds. The main building had stood empty for the past week; there'd been no new captain of the Argo, and there never would be again. But there was something in Jason's office that Michelle wanted, something she intended to carry with her from now on. No one else had to know. She would keep it secret, and guard it with her life.

She opened the door to the building and walked the short hallway to the room where the leader of the Argo had initiated her into the mysteries of his camp. There on the shelf where he'd left it, the green jar gleamed dully in the early morning light. She'd never asked Kareem why, of all the things he could have taken from the lab that had held him captive, he'd chosen this unlikely object, an empty jar of the same material that housed the immature Skaldi. Maybe it was the first thing he'd gotten his hands on when he escaped. But she couldn't help thinking it was more than that. A relic from the only home he'd known, maybe this was his collection jar, meant to carry something important. Memories. Hope. Dreams. The things we try to hold onto, even when the world tries to take them away.

She returned to the field where the final battle had taken place. Wind and time had done away with most of the ashes, but she scraped her fingers through the charred grass to collect a solid handful, then another, then another. One measure at a time, she scooped the dust of his body into the jar, filling the container nearly halfway before there was so little of him left it had all but merged with grass and soil. Then she rose, her hands black with ashes, and closed the jar.

Standing where he'd fallen, she whispered a few words of farewell. Her plight, her troth. She told him that she would remember everything. She vowed that she would keep their secret always, sealed with his ashes in the bottle-green jar. She promised that when they reached the mountains, if they reached the mountains, only then would she set his soul free.

The camp was waking around her, the sound of human voices mingling with the chorus of birdsong. Tyris's call reached her from afar, chiding her for leaving the bedroom without permission: "Diana! Where'd you go?" When the little girl caught sight of her new caregiver and best friend, she skipped down the steps and ran barefoot across the grass, her dress flapping with the wind of her movement.

Michelle smiled. She tucked the jar at the bottom of her backpack, where no one would find it. Tyris clutched her hand, and they walked back to the women's quarters.

"Can I tell you something?" Michelle asked the girl at her side.

Tyris's eyes shone. "What?"

"My real name isn't Diana."

If possible, her partner's eyes widened even more. "What is it?"

Chelle, she thought. "It's a secret," she said.

Then she caught Tyris in a hug and swung her high in the air, while the little girl laughed at the feeling of flight.

THE END

The Book of the Huntress, Volume One ends here

The hunt continues in *Dark's Dominion* (Book of the Huntress, Volume Two), due December 2020

Acknowledgments

My thanks go to my agent, Liza Fleissig, for encouraging me to write this story. Jen Rees has been my first reader for years, and her impact on *Daughter of Dust* is immeasurable: she challenged me to turn the barest sketch of an idea into the book you just read. If you've enjoyed it, you can thank not only me but her, too.

Other people helped as well. Marshall Highet gave me lessons in wilderness survival. Megan Coffey provided linguistic advice. Cameron Yeager deleted smiles. Writer friends cheered from the virtual sidelines. Kate Brauning made a suggestion or two. The members of the La Roche University NaNoWriMo club kept me honest. The residents of southwestern Pennsylvania—especially its librarians, booksellers, teachers, and students—listened to and shared my stories. I'd like to apologize to them for taking liberties with the geography of their state, not to mention for turning it into a monster-haunted wasteland.

My greatest debt is to my family—my wife, Christine, and my children, Lilly and Jonah—who gave me the space and the patience every writer needs. Now that I'm done, I owe them some quality time in the real world.

About the Author

Joshua David Bellin has been writing novels since he was eight years old (though the first few were admittedly very short). A college teacher by day, he has published numerous works of fantasy and science fiction, including the post-apocalyptic Querry Genn Saga, the deep-space adventure *Freefall*, and the fantasy-adventure Ecosystem Cycle. In his free time, Josh likes to read, watch movies, and take long nature hikes with his kids. Oh, yeah, and he likes monsters. Really scary monsters.

To find out more about Josh and his books, visit his website and sign up for his e-newsletter. He promises not to send it to you more than once a month!

joshuadavidbellin.blogspot.com

Also by Joshua David Bellin

The Ecosystem Cycle

Only those born with the psychic power known as the Sense can survive within the planetary Ecosystem. When Sarah, a seventeen-year-old Sensor, sets out to avenge her mother's death, she discovers that the Ecosystem is far more perilous than she ever dreamed.

The Querry Genn Saga

A desert world. An embattled remnant of humanity. A monstrous enemy that consumes and mimics the bodies of the living. And a boy without memory who might hold the key to survival.

Available from online merchants and selected booksellers

www.ingramcontent.com/pod-product-compliance
Lightning Source LLC
Chambersburg PA
CBHW020255200626
46816CB00001BA/304